Virginia Vineyards

LOVE
AND
WAR

USA TODAY BESTSELLING AUTHOR

ASHLEY FARLEY

ALSO BY ASHLEY FARLEY

Saving Ben

Sweeney Sisters Series

Saturdays at Sweeney's

Tangle of Strings

Boots and Bedlam

Lowcountry Stranger

Her Sister's Shoes

Magnolia Series

Beyond the Garden

Magnolia Nights

Scottie's Adventures

Breaking the Story

Merry Mary

CHAPTER 1
HAZEL

Hazel is on her way home from work at the flower shop when she passes her husband zipping down the road in the opposite direction. She glances at her dashboard clock. Where could he possibly be going at almost six thirty? They rarely spend time together anymore, and he promised to be home for dinner tonight at seven.

On a whim, she hangs a U-turn on the country highway and follows his Land Rover at a safe distance back through town on Magnolia Avenue. When traffic thins, she slows her speed to put distance between them.

They've traveled about five miles when Charles makes a sudden right-hand turn. Hazel is grateful for her Tesla's quiet engine as she follows him a hundred yards up a bumpy dirt road. When Charles parks in front of a tiny log cabin, Hazel pulls in alongside a stand of pine trees for cover. Heart throbbing in throat, Hazel grabs her cell phone and gets out of the car, crouching down as she moves closer to the cabin for a better view.

As Charles approaches the cabin, the front door swings open and his lifelong friend, Stuart Malone, steps onto the porch. Hazel watches in horror as Charles walks into Stuart's arms, not in the familiar bro hug she's seen them exchange many times but in a passionate embrace with mouths pressed together and hands on asses.

Swallowing back a wave of nausea, Hazel accesses her new phone's fancy camera and snaps a dozen images of the lovers before retreating to her car. With head pressed against steering wheel, she contemplates her choices. She can back out of the driveway, hoping to escape undetected, or she can make a dramatic exit, letting her presence be known. Starting the engine, she slams her foot on the gas pedal, and the car hurtles forward toward the cabin. She spins the steering wheel, doing several donuts in the dirt yard before zooming back toward the highway.

Hazel pounds the steering wheel and screams at the empty car. How dare Charles do this to her? Another woman is one thing, but another man is a hard pill to swallow.

She cruises through town, barely slowing at stop signs, and when she reaches the stretch of highway heading home, she increases her speed to nearly ninety miles an hour.

When they purchased Clover Hill Farm ten years ago, Hazel had imagined raising their brood of children in the rambling old farmhouse, watching them play chase through the small apple orchard and swing on a tire from a branch of the meandering oak tree in the sprawling front yard. But now, the empty rooms serve as a constant reminder of her inability to bear children.

She flies up the stairs to the master bedroom, where she stuffs random articles of clothing into a duffel bag before going to the adjoining bath for her toiletries. The sight of Charles's toothbrush in the stand next to hers makes her stomach heave. He's brushed his teeth with that toothbrush after having sex with another man.

Hazel drops to her knees and vomits into the toilet. She's been so desperate for a family, so desperate to save her marriage, that she failed to notice the signs in front of her—Charles's frequent absences, sullen moods, and diminished interest in her sexually. Will she ever be able to rid her memory of the image of Charles and Stuart in a lover's embrace?

Rinsing her mouth out, she zips her cosmetics bag into her

duffel and hurries down to the kitchen. She's filling a large tote with food when a breathless Charles explodes through the back door.

"Hazel! It's not what you think," he says, gulping in air.

Dropping several cartons of yogurt in her bag, she slams the refrigerator door shut and faces him. "Be real, Charles. I saw you kissing Stuart with my own eyes. How long has this been going on?"

Charles's shoulders slump as his eyes fall to the floor. "On and off since we were kids."

Fury overcomes Hazel as the puzzle pieces fit into place. "You used me as your cover."

His head jerks up. "That's not entirely true. I desperately wanted to have a normal life with a wife and children. I tried, Hazel. I really and truly tried."

"Not hard enough." Hazel palms her forehead. "Everything suddenly makes so much sense. I should have realized something was wrong when you refused to see a fertility specialist. Why did you give up on having children, Charles? Was it because of me? Or because of him?"

Charles answers by staring at the floor.

Hazel rakes her hands through her hair as she paces in circles around the kitchen. "You blamed your impotency on work-related stress. But it was me. I turned you off. You ruined my life, you selfish bastard." She pounds his chest with her fists. "You should've told me the truth. I could've found a husband who desires me. Someone who wanted children. Instead, you held me hostage in this house. And now my childbearing years are over."

His grip on her arms is strong. "I didn't hold you hostage, Hazel. I would've given you a divorce. But you never asked."

Hazel wrenches free of his grasp. "And I'm not asking now. I'm telling you. I'm filing for divorce. Fair warning, it's gonna cost you." She flashes her phone at him. "I have evidence of your infidelity, and I will use it to suck every red cent I can from you."

Charles freezes, his hand gripping the counter. "What evidence?"

"Pictures of you and Stuart kissing," she says, swiping through the photos she took. "I dare say, this was not your best moment."

Charles grabs at her phone. "Please! Hazel! You can't show them to anyone. Stuart is happy in his marriage. Don't ruin that for him," he begs, his tone desperate.

Hazel backs away, her phone hidden behind her back. "He can't be but so happy if he's sleeping with you, can he?" She gathers her bags and flees the kitchen.

Charles chases her out into the driveway. "Wait! Don't leave like this. Let's talk this through. You're still my best friend. I don't want to lose you."

"You should've thought about that before you betrayed me." Hazel tosses her bags into the back, slides into the driver's seat, and takes off.

When she calls Laney on the way back to town, Hazel hears music and laughter in the background. "I'm sorry to bother you. I didn't realize you were having a party tonight."

"I'm not. The girls have some friends over," Laney says about her teenage daughters. "Hang on a second. Let me step outside." The laughter and music fade. "There. That's better. I can hear myself think. What's up?"

Hazel inhales an unsteady breath. "You once offered the apartment if I should ever need it. That time has come. I caught Charles having an affair."

"Oh, honey. I'm so sorry. The apartment is all yours. You know where the key is. Stay as long as you like. I can be there in fifteen minutes if you need to talk."

"Thanks, Laney. But I need time alone tonight to think."

"I understand. I'm only a phone call away if you change your mind."

Hazel drives down the alley and parks behind the flower shop. She retrieves the apartment key from under the planter of pink geraniums and carries her bags up to the second floor, throwing open the floor-to-ceiling windows to let fresh air into the stuffy living room. She kicks off her shoes and leans against the frame of the open window. Dusk has fallen over the town, and the lights twinkle from the stores and restaurants on Magnolia Avenue below.

Reality settles on her like the weight of the earth. Her husband is gay. For ten years, he's used her as a shield to prevent his friends and family from discovering the truth. Pain grips her chest and she struggles to breathe. While she's not vindictive, Hazel desperately wants Charles to know how this hurt feels. She can hit him the hardest by going public with his dirty little secret. And the best way to reach the most people is through social media.

Laney recently appointed Hazel in charge of their meager marketing efforts. Hence the reason she purchased a new phone with enhanced camera features. Through posting pics of their most remarkable bridal bouquets and table arrangements, she's amassed a substantial following of locals, mostly women, the ideal audience with which to share her news.

Retrieving her phone from her purse, Hazel studies the images of Stuart and Charles on the cabin's front porch. She picks the one that best shows their faces and posts it on Instagram with the message: *Imagine finding out your husband isn't who you thought he was.*

Hazel powers off the phone before the urge to delete the photo gets the best of her. Charles deserves to suffer for what he's done to her. And Stuart's wife, Bonnie, has a right to know the truth.

Dropping to the floor, Hazel crosses her legs and stretches her spine. Meditation and yoga have gotten her through the lonely years at the farm. But tonight, her thoughts are too intrusive, and she soon gives up on clearing her mind.

As she unpacks her groceries, Hazel familiarizes herself with the location of items in the small but updated kitchen. Brewing a cup of lavender tea, she takes her duffel bag to the two bedrooms on the third floor. Choosing the bedroom on the front of the building, she places her tea on the nightstand and stretches out on the queen-sized bed. From the darkened room, she can see the lights of the neighborhood streets leading away from Magnolia Avenue. Once she sorts out her life, maybe she'll buy a small house on one of those charming streets.

If Laney approves, she'll stay here until she gets her feet back on the ground. The starkness of the apartment, with its all-white furnishings and wooden floors, feels like the right place for a fresh start. And the sounds from below, horns blowing and trucks back-firing, offer comfort after the eerily quiet nights in the farmhouse with only her troubled thoughts to keep her company.

Her thoughts turn to Laney—her boss, best friend, and sister-in-law—recently separated from Charles's older brother Hugh. If Laney can escape an abusive marriage, Hazel can survive the public humiliation of her husband choosing his gay lover over her. Somehow, she'll forge ahead, one day at a time, with the freedom to do as she pleases. Hazel drifts off to sleep wondering how a single woman goes about adopting a child.

CHAPTER 2
CASEY

Casey falls back against the pillows and lets out a satisfied purr. "That was amazing. Thanks to you, I'll be worthless for the rest of the day." She cuddles close to Luke's long frame. "Too bad we have to go to work."

He wraps his legs around her body. "It's Friday. Why don't we call in sick? I'll serve you banana pancakes in bed."

Casey lets out a soft moan at the thought of his banana pancakes. "I wish I could. But I can't." She wiggles free of his legs. "Dad's treating me to breakfast at the diner. I'm meeting him in forty-five minutes."

Luke lets out a disgruntled humph. "Breakfast with Daniel usually comes with strings attached. He's up to something. Any clue what he wants?"

Her skin prickles. Luke often complains about her father taking up too much of her time, about being too involved in her life. But Daniel has been a part of her life for less than a year, and Casey wouldn't have it any other way.

"He didn't say." Casey throws her legs over the side of the bed and walks naked to his closet, thumbing through the meager wardrobe she keeps at his house. "I'm tired of these clothes. I've worn everything in here at least twice. I need to switch out some of my outfits from my condo this weekend. Living like a vagabond is getting old."

He rolls onto his side, propping himself on one elbow while watching her hold dresses up in front of the full-length mirror. "Marrying me will solve that problem, you know?"

Casey doesn't flinch. He's asked her nearly every single day for the past four months but she's yet to see a ring. "I'll consider it when you make a legitimate proposal."

"A legitimate proposal sounds like a business deal."

Casey returns the gray dress to the closet and tosses the pale blue one on the bed. "This conversation is old, Luke. Let's shelve it until you're serious," she says and disappears into the adjoining bathroom.

Casey emerges twenty minutes later with makeup on and wavy golden hair dancing around her shoulders. Luke is lying back against the pillows, staring up at the ceiling with a faraway expression on his face. "What's on your mind, babe? Big day at work?"

"I'm waiting on some big news. If I hear today, I'll share it with you tonight."

"I'm intrigued. Tell me more. Is this about a potential new case?" Dropping her towel, she puts on her bra and panties and slips the dress over her head.

He shakes his head. "I'm not telling you. I want it to be a surprise."

"That's not fair." She moves around to his side of the bed, placing her back to him while he zips her zipper. "How about a hint?"

"No way! You'll have to wait. I'll make you dinner as a reward for your patience."

She looks over her shoulder at him. "Why are you torturing me? This will be the longest day ever."

"You'll survive." He smacks her bottom. "Now get going or you'll be late. And give your father my regards."

Luke is being sarcastic. He, along with the rest of the local community, lost respect for her father when he faked terminal cancer last fall. Daniel's massive stroke not long afterward did little to elicit sympathy.

She bends over and kisses Luke's lips, lingering until he pulls her on top of him. She lets out a squeal and jumps to her feet. "If we start up again, I'll never leave," she says and hurries out of the room.

On the short drive to the diner, Casey wonders about Luke's big surprise. Is it life altering? Does it have something to do with her? Is it the reason he hasn't formally proposed? They have both expressed their readiness to get married. Since last fall, Casey has been living with him in the Spanish-style hacienda at the boutique vineyard he inherited from his parents. She can hardly wait to dispose of their worn-out furnishings and make the house their own.

When she arrives at the crowded diner, Daniel is already seated at a booth, perusing the menu even though he always orders the same thing—two eggs sunny-side-up with hash browns, sausage, and the muffin flavor of the day.

Casey slides onto the bench seat opposite him. "Morning."

"Good morning to you, sunshine," Daniel says with a lopsided smile. While he's made dramatic improvements over the past few months, the telltale signs of his stroke persist. Along with the crooked grin, he has a slight limp in his right leg and moments of confusion.

Ruthie, the diner's owner, appears with a pot of coffee. "This is a pleasant surprise. What brings the two of you in this morning?" she asks as she fills their mugs with steaming coffee.

"Do I need a reason to have breakfast with my beautiful daughter?" Daniel asks.

"Nope. I just thought maybe you were celebrating a birthday. Or perhaps an engagement to a certain sexy saxophone player," Ruthie says, her pale blue eyes twinkling with mischief.

Casey blushes. "My birthday is in March, and Luke is taking his sweet time in proposing."

Ruthie winks at her. "I have a hunch you won't have to wait much longer."

Daniel places a possessive hand on Ruthie's hip. "I'm looking forward to tomorrow night. Shall I pick you up around seven?"

She brushes his hand away. "I'll meet you there. We have our first annual Spring Fling from three until six. I won't be able to get away until six thirty at the earliest."

Daniel furrows his brow. "What is Spring Fling?"

"The merchants of Magnolia Avenue are hosting a street festival. We're blocking off the road and we've invited the whole town. Restaurant owners are offering samples of their food. Ada and Enzo will offer tastings at the wine shop. And the boutiques will display their goods. It should be a lot of fun. You should stop by if you get a chance."

Daniel curls up his nose. "Street festivals aren't really my thing." While he's mellowed since his stroke, Casey occasionally glimpses signs of the old snobby Daniel.

Casey's eyes travel back and forth between the two before landing on Ruthie. "What's going on tomorrow night? Did you agree to go out on a date with him?"

Ruthie rolls her eyes. "He won't leave me alone until I do. Besides, I'm dying to attend the soft opening."

Casey cuts her eyes at Daniel, who gives his head a slight shake, warning her not to rat him out.

A waitress from across the diner calls for Ruthie's attention. "Be right there," she hollers back. She removes a pencil from the bleached blonde rat's nest on top of her head. "What can I get you two?"

"I'll have the usual," Daniel says.

Casey hands Ruthie her menu. "And I'd like oatmeal with fresh berries."

She waits for Ruthie to leave before leaning across the table. "She's gonna be furious when she finds out the opening isn't until next Wednesday."

"Not when she sees the romantic dinner I have planned. Chef

Michael is preparing his favorites. I've hired a harpist to play background music. And Bruce will pour one of our new varietals."

Casey props her elbows on the table. "What're you up to, Daniel? Why the big to-do?"

"I'm asking Ruthie to marry me. This time, I picked out an engagement ring just for her," he says, referring to his previous proposal when he tried to pawn off a ring he'd bought for Casey's mother.

Casey lowers her coffee mug. "Wait. What? Since when are you two back together?"

"We're not. She's still angry with me for the fake dying stunt. But I know Ruthie. She wants to get married. Once she sees the boulder of a diamond I bought her, she'll be putty in my hands."

"You're awfully sure of yourself. She's liable to turn you down."

"She won't," Daniel says, stirring cream into his coffee.

Casey sits back on the bench. "Why did you need to see me?"

"I'm hosting a dinner on Sunday night, and I want you to come."

Casey crinkles her nose. "You invited me to breakfast to invite me to dinner? Why didn't you just text me?"

"This isn't our usual Sunday night supper, Casey. I've invited all you kids to discuss the vineyard's future. You may not like what you hear at first. But I want you to promise you'll talk to me before you make any major moves."

Goose bumps crawl across Casey's skin. "Uh-oh. Sounds like trouble to me."

"I've thought about it for months, and I've come up with a plan that I believe is best for the vineyard. Problem is, some of you might think my method unconventional."

She studies him while he talks. His hair is now snow-white like an old man, but his skin bears the golden glow from hours spent outdoors. "So, you're expecting pushback on your plan?"

He gives his head an affirmative nod. "Probably a lot of it."

"This is about Hugh," Casey says in a deadpan tone.

"This is about all of you. I realize things have been tough these past few months. But you've grown a great deal, and I'm proud of the way you've handled Hugh. Unfortunately, things will probably get worse before they get better. I'm rooting for you, Casey. I hope you'll stick it out."

"But—"

Daniel's hand shoots up. "That's all I'm saying for now. After the meeting, if you still have questions, we'll talk more in private. Now, excuse me, I need to use the restroom."

Daniel slides out of the booth, and Casey watches him make his way toward the back of the diner. He's no longer using his cane, and his limp is only slightly noticeable.

She pulls out her phone and scrolls through social media. Her pale olive eyes pop when she sees Hazel's post from last night. She's still reading through the comments when Daniel returns. She debates whether to tell him. Over five hundred people have already liked the post. That number will probably grow as the day wears on. There's no way to keep this development from him.

"You need to see this." Casey places the phone screen-side up on the table and slides it over to him.

His expression is impassive as he examines the image. "I'm not surprised, actually. This explains a lot about Charles."

Casey narrows her eyes. "Seriously? You're not upset about this? Do you understand what that picture means?" she says, jabbing her finger at the phone.

"Of course, Casey. The stroke didn't affect my brain as much as you think. It means Charles is gay. He's probably been gay all his life. I'm only sorry he felt he needed to hide his sexuality." He hands her back the phone. "Poor Hazel. I can't imagine what she must be going through. Although I can think of better ways to handle the situation than blasting the news on social media."

When Ruthie arrives with a food tray, he stops talking while she places their plates on the table in front of them. Shaking pepper on his eggs, he says, "I don't wish this on any of them. Not the men nor their wives. And Stuart has young children."

Casey cocks her head to the side. "Who are you? And what have you done with the real Daniel Love?"

He chuckles. "Near-death experiences have a way of changing people. I've had a lot of time to think these past six months while I was imprisoned in my mind with no ability to speak. I'm doing my best to make amends for my past sins," he says, sinking his fork into an egg.

Casey sprinkles brown sugar on her oatmeal. "I believe you mean that."

"With all my heart. I've been given another chance. Before I die, I want nothing more than to see my children settled. Speaking of which, has your rascal boyfriend popped the question yet?"

Casey mixes her berries into her oatmeal. "Not officially, but he keeps hinting at it."

A smirk appears on Daniel's lips. "You won't have to wait much longer."

Casey freezes, her spoon near her mouth. "What do you know about the situation?"

He shrugs. "If I knew anything, I wouldn't tell you."

"Since when are you the greatest secret keeper on the planet?" she asks, shoveling the oatmeal into her mouth.

Daniel appears wounded. "I'm telling you, Casey, I've changed. If you'll give me a chance, I'll prove it to you."

"Does *proving it* involve your plan for the vineyard's future?"

"Yes, in a roundabout way. Considering my history, I have no right to ask this of you, but I need for you to trust me about the plan. Can you do that for me, sweetheart?"

Casey considers her words before responding. "I can try. I'll give you another chance, Daniel. But you'd better not let me down again."

He places a hand over his heart. "You have my word."

His word means little to her now. But he's her father, and she can't help but love him.

CHAPTER 3
SHELDON

Sheldon stands in the kitchen doorway watching his wife nurse their newborn son. He never realized love could be so tender, so profound.

Ollie looks up with misty eyes. Breastfeeding still moves her, even after a month. For a woman who never wanted kids, she's a natural at motherhood.

She eyes his five-pocket khakis and golf polo. "You look nice. Are you going out?"

"I'm headed over to Valley View. Gray invited me for coffee. I got the impression he wants to talk about our offer." Sheldon kisses his wife's upturned face and rubs the downy hair on his son's head.

"I hope he has some good news for us. The waiting is killing me," Ollie says, moving her infant to the opposite breast.

Sheldon raises his hands to show fingers crossed. "We'll know soon enough."

He grabs his keys from the wall hook beside the open back door and steps onto the porch where jasmine-scented air greets him. The sky is a brilliant blue and the temperature is mild. He pockets his car keys. Why waste a beautiful morning when he can walk to his meeting instead of driving?

Exiting the porch, he strolls up the driveway toward the country highway.

His life has changed for the better since marrying Ollie eight months ago. Her boutique vineyard, Foxtail Farm, now feels like home. He much prefers her comfortable farmhouse with its cheerful yellow door and black shutters to his family's stone mansion with its vast rooms and memories of his unhappy childhood at the vineyard next door. He can be himself here, without the pressure to live up to his father's high standards.

Sheldon crosses the highway and continues past the black split-rail fence with dangling wooden sign identifying the property as Valley View Vineyard. Purchasing Gray's vineyard will double the size of Foxtail Farm's real estate. Their expansion plans include converting Gray's farmhouse into a welcome center, consolidating the winemaking from both vineyards at Valley View's newly updated winery, and transforming Foxtail's rustic winery building into a space for private events and tastings.

Ollie will be heartbroken if the deal falls through. But the deal is taking longer than necessary, and Sheldon has a gnawing feeling in his gut that something has gone wrong.

The trees clear and the vineyard comes into view with rows of grapevines sloping downward into the valley. His heart races as he imagines the views from the porch-wrapped farmhouse overlooking the vineyard—not only spectacular sunrises over the valley but also prime sunsets descending beyond the mountains from Ollie's tasting room cafe.

Gray, waiting on the porch with two coffees in to-go cups, hands Sheldon a coffee. "I need to stretch my legs. Do you mind if we walk?"

"Not at all." Sheldon extends an arm. "After you."

They leave the porch and head down the dirt path toward the fields. "I'm afraid I have bad news. An anonymous party has made an offer on the vineyard."

When Gray tells him the amount, Sheldon stops dead in his

tracks. "You can't be serious. That's nearly double the value of the property."

"Isn't it crazy? It doesn't make sense."

"What do you know about this anonymous person?" Sheldon has a sneaking suspicion his oldest brother, Hugh, is the interested party.

"Not much. The individual contacted Miranda directly. According to her, the person insisted on keeping their identity a secret. I don't trust Miranda, though. I wouldn't be surprised if she knows who it is. She's determined to suck every last dime out of me. Her divorce attorney is adamant we accept this offer, but I convinced them to give you and Ollie an opportunity to match it. You have two weeks." Gray claps Sheldon on the shoulder. "I'm sorry, bro. I realize it's a lot of money. If you can even come up with half the difference, I might convince Miranda to let you have it."

Sheldon's spirits sink. "But you both agreed to our offer months ago."

Gray kicks at a pebble on the path. "In hindsight, we should've drawn up an official contract, maybe even gotten a Realtor involved. I wish I could do more, but my hands are tied."

They start walking again. When they reach the fields, instead of entering the rows of grapevines, Gray turns toward the winery. "If it were up to me, I'd sell you the vineyard today. But Miranda's being a real bitch."

"I can't figure out how you two ended up together when you're so different. You're so laid back, and she's strung as tight as a guitar string."

Gray lets out a sigh. "We were twenty-four when we met at a friend's wedding. We hadn't been together long when she got pregnant. I wanted to do right by her, and I honestly thought she was the one. We ran off to Las Vegas and got married. Two weeks later she suffered a miscarriage. Truthfully, I'm not sure she was ever really pregnant."

Sheldon tucks his chin and looks at Gray over the top of his sunglass frames. "Are you saying she faked the pregnancy?"

Gray hunches a shoulder. "Maybe. I'll never know for sure. The miscarriage devastated me. We started trying again right away. I started getting suspicious when we still hadn't conceived after ten years. Then one day in June of last year, I was rummaging through the trash looking for a bill I'd misplaced when I found an empty packet of birth control pills. We had a terrible argument, and she moved out the next day."

Sheldon's heart goes out to him. "I'm really sorry, man. That's a bummer. But you're still young. You still have plenty of time to find the right woman and start a family."

"I appreciate your sincerity, but another woman is the last thing I'm looking for right now," Gray says, and they walk the rest of the way to the winery in silence.

Sheldon admires the building, remodeled to resemble the farmhouse with white siding, copper roof, and dormer windows. "You and Miranda certainly did a bang-up job on the renovations."

Gray grunts. "A simpler plan would've worked just fine. I let Miranda talk me into this extravagance. I overextended myself trying to make her happy, and now I have to sell the vineyard my family has operated for three generations."

"That's tough, Gray. I'm sorry, man."

"That's the way it goes sometimes. I'm ready for a fresh start."

"What will you do?"

"Who knows?" Gray says, holding his hands by his sides. "I'm not really qualified for much. Maybe construction work."

"Maybe Ollie and I can figure out a way for you to stay on."

Gray's face lights up. "Doing what?"

"Managing wine production. Ollie can no longer handle everything by herself. She loves being a mother more than she expected, and she wants to try for a second child as soon as the doctor clears her." Sheldon realizes his mistake as the words leave his lips.

"Good for you, you lucky dog," Gray says, tipping his cup back and draining the last of his coffee.

"I'm sorry, Gray. I didn't mean to hit a sore nerve."

"Not at all. I'm happy for you. I'm glad things are working out for you." Gray turns back toward the house. "So, do you think you can swing the additional funds?"

"It's not about the money, Gray. I have a problem with paying more than the property is worth."

"I understand. Think about it. The ball's in your court. I won't do anything until I hear from you."

When they part in front of the house, Sheldon says, "I'll talk to Ollie, and we'll get back to you soon."

Sheldon slowly retraces his steps home as he considers how to break this devastating news to Ollie.

He's surprised to find his father seated on the screen porch with the baby in his lap. Daniel looks up at Sheldon with a crooked smile. "I approve of your choice in names."

Sheldon sits down in the wicker rocker next to him. "I loved the idea of using Ollie's maiden name, but she thought Hendrix was too big a burden for a little boy to bear."

Daniel smiles over at Ollie. "I agree. Many great men were named Henry. Kissinger and Ford and several kings of England."

Sheldon watches his father coo softly to the baby. "I'm impressed, Dad. You're a natural with him."

"Remember, son, I had four children. And I would've been a good papa to Casey if her mother had given me a chance."

The baby groans and an explosion sounds from inside his diaper. The threesome laughs and Daniel quickly hands the infant over to his mother.

"Excuse us," Ollie says and takes the baby inside for a diaper change.

Daniel rests back in his chair. "I'm sorry it's taken me so long to visit. I remember all too well what it's like to have a newborn, and I wanted to give you a chance to get settled."

Sheldon chuckles. "We've had some tense moments, but things

have gone relatively smoothly for the most part. Thank you for the gifts. Ollie appreciated the flowers, and Henry will enjoy his silver rattle when he starts teething."

"You're most welcome." Daniel crosses his long legs. "I wanted to see the baby, but I had an ulterior motive in stopping by. I'm inviting you and your siblings to dinner at The Nest on Sunday night. We have family business to discuss. Otherwise, I would include your spouses and significant others."

"About the family business . . . I'm happy here with Ollie, and I've been thinking of making my leave of absence a permanent one."

Daniel stiffens. "Can you at least hear what I have to say on Sunday before making your final decision?"

Sheldon nods curtly. "I can do that. What is this meeting about anyway?"

"I'd rather not get into it now. I'll explain everything tomorrow night. If you still have questions after you hear my plan, please speak with me in private."

"Now I'm really curious. Is Ada coming?"

"I invited Ada, but she politely declined. And that's the right choice for her. She's blissfully happy running the wine shop with Enzo and working part-time at the equestrian center. I respect and support her decision."

Sheldon studies his father. He appears healthy, and he seems less tense, more at ease with himself. "Are you feeling okay? The Daniel Love I know doesn't have an empathetic bone in his body."

"Ouch! That hurts. But I guess I deserve it. I've changed son. I've left that old self behind. You're looking at the new and improved Daniel Love."

Ollie's timely return saves Sheldon from having to respond. Try as he might, a leopard can't change its spots.

Daniel cranes his neck to look at her. "Where's my grandson?"

"He was fussing, so I put him down for his nap. Can I offer either of you some coffee or sweet tea?"

Daniel slowly rises from his chair. "Thank you, my dear. But I've taken up enough of your time." He kisses Ollie's cheek. "You're radiant, Ollie. Motherhood really suits you."

Ollie's smile reaches her aqua eyes. "If I had known I would be this happy, I would never have resisted having children."

Sheldon stands and pulls Ollie in for a half hug. "You were waiting for the right baby daddy."

"That's it exactly," she says, nestling against him.

"I hope to see a lot more of my grandson. You're welcome at The Nest anytime," Daniel says, retrieving his cane from the chair's arm and crossing the porch to the door.

Daniel hasn't yet reached his car when Ollie asks, "Well? The suspense is killing me. What did Gray say?"

Ollie's expression tightens as Sheldon relates his conversation with Gray. "Do you think Hugh is the anonymous party?"

Sheldon presses his lips into a thin line. "The thought crossed my mind."

Ollie paces in circles around Sheldon. "Ugh. This is so infuriating. I want that property, Sheldon. Do you think the bank will loan us the extra money?"

"You're making me dizzy. Let's sit down." Sheldon pulls her back to the chairs. "I have the money, but paying more than the property is worth is a poor business move."

"I don't think of it as a business decision." Ollie gets up again and goes to stand at the railing, looking out over the vineyard. "I think of it as our future. God willing, we'll have many more years to work this land. We're building something special here for our children. Our new rosé is getting noticed. If it takes off like I think it will this summer, we'll make the money back in a year." She turns to face him. "Loan me the money, Sheldon. I'll pay you back with interest. I can't pass up this opportunity. Valley View is right across the road. The opportunity is ideal. We'll never get another chance like this again."

Standing, Sheldon goes to her, taking her by the arms. "We're in this together, Ollie. If you really want to counter the offer, I'll gladly put up the money. But let's not rush into anything. Dad invited me to dinner with my siblings on Sunday to discuss the vineyard. He's got something up his sleeve, and I'd like to hear what it is before we make a final decision."

"Hmm. Interesting. Any idea what that's about?"

"Knowing him, he'll try to rope me into returning to Love-Struck. Either he'll make an offer I can't refuse, or I'll be able to take my permanent leave with a clear conscience."

CHAPTER 4
HAZEL

arly Friday morning, Hazel is seated at the worktable, drinking coffee and staring off into space, when Laney barges through the back door, her arms laden with poet's laurel stems.

"I robbed my neighbor's garden," Laney says, filling a bucket with water. "We have Beverly Walker's dinner party this weekend. With twelve-foot ceilings in her dining room, the pair of arrangements for her breakfront should be massive. I figured the poet's laurel will make for great filler."

"And last forever." Hazel gets up from the table to help her boss stuff the greenery in the bucket.

Laney straightens with one hand on her lower back. "Why don't you get started on these arrangements, and I'll work the front today."

Hazel breathes a sigh of relief. "That would be great. I'm in no mood to interact with the public."

Laney gives Hazel's shoulder a gentle squeeze. "I know you have a lot on your mind, honey. I was in your shoes not so long ago, and I'm here for you when you're ready to talk."

Hazel nods as tears blur her vision. She turns away from

Laney, gathering several blocks of oasis and placing it in the sink to soak.

The morning passes in a whirlwind of activity with last-minute orders for birthday and anniversary arrangements. At lunchtime, Laney puts the Closed sign on the front door and goes next door to the diner for takeout. When she returns, she places two Styrofoam containers on the worktable and plops down on a stool. "What a morning. Seems like everyone in town was born or married this weekend."

Hazel jabs a pink peony in the arrangement she's working on. "April is a popular time for weddings. I'm surprised we don't have one this weekend."

"This is the calm before the storm. We're booked every weekend from now until Labor Day." Laney pats the seat beside her. "I got your favorite Cobb salad. Sit down and eat. You've been going hard all morning."

"Thanks, but I'm not hungry," Hazel says, clipping a stem of a green hydrangea.

"At least rest your legs for a minute. You can keep me company while I eat," Laney says, drizzling dressing on her salad.

Hazel sets down her clippers, wipes her hands on her apron, and lowers herself to the empty stool. She'll have to talk about Charles eventually. Might as well get it over with. "Did you see my Instagram post?"

"No," Laney says, jabbing at her salad with her fork. "But I've been hearing about it all morning from the customers. You really gave the gossipmongers something to talk about."

Hazel lets out a humph. "I'm sure they're thrilled to have juicy scoop about a Love family member."

"Believe it or not, only one woman made a catty remark. The others all expressed their concern for you. They say you deserve an award for sticking it to Charles with your social media post. What happened to you, Hazel, is every woman's worse nightmare."

Laney's words boost Hazel's spirits. "I acted out of rage. Not my finest moment. I don't consider myself a vengeful person, but I feel somewhat vindicated since learning Charles betrayed me for the entirety of our marriage."

Laney's slate-blue eyes go wide. "You mean, he's been carrying on with Stuart for that long?"

"Since they were in high school. Charles claims they tried to lead normal lives by getting married and having families. At least Stuart did. Charles gave up on the children part." Hazel drags a hand down her face. "Why am I having such a difficult time accepting my marriage is over when I knew it was coming?"

Laney places a hand on Hazel's arm. "You've suffered a devastating blow. Your emotions must be all over the place. At least now you know the truth about Charles. As hard as it is, you can work toward moving on with your life."

Hazel's lip quivers. "Divorce is so final. An admission of defeat. I tried so hard."

Laney wraps an arm around Hazel, pulling her in close. "You didn't fail Charles. He failed you. You have nothing to be ashamed of or to feel guilty about. You gave your marriage a hundred percent. This isn't on you. It's on him."

Hazel pushes away from Laney. "I know that deep down. It's just hard for me to accept it."

"You will. Give it some time. What can I do to help you?"

Hazel grabs a napkin and wipes her runny nose. "If possible, I'd like to rent your apartment until I figure out my life."

"That's a given. I told you last night to stay as long as you'd like. What else?"

"Have you been satisfied with your . . . um, divorce attorney?"

"Yes! Candice Wright is wonderful. I'll share her contact information with you." Laney picks up her phone, and seconds later, Hazel's phone pings with the incoming text.

"Thank you. I'll call her this afternoon."

Laney's thumbs fly across her phone's screen. "I'm sending Candice a text, asking her to be on the lookout for your call."

Hazel opens her salad container. "You're right about the

emotions. I'm overcome by a tsunami of feelings, ranging from intense anger to extreme sorrow. I'm sad to be losing my best friend. On the other hand, Charles has been so distant these past few years, I can't remember the last time we really connected."

"You deserve better, Hazel. I hope you realize that."

Hazel lifts a shoulder. "I wanted so much to have a baby. I have an immense hole in my heart that only a child can fill." She mixes her salad ingredients with her fork. "I've been thinking about adopting a baby. You're a mother. Do you think I can handle raising a child on my own?"

"Absolutely. Women do it all the time. After working with you for six months, I'm certain you can accomplish anything you set your mind to. You're organized and creative, and you tackle every task with determination."

"Thanks for your vote of confidence." Hazel stabs a slice of deviled egg. "I only wish I had my family's support. My parents are too old to help with a baby. I'm not close to them anyway. And my sister lives in Chicago. But I'm not interested in moving. Lovely is my home now."

Laney places a hand on Hazel's arm. "I don't have any family to speak of either. But we have each other. As Love divorcees, we have to stick together."

Hazel offers her a sad smile. "Your support means more than you know. Do Ella and Grace like to babysit?"

"They love it! They're both regulars for several families with young children. Not to mention, they're thrilled to finally have cousins. They can hardly wait to sit for Henry when he's a little older."

Hazel stretches her back tall with shoulders squared. "Okay then. It's now or never. If I wait any longer, I'll be too old to chase a toddler around. Do you have any clue how one goes about adopting a child?"

"No, but I'm sure we can figure it out if we put our heads together."

While they eat, they discuss the pros and cons of traditional adoption versus other alternatives such as finding a baby in another country or parenting a foster child.

"Have you given up on having your own child?" Laney asks, wiping her mouth with her napkin and closing her salad container. "You could get a sperm donor."

"Charles would never consent to me seeing a fertility specialist. Wait a second," she says her face lighting up. "What if I'm not the one with the problem? Charles could have a low sperm count, which means there's a chance I can conceive."

"Sounds to me like that's the place to start."

Hazel's smile fades. "I don't know. There are so many unwanted children in the world. What if a higher being is calling me to adopt?" She experiences the first glimmer of hope as she gathers their salad containers and takes them to the trash can. Maybe there's a reason she could never conceive. Maybe she was meant to adopt a poor child in desperate need of a home.

There's a knock at the back door, and Laney accepts a delivery from the UPS driver. "Wonder what this is," she says, placing the large box on the worktable. "Did you order something from Bud and Vase Floral Supplies?"

"Yep! I was worried they wouldn't get here in time." Hazel rips open the box and removes a tiny, square, blue glass vase. "Aren't they adorable? I ordered fifty. We can create miniature bouquets and pass them out at Spring Fling tomorrow."

Laney holds the vase up to the light, admiring the cobalt-blue glass. "Brilliant idea." She hands the vase back to Hazel. "Speaking of Spring Fling . . . Ella and Grace have a lacrosse tournament in Charlottesville tomorrow. Since we don't have a wedding this weekend, I was hoping to leave around noon to go to the game. After everything that's happened with Charles, I understand if you're not up to working the Spring Fling. I can probably find someone else to fill in for us."

Hazel dismisses her with a wave. "Don't do that. I'm grateful for the distraction. I'm dreading my first weekend alone."

Hazel plans to work Saturday and collect the rest of her

belongings from the farm on Sunday. Her days will be filled. Question is, How will she spend her evenings? There's a new movie she's been wanting to see. Is it weird for people to go to the movies alone? Maybe she'll drive over to Hope Springs where she doesn't know anyone.

Hazel spends the afternoon creating flower arrangements for weekend events, while thoughts of babies preoccupy her mind. Around four thirty, she takes a break to schedule two appointments—one with the divorce attorney and the other an adoption counselor. She's not ready to pursue the process of artificial insemination with a sperm donor just yet. She'll put that option on the back burner for now.

At closing time, Hazel drives to the grocery store and loads up her cart with food and supplies for the apartment. Charles's Land Rover is parked behind the floral shop when she returns.

He opens her door for her. "We need to talk."

She slides out of the Tesla to face him. "There's nothing left to say, Charles. Our marriage is over."

"Ours may be, but Stuart is trying to save his."

"Stuart's marriage has nothing to do with me." She grabs an armload of groceries from the back and hurries up the stairs to her apartment.

Charles follows her with two more bags. "Your Instagram post hurt a lot of people, Hazel. Not only Stuart but his wife and children as well. You need to tell people you photoshopped that image."

"I'll do no such thing," she says, snatching the bags from him and dropping them on the counter.

"Please, Hazel. I'm begging you."

Hazel studies her husband's face. Bruises underline his eyes and beads of sweat dot his forehead. "What's this really about, Charles? If I didn't know better, I'd think you were afraid of losing Stuart?" When he refuses to look her in the eyes, she says, "That's it, isn't it? You're more concerned about your gay lover than your wife of ten years. You're pathetic." Taking him by the arm, she marches him back across the living room. "Get out of my apartment. I never want to see you again. If you need to communicate with me, contact my divorce attorney, Candice Wright."

He gawks at her. "You've already hired a divorce attorney?"

"Damn right! Now leave!" She gives him a shove toward the stairs. "Before I call the police."

Charles stumbles, grabbing onto the railing. When he rights himself, he hurries down the stairs without looking back.

"Coward!" she calls after him. Hazel gives herself a pat on the back for standing up to him. For the first time in ten years, she feels like she has control of her life again.

CHAPTER 5
CASEY

Casey arrives home from work on Friday to find a picnic basket waiting by the door and Luke emerging from the kitchen, carrying a small cooler with his saxophone case slung over his shoulder.

His face lights up at the sight of her. "Good! You're here. Change clothes so we can get this show on the road."

"I can see we're having a picnic, but where are we going?" she asks, walking backward down the hall toward the master bedroom.

"You'll have to wait and see. Now hurry!" He flaps his hand as he shoos her on. "I'll put this stuff in the truck and wait for you outside."

Five minutes later, wearing faded jeans and a pink T-shirt, Casey climbs into the passenger seat of his pickup truck and they head off down his curving driveway.

"Give me a hint where we're going," she says, stuffing her feet into hiking boots.

Luke shakes his head. "No way. It's a surprise."

"Have I ever been there before?" she asks, tying her shoelaces.

"I don't think so. At least not with me. Now stop asking so

many questions," he says and turns up the volume on his country music station.

Luke turns left, away from town, and drives five miles to the overlook.

"Some surprise," Casey says with an eye roll. "I've been here with you dozens of times."

"We're not picnicking at the overlook, Casey. Come on."

They get out of the truck and unload their gear from the back. Fifty feet away from the parking area, he ducks into a wooded path, and they walk a quarter mile down the trail until the trees clear and a rocky stream comes into view. Beside the stream, a table is set with a white linen cloth and candles and a small bouquet of wildflowers.

This is it, Casey thinks. *He's finally going to officially propose.*

She drops the picnic basket beside the table. "Wow! I'm impressed, Luke. You really outdid yourself."

He grins. "I had a lot of help from Mother Nature."

Casey picks up the vase of flowers and holds them to her nose, inhaling the sweet scent of honeysuckle.

"Those are courtesy of Laney's Bouquet."

"I figured. Hazel and Laney do such a nice job." Casey returns the vase to the table. "Speaking of Hazel, I assume you heard about Charles."

"Duh. The news is all over town. In this day and age, who waits until they're thirty-eight years old to come out of the closet?"

"Someone who wishes they were straight."

"I didn't think about that. I guess we should hand it to him for trying." Luke removes a bottle of expensive Champagne and two glasses from the cooler.

"You bought the good stuff. What're we celebrating?"

"Us." He pops the cork and fills two glasses, handing one to her.

Clinking her glass to his, she says, "To us."

Luke sets his glass on the table and removes his saxophone

from its case. "I wrote a new song for you." He brings the mouth-piece to his lips and beautiful music fills the forest around them.

Luke has written plenty of songs for her. But this one is slow and smooth, more soulful than the others. By the time the song ends, her eyes are brimming with tears.

"That was lovely," she says, dragging her fingers under her eyes. "What's it called?"

"Marry me, Casey," he says, returning the saxophone to its case.

She laughs. "Is that the name of the song or a question?"

"Both." He removes a ring box from his pocket. "I'm legitimately proposing this time." He opens the ring box to reveal a stunning diamond encased in a halo of smaller diamonds.

Casey's pale olive eyes widen as she presses her hand to her mouth. "It's gorgeous, Luke."

"The diamond belonged to my mother. I had it reset for you." He places the ring box on the table. "Before I ask you to marry me, I need to tell you something about that big news I mentioned this morning."

Casey furrows her brow. "Are you imposing conditions on your proposal?"

"Something like that. Let's sit down," he says, pulling a chair out for her. Once she's seated, he removes a bag of celery sticks and a container of hummus from the picnic basket before taking the chair opposite her.

She picks up the black velvet box and examines the ring. "Can I try it on?"

"Not yet!" He snatches the box from her and snaps it shut. "I don't want to see it on your finger unless you're planning to keep it."

Her neck hairs stand to attention. "You're scaring me, Luke. What's going on?"

"I've been offered a job on the legal staff at the EPA."

Casey shakes her head, unsure she heard him correctly. "You mean the Environmental Protection Agency in Washington, DC?"

Luke's demeanor changes, and his body goes rigid. "What do you think? I'm an environmental attorney. This is my dream job, Casey. I can't turn it down."

Her stomach sours, and she slides her Champagne glass away. "Why would you look for a job in DC without talking to me first?"

"I didn't go looking for it. A recruiter approached me. I thought you'd be excited about us starting a new life in DC as a young married couple. You're a graphic designer. You can get a job anywhere."

Casey lets out a grunt. "I'm not just a graphic designer, Luke. I'm part owner in Love-Struck Vineyards."

"But I thought you wanted to get away from Daniel."

"You're the one who has a problem with Daniel. He and I may have had our differences in the past, but I'm not ready to give up on him yet. I grew up an only child of a single mother. Why would I leave my father and siblings when I just found them?"

Luke slumps as he deflates. "We can work this out, Casey. I'll commute on the weekends if I have to."

"Meanwhile, I'll be living in your parents' house alone, Monday through Friday. What happens when we have children?"

"I'll be able to work remotely some," Luke offers.

"What does *some* mean? A couple of days a month? Washington is nearly three hours away. That *commute* will get old fast."

Luke looks away from her hostile glare. "It's a career maker. After five years with the EPA, I can write my ticket anywhere."

"Your ticket to another big city. I grew up in New York, Luke. One of the many things I've realized about myself since coming to Virginia is that I'm not a city girl." Casey jumps to her feet, dumps her Champagne into the stream, and returns the vegetables and hummus to the cooler.

Luke scrambles out of his chair. "What're you doing?"

"Packing up. I wanna go home. To my condo."

He grabs her arm. "Come on, Casey. Don't be like this. Let's talk this through. I want you to be my wife. I asked you to marry me."

"Correction. You told me the name of your song. You didn't officially pop the question."

"You're being difficult, but whatever." He drops to one knee. "Will you marry me, Casey?"

Casey stares down at him. She hears fear and uncertainty in his voice, but no sincerity. Anger and sorrow collide, and she is too emotionally wrecked to respond. Jerking her arm free, she gathers up the cooler and picnic basket and storms off down the wooded path to the truck.

Luke follows a few minutes later with the folded table and chairs, his saxophone dangling from one shoulder. She fights back tears. What has she done? What if she never again hears him play his lovely instrument?

He slides into the driver's seat, and they head back toward town. "I'm sorry, Casey. I didn't realize you'd be so upset. I thought you'd be happy for me."

"Then I guess we don't know each other as well as we thought, because I have no interest in living in a city filled with crime and corrupt politicians."

"You're being melodramatic. DC has much to offer."

Casey tosses up her hands. "So now I'm being melodramatic. I'm not your puppet. I'm a real girl with genuine feelings."

He tightens his grip on the steering wheel. "I can't talk to you when you're like this."

When they reach his house, Casey gets out of the truck and marches over to her convertible. Luke catches up with her, preventing her from opening the driver's door. "Come inside with me. We'll drink some wine and have a civilized conversation."

"I'm sorry, but I need to be alone right now." Shoving him out of the way, she gets in her car and speeds off, fighting back tears during the short drive through town.

Casey hasn't been to her condo in weeks, and the air inside smells musty. She'd been beyond excited when she purchased the third-floor unit last summer. But then she'd started dating Luke and spending all her time at his vineyard. As she wanders around the rooms, she feels like a guest visiting a stranger's home. The refrigerator shelves are empty, and there's no toothbrush in the holder in the bathroom. She bought the condo with high hopes of being a young professional woman living on her own. If Luke moves to Washington, that's exactly what she'll be. All alone and starting over.

She can't be here right now. She leaves the condo and drives out to Love-Struck Vineyard. She passes through the stone columns and parks in front of the main building, which houses administrative offices on the second floor and their swanky new bistro on the first.

Casey skirts the new stone terrace with its clusters of fire pits and crosses the lawn into her father's backyard. She pauses in the rose garden to inhale the sweet fragrance of the season's new blooms before continuing on to the fly-fishing stream. A sense of calm settles over her as she leans against the railing of the old wooden footbridge.

She's grown accustomed to living with Luke, taking leisurely strolls around his property in the evenings and hearing the birds sing in the morning. Having coffee on his patio in the morning and a glass of red wine before bedtime at night.

After a rocky start, Casey's relationship with Luke has been nothing short of bliss. They hardly ever argue, and the sexual chemistry between them is spectacular. And they agree on all the important issues most couples argue about. At least until now. Luke gave no indication he was unhappy with his job. Why would he consider such a drastic move when everything was going so well?

Casey's chest tightens, and she finds it difficult to breathe. How will she survive without Luke in her life?

She hears rustling in the woods and Daniel appears with his fly-fishing rod. "Casey, what a pleasant surprise. I didn't know you were here."

Her emotions reach the surface, and she bursts into tears. "Luke asked me to marry him," she sobs.

Daniel drops his fishing gear and takes her in his arms. "I take it these aren't tears of joy. What happened? I thought you wanted him to propose."

She buries her face in his chest. "He was offered a job in DC. Sounds like he's going to accept it. He wants me to go with him."

Daniel strokes her hair until her crying fit subsides. He removes a linen handkerchief from his pocket and hands it to her. "There now. That's better. Let's go up to the house and have some of Marabella's herbal tea."

Casey mops up her tears and blows her nose. "Since when do you drink herbal tea?"

"Since my stroke. Her tea is good for whatever ails you."

"Even broken hearts?" Casey asks, helping him gather his fishing gear.

"Don't give up on Luke just yet." Daniel takes hold of her hand as they walk. "He invited me to lunch last week. He asked for your hand in marriage, but he didn't mention a move to DC."

Casey smiles to herself. At least Luke did one thing right by asking her father for her hand. Especially when he dislikes him so. "He didn't get confirmation about the job until today. I told him I don't want to leave Lovely, and I certainly don't want to live in Washington. But he didn't offer to turn down the job. He expects me to choose him over my career, yet he won't do the same for me."

Daniel squeezes her hand. "Give him some time, sweetheart. Your response probably took him by surprise. He'll come around."

"I'm not so sure about that, Dad."

Daniel gives her a quizzical look.

"What are you looking at? Do I have nose boogers?" she asks, wiping her nose again with his handkerchief.

"You just called me Dad."

She smiles. "I didn't realize it. I hope you don't mind."

"Mind? I'm overjoyed." Dropping her hand, Daniel places an arm around her waist, pulling her close.

Casey takes in the scenery as they continue up the hill to the house. She notices construction on the bungalow next door is nearing completion. Daniel was originally building the house for Casey, but when she moved to her condo in town, he talked of letting Bruce, his new winemaker, move in.

"Have you decided who will live in the new house?" she asks.

"That's one thing I want to talk to you all about on Sunday night."

They continue on to Daniel's sprawling stone mansion, known as The Nest for generations of Loves before them. Casey had lived there for several months when she first came to town. While she appreciated the luxury resort setting, her father's overbearing presence soon made her feel trapped.

They climb two sets of stone stairs, past the pool to the second-level terrace. Daniel motions her to a grouping of lounge chairs. "Wait here while I put away my gear."

Casey settles in to watch the sun set over the mountains. Daniel returns with two cups of steaming tea. He turns the gas fire pit on to warm them against the evening chill and sits down in the chair next to her.

Casey stares into the flames as she sips the tea. "Am I wrong to be upset with Luke?"

"You can't help how you feel, sweetheart. Luke threw you a curveball. Perhaps you'll see things differently in the morning."

She shakes her head. "I doubt I will. I'm happy here. I don't want to leave."

"Then you're going to have to stand your ground. I'm proud of you for choosing what's best for you."

Father and daughter sit in silence while they drink their tea. "This stuff really works." Casey rests her against the back of the chair. "Not only do I feel calmer, I can hardly hold my eyes open. I'm not sure it's safe for me to drive back to town."

"Why don't you sleep here? You can have your old room."

"I might just do that. I'd feel better knowing you are close by."
Slowly rising from her chair, she kisses the tips of her fingers and
touches them to his cheek. "I'm glad I ran into you. Thanks for
talking me off the ledge. I'll see you in the morning."

On her way through the kitchen, she puts her cup in the dishwasher before ascending the back staircase to her corner room on
the second floor.

When she moved out, she'd left some clothes here for occa-
sions like these. Changing into her pajamas, she stands at the
window, looking up at the starry sky. Even though she didn't
grow up here, this vineyard has come to mean a lot to her, and
she's not sure she can give it up. Not even for Luke.

CHAPTER 6
RUTHIE

Ruthie uses her body as a shield to protect the fresh platter of cheeseburger sliders from the town's new, sexy playboy. When Davis tries to reach behind her for a slider, she smacks his hand away. "Stop that! You've already had three. Save some for others."

Davis presses his hands together under his chin. "Please, Ruthie. Just one. Then I promise I'll go away."

Ruthie doesn't want him to go away. She enjoys flirting with him, even if he is ten years younger than she is. The new owner of the local hardware store is positively swoon worthy, with chestnut wavy hair, chiseled features and ice-blue eyes.

"Fine. You may have one more." She steps out of the way of the platter.

He grabs a slider, stuffs it into his mouth, and raises his pointer finger. "One more," he says with food in his mouth.

"Absolutely not." She grabs his arm and pulls him away from the food table. "Go mooch off some other unsuspecting merchant."

"None of them are as pretty as you." Placing a hand on her hip, he presses his body to hers. "Stop denying our attraction and have dinner with me."

"I've told you a million times, I'm old enough to be your mother."

He fingers a lock of hair off her forehead. "That would mean my mother gave birth to me at age ten. Which she obviously did not. Besides, I'm attracted to older women. How about next Wednesday night? I have tickets to Vino Bistro's grand opening."

Ruthie raises a manicured eyebrow. "But the opening is tonight."

"No. I'm pretty sure it's Wednesday." Davis tugs his wallet out of his back pocket and removes two printed tickets. "Yep. Wednesday. See?" He hands her the ticket.

She lowers her pink readers from the top of her head and scans the printed information. Sure enough, the grand opening is scheduled for Wednesday. Maybe the restaurant is having a soft opening tonight. Or maybe Daniel is up to his old tricks.

Ruthie hands him back the tickets. "Seriously, Davis. I just got out of a long-term relationship. I'm not interested in starting up with someone new." Which isn't entirely true. She's looking for a man to grow old with, someone to share her golden years. Their age difference makes Davis a poor candidate for the position.

"And I'm just the new guy in town looking for companionship. One date. No strings attached. I promise."

She's finding it increasingly more difficult to deny his infectious charm. Why not go on one date with him? Besides, the grand opening sounds like fun. "Okay. One date, no strings attached."

He fingers an X across his heart. "You have my solemn vow. By the way, a group of us are heading over to the Blue Saloon for drinks later. Care to join us?"

"I can't. I have a date," she says, busying herself with collecting empty trays from the food table.

"I'm jealous. Who's the lucky guy?"

"I never kiss and tell," Ruthie says, and saunters toward the diner with hips swaying for his benefit.

When Spring Fling ends at six, Ruthie rushes home to change into a black wrap dress before driving out to Love-Struck. While dim lights burn from inside the bistro, the parking lot is empty. Daniel must have his dates mixed up. She read somewhere that confusion following a massive stroke is normal. She's backing out of the parking space to leave when Daniel emerges from inside.

He holds up his hand to stop her and approaches the car. She rolls down the window. "Where is everyone? Isn't the opening tonight? Or is it Wednesday?"

A devilish smile tugs at the left side of his lips. "We're having our own private soft opening tonight." He opens her door and helps her out of the car. "I've arranged a special evening in your honor. We'll be the first to sample Chef Michael's tasting menu, and Bruce will pour the first bottle of our new Brut Blanc de Blancs. For your listening pleasure, a harpist will serenade us with romantic music." He offers her an elbow. "Shall we? Our table is ready on the terrace."

Ruthie inspects the new decor as they pass through the inside dining area. A white marble bar takes up the far wall, while a combination of tables with cream chairs and booths with sapphire-blue upholstered benches occupy the rest of the room.

They emerge through sliding doors to the stone terrace where the harpist is playing soft music from a remote corner. Daniel leads her to their table, which is set with linens and candles and positioned near a burning fire pit.

He pulls her chair out, and she smiles up at him as she sits down. "This is very tasteful, Daniel. You've outdone yourself."

"Casey helped a lot. She has exquisite taste," Daniel says, taking the chair opposite her.

Bruce appears with his bottle of bubbly. He greets Ruthie with a smile but says little as he fills two Champagne flutes.

Daniel waits for Bruce to leave the table before proposing a toast. "To us."

Her smile fades. "There is no us, Daniel." Instead of clinking his glass, she brings hers to her lips and sips.

Daniel appears wounded. "Of course, there's an us. We have history, Ruthie. You can't erase the ten years we spent together."

"Our relationship was one of convenience. *Your* convenience. I was the dirty little secret you kept hidden." Anger surges through her, and she extends an arm at the empty tables around them. "Apparently nothing's changed, because here we are alone in your restaurant. God forbid anyone see us together."

"You're mistaken, Ruthie. I saw this as an opportunity to wow you, to show you how much you mean to me."

"Really?" She folds her hands and rests them on the table. "Then who are you taking to the official grand opening on Wednesday?"

"I was going to ask you to be my date."

Ruthie softens. He went to a lot of trouble to impress her, and she doesn't want to spoil the evening by telling him she already has a date for Wednesday. "I'm sorry. I didn't mean to jump down your throat. Can we try to enjoy ourselves without talking about us?"

"I would like that." Daniel's gaze shifts to something behind her. "And here comes our first courses now."

Chef Michael arrives with samples of the bistro's appetizers—artichoke ravioli, peach burrata salad, and fried green tomatoes. Next up, he serves reduced portions of entrees—swordfish and duck breast and hanger steak—followed by a platter of desserts—orange sponge cake and key lime Brulé. Throughout the meal, Bruce hovers nearby, keeping their glasses filled with the vineyard's newly formulated wines.

They are both tipsy by the time they finished eating. Ruthie waves her wineglass in the air. "I deem Vino Bistro an enormous success. The food was delizioso, as are your new wines. Thank you for allowing me the honor of taking part in your soft opening," she says with a giggle and a hiccup.

"The honor was all mine." Daniel gets up from his chair and

helps Ruthie to her feet. "Neither of us should drive right now. Why don't we go sit by my pool while we sober up?"

"What time is it?" Ruthie grabs his arm to look at his watch. "How is it only nine o'clock? It feels much later. I can stay for a few minutes." She wags a finger at him. "But I'm warning you, Daniel Love, I am not spending the night with you."

"Fair enough," he says, and they start off across the lawn toward his house.

They reach the pool, kick off their shoes, and stretch out on lounge chairs, staring up at the half moon.

Ruthie lets out a contented sigh. "This is nice."

"Yes, it is. There's something I want to talk to you about. Move over," Daniel says, nudging Ruthie to make room for him on her chaise lounge.

"Uh-oh. Should I be worried?" Ruthie asks as she slides over.

"Not at all." He places an arm around her, drawing her in close to snuggle.

Ruthie has missed the feel of his body next to hers. She's missed his insatiable hunger for sex. And she's missed lounging in bed with him on rainy Sunday mornings. But she has not missed all the other lonely nights of the week and the constant worry that he was out with someone else.

Daniel kisses her forehead. "I screwed things up for us. I was a real jerk to you. But I learned a lot about myself during my illness, and I'm a different man now. I'm lucky to be alive, and I want to enjoy the rest of my days to the fullest. I can only do that with you, Ruthie." His free hand produces a black velvet ring box.

Ruthie sits up straight. "Is that what I think it is?"

"Yep." He opens the box, revealing the biggest, most sparkling diamond Ruthie has ever seen. "No more secondhand rings. I bought this one especially for you."

Ruthie jumps to her feet. "What is wrong with you? That stroke affected your brain worse than I thought. We're not even together anymore and you're proposing marriage." She strides across the deck and sits down on the edge of the pool with her feet dangling in the water.

Daniel comes to sit beside her. "I'm confused. I thought marriage is what you wanted."

"Once upon a time, I wanted nothing more than to be your wife. But I don't know what I want anymore." Ruthie has worked all her life, and she's ready for some time off. She could lead a life of wealth and privilege with Daniel. But he's seven years older, and he's suffered a massive stroke, which places him at risk for health complications in the years ahead. Ruthie yearns to travel, to see the world. Or at least the country. She can't do that if she's married to an invalid.

"Do you still have feelings for me, Ruthie?"

"My feelings for you aren't the issue." She shifts her body toward him. "The years we spent together were both the best and the worst of my life. I loved being with you. But I was miserable when we were apart. Your refusal to allow me to be a part of your life had a negative impact on me. My self-esteem is finally recovering, and I've enjoyed my freedom these past few months. I'm having fun dating around."

His mouth turns downward. "Are you serious about any of these other men?"

"All of them are a good time, but none of them are you," she says, her tone soft and genuine.

"So, there's still hope for me?"

His sincerity tugs at her heartstrings. She's never seen this vulnerable side of him. "Of course, there's hope. Somewhere down the road, maybe. Just not right now."

He runs his finger down her cheek. "Then I'll have to court you with flowers and chocolates and elaborate dinners."

"That will definitely help. As long as you understand I don't want to be exclusive."

"I understand." He closes the ring box and sets it on the pool deck beside him. "I'll keep this in a safe place for now."

Ruthie lifts her feet out of the water and stands. "I should go."

Daniel gets up with her. "Are you okay to drive?"

"Your proposal sobered me right up. Truth be told, I didn't drink that much. I mostly just sipped."

"Then I'll walk you to your car," he says, offering her his elbow.

Ruthie has a bad premonition as they walk in silence back to the parking lot. Is she making the wrong decision in turning down his proposal? Then again, after all he's put her through in the past, how can she consider marrying him when she still has so many reservations?

CHAPTER 7
HAZEL

When Spring Fling ends, Hazel migrates with a large group of merchants and locals to the Blue Saloon to hear a popular country music band. The hotspot is loud and crowded, and she immediately wishes she hadn't come. She attempts to strike up a conversation with women she knows by name but doesn't consider friends. When they ignore her to the point of rudeness, she decides to leave and starts toward the door. A hand on her shoulder stops her.

"Leaving so soon?"

Hazel turns to face an attractive man whose sexy smile warns her he's trouble. "I made a mistake in coming. This isn't my scene."

"You only just got here. You haven't given it a chance. Have you ever heard of the Lonerock Boys?"

Hazel shakes her head.

"They're amazing. You must stay for at least one set. They'll be taking the stage any minute. I'll buy you a drink while we wait."

Hazel considers her options. Letting a nice guy buy her a drink or going home to her lonely apartment. "Why not? One drink won't hurt. I'll have a white wine, please." She's not a big drinker, and even though her husband's family owns a vineyard, she knows little about wine.

"Chardonnay or pinot grigio?"

"Either is fine."

"Then we'll go with the pinot grigio. The house Chardonnay is too oaky for my tastes."

Hazel watches him worm his way to the bar. She's certain she's never seen him before. She would remember a face like his. Maybe he's a tourist.

The mystery is solved when he returns with her wine. "I've seen you at the flower shop. Are you Laney?"

"No. I'm Hazel, her assistant. And you are?"

"Davis Warren, the new owner of the hardware store."

"Right. I didn't recognize you without your tool belt," she teases.

He laughs at her corny joke, setting her at ease. Hazel takes a sip of wine and then a gulp. The wine is crisp and dry and refreshing after standing for hours in the afternoon sun.

"Your name rings a bell. Wait a minute." Davis wags a finger at her. "You're the Hazel who dropped the social media bomb on your husband this week."

Her face warms. "Unfortunately. I was hurt and angry. Not my finest hour."

"Who can blame you after making a discovery like that?"

Hazel hears loud laughter behind her. When she turns around, the women she tried to talk to earlier are all staring daggers at her. They go silent and the prettiest in the bunch—a redhead Hazel thinks is Beth Jordan—says Hazel's name in a whisper loud enough for her to hear.

The wine gives Hazel courage to confront her. "Are you talking to me?"

"I'm talking *about* you." Beth breaks free of the group and approaches Hazel. "How dare you show your face in public after what you did to Bonnie?" she says, the flecks in her green eyes flashing yellow with anger.

"I never meant to hurt Bonnie. She got caught in the crossfire."

"Hurt her? You ruined her life."

"Stuart ruined his wife's life, not me."

Beth jabs a finger at Hazel. "You butted your nose in their private business. And it's costing them their marriage."

Davis moves closer, insinuating himself between the women. "Don't you think Bonnie has a right to know her husband is gay?"

Beth looks from Hazel to Davis and back to Hazel. "Who's this? Your new lover? You didn't waste any time, did you?"

Davis glares at her. "I'm her friend, not that it's any of your business. She's going through a difficult time. Put yourself in her shoes. What would you do if you found out your husband is gay?"

Beth coughs up a laugh. "Trust me, my husband is definitely *not* gay," she says, spinning on her heels and returning to her group.

Hazel's throat tightents. "I can't believe this. Why is the whole town against me when I'm the victim?"

Davis rests a reassuring hand on her back. "I wouldn't worry too much about what those callous women think."

"Those callous women are Laney's clients. This could negatively impact the business at the flower shop."

"Those women won't let a little thing like you prevent them from buying flowers if they want them bad enough."

Hazel giggles. "That's a good point."

When they hear the band strike up on the back deck, Davis grabs refills from the bar and leads Hazel outside to a table for two. The second glass of wine goes down more smoothly, and when the band takes its first break, Hazel finds herself telling this perfect stranger about her marital problems.

He's surprisingly understanding for someone who's never been married. "Isn't it better to find out now while you still have your whole life ahead of you?" he asks.

My whole life minus my childbearing years, she thinks and excuses herself for the restroom.

When she comes back, a third glass of wine is waiting for her on the table. She can't remember ever drinking so much in one night. But she's had a tough couple of days. Where's the harm in blowing off some steam?

Returning to the stage, the band starts off their second set with "Family Tradition," one of Hazel's all-time favorite country tunes.

"I love this song!" Guzzling down some wine, Hazel pulls Davis to his feet and leads him into the crowd. He's an exceptional dancer, and for the next several songs, he swings Hazel around the dance floor. When the band slows its tempo with another of Hazel's favorites, Davis hooks an arm around her waist and draws her close. She presses her nose to his chest, inhaling his intoxicating dark scent of patchouli.

———

Hazel wakes the following morning with a pounding headache. Groaning, she brings her hand to her eyes, shielding them from the blinding sunlight streaming in through the windows. She surveys the room—the wooden floors and brick walls and mounted billfish hanging above the burgundy leather sofa where she slept. This isn't her apartment. Where is she?

Last night comes crashing back to her. The Blue Saloon and three glasses of wine. She remembers dancing to "Strawberry Wine." After that, her memory is a dark pit of nothingness. So, this is what they mean by blackout drunk?

Every muscle in her body aches as she eases into a sitting position. She may be fully clothed, but she recognizes the telltale soreness that only comes from having sex. How could she have sex with a virtual stranger? And why is she sleeping on the sofa?

Hazel slowly rises and tiptoes past the adjacent kitchen and down a hallway. She peeks through a cracked door at Davis, who is lying naked on top of the covers in a king-size bed.

Returning to the living room, she drops to her knees and crawls around on the floor until she locates her sandals beneath the sofa. She grabs her purse from the table beside the door, slips out of the apartment, and hurries down the stairs. With head lowered, she stares at the ground as she walks down Magnolia Avenue to her apartment.

Hazel takes a long hot shower, scrubbing every inch of her body, and dresses in yoga pants and a baggy sweatshirt. Wrapping the bed comforter around her, she goes to the kitchen for hot tea and curls up on the sofa. She racks her brain, but she can't remember a single blurry detail. Did she drink more than the three glasses of wine? Did they leave the Blue Saloon after the slow dance? She's never had casual sex before, never a meaningless hookup in college or a one-night stand during her young adult years before she met Charles. Did Davis take advantage of her? Or was she a willing participant? She screwed up big time. She's inexperienced when it comes to the modern world. She was raised by staunch Baptist parents, and she's remained faithful to those conservative values all of her life. Shame burns inside of her, and she jumps to her feet, throwing open the window.

What if word gets out of her indiscretion? The callous women from the Blue Saloon will gleefully spread the gossip all over town. Charles will use it against her in their divorce, and Laney will fire her in order to salvage her reputation.

Hazel walks her mug to the kitchen and returns to her bedroom, crawling into bed and pulling the covers over her head.

CHAPTER 8
SHELDON

Sheldon is the last to arrive for dinner at The Nest on Sunday evening. He parks in the circular driveway and enters the stone mansion, passing through the center hallway to the back terrace where a rectangular table is set for five. His father and Casey are engaging in conversation with their heads pressed together while Charles and Hugh huddle together on the opposite side of the terrace, silently staring out at the vineyard.

Sheldon goes to the bar cart for a glass of the vineyard's new varietal, Cherish, a delicious red blend with notes of blueberries, blackberries, and plums.

Stemless wine glass in hand, he joins his father and Casey. "Why the serious faces? Did something happen?"

"I'll tell you later," Casey says to Sheldon before turning to their father. "Please, can we get on with it now? I have some work I need to do tonight."

"Sure thing!" Daniel motions everyone to their seats at the table. He's at the head with Sheldon and Casey on one side and Hugh and Charles on the other. After a quick blessing, he gestures for the hovering server to bring their food. "As you know, tonight is Marabella's night off. I asked Chef Michael to prepare our meal. I hope you find it to your liking."

The plates feature two silver-dollar-size crab cakes, thin slices of beef tenderloin, tender asparagus, and warm cheddar muffins. Daniel typically offers several courses at his dinner parties. Sheldon views the single-plate meal as a sign his father intends this so-called meeting to be short and to the point.

Daniel forks a crab cake into his mouth, sets down his utensil, and wipes his lips. "At the end of June, I will resign as head of Love-Struck. I will announce my successor at our Fourth of July party. My dream has always been for my children to run the vineyard together. I've given you plenty of opportunity to work as a team. And you've failed."

The Love siblings erupt into loud bickering.

"Quiet!" Daniel clangs his knife against his water glass and silence settles over the table. "Thank you for proving my point."

"But, Dad . . ." Hugh objects, his face covered in perspiration. "I'm the obvious successor. Not only did I nurse you through your recovery, I've basically been running the vineyard these past six months."

Daniel's facial muscles tighten. "With a lot of help from Casey."

Hugh mops his face with his linen napkin. "But practically no help from Charles. And Sheldon has been completely MIA."

"We've all had a lot going on in our personal lives, Hugh. Including you with your divorce and legal battle. That's why we're starting over, on a level playing field." Daniel picks his fork up and returns to eating.

With fire in his eyes, Hugh says, "What exactly does that mean?"

"The clock starts ticking tomorrow morning at eight. Each of you will have until June thirtieth to prove you're the best candidate to run the vineyard."

Casey, who has barely touched her food, says, "So this is a competition."

"Exactly," Daniel says, tipping his glass of red wine at Casey. "You're applying for the prominent position as president and CEO of a prestigious vineyard."

"What happens to the losers?" Sheldon asks.

"None of you are losers, Sheldon. I will give the new head half of my shares of stock, making him or her the majority shareholder. If you so choose, the rest of you will keep your jobs and your shares and remain on the board of directors."

Hugh pushes his plate away. "This makes no sense, Dad. We're your children. You know everything about us, including our work ethics. How do you expect us to impress you?"

"Figure it out! That's what this little exercise is all about. I want to see which of you has the talent and resources to manage the vineyard in the manner I deem appropriate."

Hugh gets up from the table to get more whiskey from the bar. "Who gets to live in The Nest?"

"The head of the vineyard will live here, as has always been the case." Daniel looks over at the new house on the next lot over. "I'll be moving next door. The smaller floor plan and first-floor master bedroom are better suited for someone my age."

Hugh plops back down in his chair, slamming his drink on the table with a splash. "This is not fair, Dad. I'm the oldest child, and I've been living here since October. The Nest is rightfully mine."

"Nothing is rightfully anybody's, Hugh. You took it upon yourself to move in here after my stroke. After your wife kicked you out of your house. If I don't choose you as the new head, you'll have to move elsewhere."

Charles drops his fork and sits back in his chair with arms crossed over chest. "I don't want to play your game. I'm out."

Hugh barks out a laugh. "As in out of the closet? We know. Your wife told the entire world about your affair with Stuart."

Charles scowls at Hugh. "Then why didn't you say anything? Because you disapprove of me being gay?"

"I resent that, Charles. You know I'm not a homophobe. But

I'm not throwing you a coming out party either. It's your life. You're free to live it however you want."

Charles stands abruptly, knocking over his chair. "Damn straight I am. I don't care what any of you think. It's ironic our last name is Love, because there's no love in this family. You're all self-absorbed narcissists. And I want nothing more to do with you. Effective immediately, I'm resigning from my job."

"You weren't doing anything anyway," Hugh says, rattling the ice cubes in his glass. "Name your price, and I'll buy your shares."

"No way! My shares aren't for sale. I'll remain on the board. I need the income from the dividends."

"What will you do, son?" Daniel asks in a concerned tone.

"I have an idea for a business venture. I'll let you know if it works out." Charles rights his chair and leaves the terrace without another word.

Sheldon's heart goes out to his brother, and he's tempted to go after him. Heck, he's tempted to follow Charles's lead. He doesn't need this headache. But he promised his father he wouldn't make any rash choices without speaking to him in private first.

"One down, two to go," Hugh says with a smirk as he drains his whiskey.

Casey casts a menacing glare at him before looking over at Daniel. "I'm sorry. But I have an excruciating headache. I'm going home."

"I understand, sweetheart. A good night's sleep will do you good." When she picks up her plate to take it to the kitchen, Daniel says, "Don't worry about that. The server will get it."

Sheldon jumps to his feet, abandoning his plate. "I'm leaving too. I need to help Ollie with the baby," he says and hurries after Casey.

He catches up with her in the hallway inside. "Can you believe what just happened?"

"I can, actually. Nothing surprises me anymore." She lifts her hand to her temple. "But I can't talk about this right now. This headache is making me nauseous."

They reach the driveway and he opens her car door for her. "Are you all right, Casey? I can tell something is bothering you other than the headache."

"Just some stuff with Luke. I'll tell you about it tomorrow. Maybe I'll stop by Foxtail for coffee before work."

"That would be great. We have much to discuss." As he watches her taillights disappear down the road, Sheldon considers going back inside. He has questions for his father, but none he can ask in front of his brother. Besides, he wants to talk it over with Ollie before he does anything.

But when he arrives home, Sheldon finds both Ollie and the baby asleep in the hammock on the porch. Taking Henry from her arms, he carries him up to his nursery, changes his diaper, and puts him in the crib. When he returns to the porch, Ollie has moved to a wicker rocker and is drinking a glass of milk.

"How was dinner?" she asks.

"Strange. As predicted." When he tells her about Daniel's competition, Ollie rolls her aqua eyes.

"In other words, he's waging a war among his children."

"For once, I agree with Charles. I don't want to play Dad's game."

"So you're just gonna walk away?" Ollie says in a tone of disbelief that surprises Sheldon.

"Isn't that what you want?"

"Not necessarily." She finishes her milk and sets down the glass. "I've been thinking about this a lot lately. Our son is a Love. That land is his birthright. It's not fair to keep him from it because of my animosity toward your brother. It would definitely make things easier if Hugh were out of the picture."

Sheldon frowns. "In order to be considered for the head position, I would have to return to Love-Struck."

"I love having you working here with me." She leans across the chair's arm and rests her head on his shoulder. "But we need to think about what lies ahead. Who knows if we'll ever be able to buy Valley View? This might be our only opportunity to expand."

"So you're suggesting we merge Foxtail Farm and Love-Struck?"

Ollie straightens. "I don't know what I'm suggesting, Sheldon. I'm thinking out loud."

Sheldon strokes his scruffy chin. "I have to think about Casey."

"Of course, you do. Talk to her. I'm confident you two can develop a plan of attack. You have to be absolutely certain. Because once you walk away from your family's vineyard, you can never go back."

Sheldon settles back in his chair. His wife is right. Daniel has threatened retirement before, but something tells him his father means business this time. Hugh will destroy Love-Struck if he gets control. And Sheldon can't let that happen. He's confident Casey will put forth her best effort, but he's not sure Casey can handle Hugh on her own. She'll need a strong advocate in order to beat him at what will surely become a vicious battle. Sheldon will fight for the vineyard now and figure out where he fits into the puzzle later.

CHAPTER 9
CASEY

Casey's headache medication does the job, but she'd barely touched her dinner, and her stomach is now rumbling. An inspection of the meager contents of her refrigerator reveals only a carton of Greek yogurt and a block of moldy Manchego cheese. Takeout is her best option, but is anything open on Magnolia Avenue on Sunday night? She changes into walking shoes and ventures out.

As she strolls up the avenue, she contemplates the colossal shit show Daniel has put into motion. Charles removed himself from the situation, and Sheldon, because his allegiance is now to Ollie and Foxtail Farm, will probably do the same. Which will leave Casey to battle it out with Hugh alone. Daniel failed to establish rules of engagement, and Hugh will undoubtedly play dirty. The potential for danger is real.

Casey admires a white halter dress on a mannequin in the window at Faith's Fashions, a new women's boutique. She's imagining herself onstage at the Fourth of July party, accepting her new role as vineyard head, when she senses someone behind her.

She cranes her neck to find Luke smiling down at her.

She returns her attention to the dress. "What're you doing here?"

"Looking for you. I assumed you needed the weekend to consider my proposal." He rakes his hands through his sandy cropped hair. "It's been a long couple of days, and I couldn't wait any longer. I need to know where things stand with us."

Casey turns toward him. "I spent the three years prior to coming to Lovely nursing my dying mother. You have no idea what it's like to watch your only parent, your only relative, wither away from cancer, knowing you'll be all alone in the world when she's gone. But it turns out I'm not alone. I discovered a father and siblings and a job I love in Virginia. How can you ask me to choose between that new life and you?"

"Because you're my person. We're meant to be together. Couples make sacrifices for each other. That's part of being in a relationship."

"I have more at stake than you. Why don't you make the sacrifice and turn down the job offer?"

His silence is his answer.

"That's what I thought." Casey leaves him standing in front of the window and goes to sit down on a nearby park bench.

Seconds later, he slides onto the bench beside her. "I don't want to lose you, Casey. I'm certain we can make a long-distance relationship work."

What if she breaks up with him and Daniel appoints Hugh to take over the vineyard? As bad as things have been these past months, she doesn't think she can work for Hugh. "Everything is way more complicated now than it was when you proposed." She tells him about Daniel's competition to find a new head for the vineyard.

"Whoa," Luke says, sagging against the park bench. "I can't believe Daniel would do that to his own children. He's clearly not thinking straight. Is it possible he's having residual confusion from the stroke?"

Casey shakes her head. "Not at all. He appeared calm and confident. He knows exactly what he's doing."

Luke crosses his legs, resting one arm on the back of the bench.

"So, Charles is out. If Sheldon bails, you'll be competing against Hugh, a man with no scruples. He'll eat your lunch, Casey. And he has a head start against you."

Casey jerks her neck back to look at him. "What's that?"

"He was raised at Love-Struck. The land is in his blood."

His words strike a nerve with Casey. She's all too aware of her siblings' lifelong association with the vineyard. "If anything, Daniel's trying to get rid of Hugh. He's tolerating him, because Hugh helped him through his recovery. But Daniel doesn't approve of the way he's been handling the vineyard."

"So he says. Did you ever think maybe Daniel's trying to let you down easy?"

Casey jumps to her feet. "Whose side are you on here?"

Luke stands to face her. "Yours, of course. But you need to be aware of what you're up against. I only want what's best for you."

"Correction. You want what's best for *you*." She digs her finger into his chest. "I'm disappointed, Luke. I never knew you were so self-absorbed. Better that I'm finding out now before it's too late." She whirls around and storms off, calling over her shoulder, "Go live your life in DC. But stay the hell out of mine."

When she hears his footsteps approaching from behind, Casey increases her pace and beats him back to her building in time to lock the door on him. She takes the elevator to the third floor and collapses on her sofa, inhaling and exhaling gulps of air until her breath steadies.

But she can't shake the nagging feeling of impending doom. Does her lack of history with the family's vineyard put her at a disadvantage? Is she giving up a life with the man she loves for a chance at a job she'll never get?

———

After a restless night's sleep, Casey arrives at Foxtail Farm early to find Sheldon on the porch, feeding the baby breast milk from a bottle.

"Where's Ollie?" Casey asks, running her hand over the top of the baby's soft head.

"I insisted she sleep in. She and the baby had a rough night."

She lets out a sigh. "That makes three of us. I need some caffeine. Do you mind if I grab some coffee?"

"Not at all. Help yourself."

In the kitchen, Casey pops a Nantucket Blend K-cup in his Keurig, waits for it to brew, and adds a splash of almond milk from the fridge. Returning to the porch, she sits down in the chair next to Sheldon and blows on her coffee. "Daniel's big announcement was unsettling."

"That's putting it mildly. I thought I was done with Love-Struck. But now I'm not so sure," Sheldon says, his expression grim.

"Really? I figured you'd hightail it out of there as fast as possible."

Sheldon stares down at the baby in his arms. "My perspective on life has changed since Henry was born. If I walk away, I'll be giving up my son's birthright. On the other hand, I'm not sure I want to go back to Love-Struck. I'm the happiest I've ever been. The work I do at Foxtail is more hands-on. I enjoy being outdoors, and I certainly don't miss the family drama."

"Sounds like you've made your choice."

"Not yet. I promised Ollie I'd talk to you first. Are you prepared to duke it out with Hugh?"

"Bring it on! I'm not afraid of Hugh," Casey says with more conviction than she feels. "Luke is the problem. He finally proposed, but he wants me to move to DC with him." She tells him about Luke's new job in Washington. "Luke thinks we can make a long-distance relationship work, but I'm not so sure. He's being a real jerk. I'm thinking about taking a break."

"There's nothing wrong with clearing your head while you sort out your professional life."

"I feel selfish putting my career before Luke."

Sheldon cuts his eyes at her. "Why? He's doing the same thing to you."

"True. But that doesn't make it right." Casey stares down at her lap. "I refuse to work for Hugh if he gets the head job. I could potentially lose my career and the man I love."

"Then don't let Hugh win. Daniel will appoint you as head, and Luke will come running back with his tail between his legs when he realizes he can't live without you."

"This isn't a romance novel, Sheldon. Not everyone gets their happily ever afters."

"Maybe not, but I'm confident you will," Sheldon says with a genuine smile.

The baby makes a loud sucking noise when all the milk is gone from the bottle. "Can I hold him?"

"Sure! But he needs to burp." Sheldon drapes a cloth diaper over Casey's shoulder and shows her how to rub the baby's back until he burps.

Reclaiming his chair, Sheldon says, "You realize Dad is letting us do his dirty work?"

"By getting rid of Hugh," she says, gently patting Henry's back.

"Dad knew Charles was on his way out. And he senses I am too. He asked me not to make any major decisions without talking to him first."

"Right. He said the same thing to me." When the baby burps, Casey wipes his rosebud mouth and cradles him in her arms.

"You're a natural," Sheldon says.

Casey smiles down at the baby. "I used to babysit a lot. When the time is right, I can't wait to have children."

Sheldon hunches a shoulder. "Who knows? Maybe your children will grow up in The Nest."

"The Nest is *your* childhood home, Sheldon. Do you honestly have no aspirations of living there?"

"None. I have some happy memories from my youth. But because of my parents' tumultuous marriage, I have plenty of bad ones too. This family needs fresh blood, and you're it." Sheldon smiles softly at her. "I can totally see you at the helm. You've come into your own these past few months. You're poised and assertive and you interact well with the public."

"Thanks for your vote of confidence." A thought strikes Casey. "Hey! Why don't you and I join forces against Hugh? I would love to have you on my team."

"I'm not sure Dad would go for it, but we can certainly ask him. I'm talking to him later this morning."

"Me too. I have serval questions for him. What would that mean for your expansion plans if you came back to Love-Struck?"

"We've temporarily put those on hold," Sheldon says. "An anonymous person has offered a considerably higher price for Valley View. Ollie and I are deciding whether to counter."

Casey lets out a humph. "I'll bet a month's salary the anonymous person is Hugh."

"I'm not touching that bet." The baby fusses, and Sheldon takes him from her.

Casey stands. "I need to get to work."

Sheldon walks her to the porch door. "Why don't you come back for dinner? We can compare notes about our conversations with Dad."

"As long as I can bring takeout. I'd hate to make extra work for Ollie."

Sheldon kisses her cheek. "Don't worry about it. I'll throw something on the grill. I promise we'll keep it simple."

"Sounds good," Casey says and heads off to her car.

Sheldon calls out after her, "Watch your back today. You're in enemy territory now."

Sheldon's words ring in her ears on the drive over to Love-Struck. If anyone is in enemy territory, it's Hugh. Casey's mother kept her from her father for twenty-seven years, denying Casey her birthright. But she's as much Daniel Love's child as Hugh and Sheldon. She may not have grown up at Love-Struck, but the vineyard is now a vital part of her life. She has a right to be president. And she will fight tooth and nail to win the position.

CHAPTER 10
SHELDON

I t's late morning by the time Sheldon finishes his chores, showers, and drives over to Love-Struck. He lets himself in the front door. "Dad!" he calls out, his voice resounding throughout the vast hallway.

An apron-clad Marabella emerges from the kitchen at the end of the hall. "What're you doing here, you rascal?"

"I came to see you." Moving toward her, Sheldon engulfs her thin frame in a bear hug, swinging her around until she explodes with laughter.

"Put me down, you naughty boy," she says, smacking him on the back.

Sheldon sets her on the floor and kisses her cheek. "I miss you, Marabella."

"And I miss you, Sheldon. How's that baby?"

Warmth floods Sheldon at the thought of his son. "He's amazing. Who knew parenting could be so wonderful?"

"And it only gets better as they grow. Is your daddy expecting you?" she asks, turning back toward the kitchen.

"No." Sheldon steps in line beside her. "But his car's in the driveway. I assume he's here."

"Somewhere." Marabella waves her hand over her head, insinuating his father could be anywhere.

Of all the rooms in the house, Sheldon's fondest memories took place in the kitchen with Marabella. The French chateau theme doesn't feel outdated, even though the kitchen hasn't been renovated in decades. The lingering aromas of cinnamon and butter tempt his nose as he moves to the back door and looks out at the terrace. His father isn't in his usual place, drinking coffee and reading the paper at the small iron table.

He turns to face the kitchen. "Does Dad go to the office much these days?"

"Most afternoons. He's been taking some tennis lessons in the mornings, and he spends a lot of time walking the grounds, regaining his strength. He's also been working with a decorator to fix up his new house next door."

"Good! I'm glad he's staying busy."

"He may be upstairs if you want to check." Marabella removes a slab of bacon from the refrigerator. "But once he gets a whiff of this bacon, he'll come running. Can I fix you a BLT? You're looking kinda skinny these days."

"Thanks, but I can't stay long. I'll check Dad's room." Sheldon darts up the back stairs and down the long hallway to Daniel's room. But his father isn't there. He's retracing his steps to the stairs when, through one of the guest bedroom windows, he glimpses Hugh and a young woman in the courtyard driveway out front. He enters the bedroom and looks out the window. He only knows one woman with white-blonde corkscrew hair. Gray's wife, Miranda Wells.

Sheldon's anger flares as he watches the couple enter the adjacent wing—the children's wing where Sheldon and his siblings lived with a long stream of nannies when they were growing up.

Leaving the window, Sheldon makes his way through a secret passage and two hidden doors from the main house to the children's wing. As he nears Hugh's bedroom, he hears loud voices. "I'm not playing games, Miranda. I want that property."

"I can only do so much, Hugh. Your brother made the first offer, and Gray insists we give him a chance to counter. For once, I agree with him. It only seems fair."

"I nearly doubled Sheldon's offer. What's *fair* is for me to get Valley View Vineyard. You'd better figure something out if you want me to keep your dirty little secret."

When she speaks again, Miranda's tone is low and angry. "You better not threaten me if you want me to keep *your* dirty little secret."

Sheldon ducks into a linen closet as Miranda is storming out of Hugh's room. He cracks the closet door and watches Hugh follow on her heels. His brother's face is pasty with beads of sweat dotting his forehead, and he's gripping something in his right fist. Are Miranda and Hugh sleeping together? They didn't sound like lovers. And what dirty little secrets do they know about each other?

He waits until the coast is clear before exiting the children's wing through the back door. When he goes around the corner of the house toward the terrace, he spots his dad coming up from the pool level. "Dad! I've been looking all over for you."

Daniel reaches the top step. "Hey, son," he says, slightly out of breath. "What's up?"

"You asked me to talk to you before I made any drastic moves."

"And since you're here, I assume you're about to do something drastic. Let's take a walk. I've been lounging by the pool, reading the paper, and I need to stretch my legs."

When Daniel motions him toward the lawn, Sheldon hesitates. "Marabella is making you a BLT. Would you rather talk while you eat?"

Daniel looks toward the kitchen, as if considering it. "Lunch can wait. I'd prefer to have this conversation in private."

As they cross the yard toward the winery, Sheldon says, "You and I both know Hugh is toxic. He ruins everything for everyone. If you appoint him as president, he'll ruin the vineyard too."

"Then it's up to you to save it." They reach the Vino Bistro terrace and sit down side by side on the knee wall. "This vineyard is in your blood, son. If you care about it at all, you'll fight for it."

"I do care about Love-Struck. That's why I'm trying to figure out how best to handle the situation. I never realized how unhappy I was with my job here until I started working with Ollie at Foxtail Farm."

"Happiness isn't everything, Sheldon. Great satisfaction can be obtained by honoring one's family commitments."

Sheldon hangs his head. "I have my own family now, Dad."

"Indeed you do. But you're a smart young man. If you put your thinking cap on, I'm certain you can figure out a way to satisfy all your obligations."

Sheldon raises his gaze. "Will you let Casey and me compete as a team?"

Daniel hesitates before answering. "Sorry, son. This is an individual competition. My goal is to have the most competent person running this vineyard."

"Would I have to return to Love-Struck full-time in order to be considered?"

"You'd have to put forth your best effort, and working part-time isn't your best effort. Besides, if I were to promote you to head, I would expect you to be here full-time from now on."

"I figured as much. Even if Hugh is out of the picture, I'm not sure I can see myself ever coming back full-time. I'm invested in the success of Foxtail Farm."

Daniel shrugs. "That's your choice. But you're taking an enormous risk in letting Casey battle it out against Hugh. She's come a long way in a short time, and I have the utmost of confidence in her, but Hugh will be a fierce opponent."

"An unethical, conniving cheat," Sheldon blurts, and Daniel doesn't respond. "What if I coach Casey on the side?"

Daniel lifts a shoulder. "Where she gets advice is none of my concern. I've been telling you children how to do things all your lives. This time, I'm letting you figure it out for yourselves. You're adults now. I've educated you to the best of my ability. You have to make the choices that are right for you. I'll respect whichever paths you take, and I promise not to interfere with your choices."

Sheldon stares out across the rows of grapevines, stretching as far as his eyes can see. Can he really walk away from all this? As an adolescent, he rode his dirt bike on the trails around the property. He fished the trout stream and got laid for the first time beside the pool. In high school, he worked during the summers as a field hand, and since graduating from college, he's been involved in every aspect of management. The ties binding him to Love-Struck are tight. But the force luring him to Foxtail is stronger. "If Casey gets the job, can she designate me as her vice president?"

"That would be up to Casey. What happens after the new head takes over is also none of my concern. I'll be drinking fruity cocktails on an exotic island by then."

Sheldon casts his father a quizzical look. "You're serious about retiring this time, aren't you?"

A solemn expression comes over Daniel's face. "My stroke taught me many valuable lessons. I've dedicated my life to this vineyard. It's time for one of you to take over."

"Unfortunately, it won't be me." Sheldon slowly rises. "I'm out of the contest, Dad, but I'm not out of the picture."

Daniel places his hands over his ears. "I can't hear this." But his lopsided grin is the approval Sheldon needs. And the direction he came for.

Sheldon helps his father to his feet. "Let's get you home. Your BLT awaits you."

Daniel loops his arm through Sheldon's as they start off back across the lawn. "I always hoped you would be the one to follow in my footsteps. But your happiness is the most important thing. I'm glad you've found that with Ollie."

Sheldon leans in closer to his father. "Thanks, Dad. It really means a lot to hear you say that."

When they reach the terrace, they part ways, and Sheldon

continues around the house to the courtyard. He experiences a pang of regret as he drives away. But the moment is fleeting when he envisions Ollie at home with their infant son. Casey is the most logical candidate to be president. But it's Sheldon's responsibility to see that she outmaneuvers Hugh and not the other way around.

CHAPTER 11
CASEY

C asey is working at her desk after lunch when Luke appears in the door with two coffees from Delilah's Delights. "I brought you your favorite Chai Latte," he says, raising one cup. "I thought you might need a pick-me-up."

She leaves her desk and takes the drink from him. "That's thoughtful of you. Why aren't you at work?"

"Obviously you haven't been reading my texts."

"Sorry. I've been busy." Casey has noticed his long stream of texts cross her phone's screen over the course of the last several hours. She just chose not to read them. In her mind, there's nothing left to say.

"Can we talk for a minute?" Without waiting for her response, he crosses the room to the seating area, lowers his tall frame to the sofa, and pats the cushion beside him.

The memory of them making love on the sofa on a snowy afternoon in late January flashes before her, and she chooses to sit in a club chair instead. "I can only spare a minute. I have a busy afternoon ahead."

"Okay . . . well . . ." Leaning forward, he plants his elbows on his knees. "I turned in my resignation this morning. Because I don't have any major cases pending, the partners congratulated me and sent me on my way. The EPA is eager to have me onboard. I'm heading to DC tomorrow. My first day is Wednesday."

Pain rips across Casey's chest as her heart tears in two. "So you're going through with it. I'd hoped maybe you'd reconsider. Why are you here instead of at home packing?"

"Because I hate leaving town with things so unsettled between us."

Casey's eyes travel to the watercolor landscape she painted of the vineyard hanging above the sofa. They replicated the painting for their Viognier label. Her heart resides here now. With a jolt to her system, she realizes she yearns to be head of Love-Struck Vineyards more than anything else in the world. "Things are plenty settled. You're following your career, and I'm fighting for mine."

Luke rubs the back of his neck. "You know what I mean, Casey. Are we together or not?"

"How can we be together when you're in DC and I'm here?" Seeing how much her words pain him, she softens her tone. "I think it's best for us to take a break."

Luke presses his lips thin. "By taking a break, do you mean we should see other people?"

"You'll be free to do whatever you want. I'll be working around the clock for the next two months. I won't have time to date. Not that I would anyway. I'm not interested in anyone else."

"What happens after Daniel declares the winner of his little contest?"

"That depends on whether the winner is me. Maybe by then you will have discovered you hate city life."

"I grew up in Richmond, Casey. Washington can't be that different."

"And I grew up in New York City. Trust me, it's vastly different." She jumps out of the chair and strides over to the door, signaling that she's ready for him to leave. "I need to get my stuff from your house. I'm having dinner with Sheldon tonight, but I can stop by on my way to work in the morning."

Luke closes the distance between them. "Can we at least stay in touch?"

Casey lowers her gaze to the floor. "I'm not sure that's a good idea. I think a clean break is best for now. Goodbye, Luke."

Fighting back tears, Casey follows him out into the hallway. When he turns right, toward the exit, she goes left to Daniel's office and knocks lightly on his open door.

Daniel looks up from his computer. "Hey there, sunshine."

"Hey, Daniel. Do you have a minute?"

"For you? Anytime. Come on in," he says, waving her in.

Casey enters the office and sits down in a straight-back chair in front of his desk.

"What's up, sweetheart?"

"I have a question for you about the contest for head position."

He holds his hands out, palms up. "Let's hear it."

"Do I have early strikes against me for not having been raised on the vineyard?"

Daniel looks her straight in the eye. "None at all. As I explained last night, we are starting on a level playing field."

"Does that mean you're going to overlook all the awful things Hugh has done in the past?"

He gives her a solemn nod. "I'm going to try."

Even if he starts out with a blank slate, with Hugh's proven track record, it's only a matter of time before he screws things up. Casey sits up straight, the top of her head reaching for the ceiling. "I'm in. And just so you know, I aim to win."

Daniel gives her a thumbs-up. "Excellent. I applaud your positive attitude. How do things stand with Luke?"

Casey falls back in her chair. "We're taking a break. He's moving to Washington this week. If I'm without a job come July fourth, I may join him." She slips in this tidbit of information to make certain her father gets the message—if she doesn't get the head job, she won't be staying in Lovely.

"Regardless of the outcome, Casey, you'll still have your job."

Daniel leans forward. "And speaking of July Fourth. We need to start planning the party. I want the same as last year on steroids. I want everyone who's anyone to be here when I announce my successor."

"I'll put our new event planner on it right away. Have you met Millie?"

"Not yet. Please tell me she's better than Sonia."

Casey laughs. "Stop dissing Sonia. She works hard. She's just inexperienced. Millie, on the other hand, was head event planner for forty years at the Commonwealth Country Club in Richmond."

"How on earth did you get her?"

"I'll let her tell you." Casey flashes her phone. "If you have a minute, I'll call her in."

"Sure. Why not? We can outline our expectations for the party."

Casey thumbs off the text, and Millie responds immediately. *On my way.*

A few minutes later, Daniel's pale olive eyes grow wide when Millie Mathis enters his office and extends a hand to him. She's handsomely elegant with silver hair, high cheekbones, and almond-shaped eyes the color of the deep ocean.

With an appreciative eye, Daniel watches Millie cross her tanned, shapely legs. When Daniel and Millie launch into a conversation about friends they have in common, Casey excuses herself and leaves his office.

She spends the rest of the afternoon at her desk, mulling over concepts for a new marketing campaign and contemplating the talents and resources she can use to outshine Hugh. It's nearly seven o'clock when she gathers her things and leaves her office. At the late hour, she's surprised to see the light on in the break room down the hall. When she goes to turn it off, someone grabs her from behind, clamping a hand over her mouth and knocking her tote bag to the floor.

Hugh's breath is hot near her ear. "Make a sound, and I'll snap your neck. You're playing with fire, little girl. Walk away now, before you get burned."

Anger conquering her fear, Casey kicks him in the shin and sends an elbow jab to his ribs. When he loosens his grip on her, she grabs a pair of scissors off the table and spins around to face him. "Did you just threaten me?"

"Damn straight I did. You need to walk away from this competition before you get hurt."

She grips the scissors over her shoulder, prepared to ram them into his heart. "If you touch one hair on my head, I will go straight to Daniel."

Hugh burst into maniacal laugher. "That's right, little girl. Go run to your daddy. Being a tattletale won't score you any points."

Adrenaline pumps through her, and she gets close enough to his face to smell booze on his breath. "You're afraid he'll take my word over yours. You can threaten me all you want, but I will not back down. I'm in it to win it. Game on, Hugh."

Tossing the scissors on the table, she snatches up her tote bag and hurries from the room. With her heart pounding against her rib cage, she flees the building, gets in her car, and speeds off. On the drive to Foxtail Farm, the adrenalin fades and fear sets in. By the time she arrives, her body is shivering uncontrollably.

She spots Sheldon at the grill in the backyard and rushes over to him. "I can't do this. I'm in over my head."

Sheldon wraps his arms around her, holding her tight. "Good grief, Casey. You're shaking all over. What happened?"

She pushes him away, inhaling deep gulps of air until she calms down enough to relate her encounter with Hugh.

Sheldon tenses, his fists balled at his sides. "That rotten bastard. I'm gonna kick his—"

"Sheldon! No!" Casey grabs him by the arm. "That won't help anything. Besides, I shocked him by standing up to him. But he's right about one thing. Being a tattletale won't earn me any points with Daniel. He's looking for someone who can handle the stress of running the vineyard. Someone who can stand on her own two feet, not run to him every time there's a problem."

Sheldon lets out a sigh. "You might not have any choice, Casey. Hugh is dangerous. You saw what he did to Laney's face."

Casey grimaces, remembering the beating Hugh gave his wife when she tried to leave him. "That was horrible. Whatever happened to those assault charges anyway?"

"I don't know. But I intend to find out." Sheldon opens the grill and begins brushing the grates with a wire brush. "I have a hunch Hugh is dealing with some underhanded stuff," he says, and then tells Casey about the conversation he'd overheard earlier between Hugh and Miranda at The Nest.

Casey slumps against the wooden fence. "So Hugh and Miranda are friends, which means Hugh is likely the anonymous party who made an offer on Valley View."

"I'm out of the contest. My primary focus right now is taking ownership of Valley View. When I spoke to Dad today, he refused to let you and me partner up. However, he didn't disagree with me coaching you behind the scenes." Sheldon turns the grill on to preheat and lowers the lid. "While he would never admit it, I honestly believe Dad wants Hugh gone. All you have to do is toe the line, and you're a shoo-in for the job."

Casey sighs. "It's gonna take a lot more than that. I have a few tricks up my sleeve, though. I plan to wow Daniel with my new publicity campaign."

"I have a trick or two up my sleeve as well. Getting dirt on Hugh is at the top of the list," Sheldon says with a devilish grin.

She smacks his arm. "You're enjoying this."

"Hugh has hurt a lot of people over the years. He deserves what's coming to him."

"Promise me no one will get hurt, Sheldon."

"As long as you promise me you'll tell Dad if Hugh threatens you again."

"Deal." She holds out her hand, and they shake on it. "If I were to win the position, do you see yourself playing a major role at Love-Struck in the future? The vineyard would benefit from your experience."

Sheldon places a hand on top of her head. "One step at a time, little sister. Let's get you promoted first. Then we'll talk. A lot depends on what happens with Valley View."

Ollie, the baby nestled in the crook of one arm, emerges from the house with a covered casserole dish in the opposite hand. "Hey there, Casey. I didn't know you'd arrived."

Taking the dish from her, Sheldon forks the pork tenderloins onto the grill. And while the meat cooks, the three of them devise a plan to attack Hugh on multiple fronts.

CHAPTER 12
HAZEL

Hazel stays in constant motion to avoid thinking about Davis. There's always plenty to do at work to keep her mind occupied. During her free time, she practices yoga, walks endless miles around town, and deep cleans the apartment from top to bottom. The nights are the most difficult, long sleepless hours plagued by visions of things she might have done with Davis on Saturday night. She yearns to pretend nothing happened. But the fingertip size purple bruises on her butt cheeks and hips are a constant reminder something did.

She thinks a lot about Charles. She's only lived with her shameful secret for a few days. He's spent his life hiding his. How difficult it must have been for him to desire a normal life with a wife and children with his body constantly betraying him.

Hazel isn't the only one out of sorts. Laney has been ill-tempered all week, vacillating between uncharacteristic snippiness and brooding silence. On Wednesday afternoon, Laney and Hazel are creating arrangements for the Vino Bistro opening when Hazel broaches the subject. "I can tell something's bothering you. Anything you want to talk about?"

Laney snips a hydrangea stem at an angle and jams it into the oasis. "It's Hugh. He's three months behind on mortgage payments, and I haven't seen a dime from him for child support."

Hazel looks up from her work. "Can't the judge make him pay?"

"Not if he doesn't have the money. He claims he overextended himself by hiring high-powered attorneys to represent him for the assault charges." She drops her clippers on the table. "He got what he paid for, I guess. Those attorneys kept him out of prison. It infuriates me that we're legally separated, and he's still controlling my life."

"I'm sorry, Laney. Will you have to sell the house?"

"Yes! And I'll be glad to get rid of it, honestly. There are too many terrible memories of Hugh in that house. Besides, selling it will make me financially independent. Which has always been my goal."

"If you need to move into the apartment, I can find somewhere else to live."

"I can't ask you to do that. Besides, I already have a solution." Laney spins the lazy Susan, inspecting her creation one last time. "A young couple down the street from me is looking for a bigger house for their expanding family. Their home is half the size of mine, but it has a small pool."

Hazel smiles. "A house swap! How convenient."

"Isn't it? The girls are thrilled about the pool. We're negotiating the deal. Fingers crossed," Laney says as she rakes discarded stems and leaves from her workstation into the trash can. "What about you? How are you holding up?"

Hazel's lips turn downward. "I'm hanging in there, taking it one day at a time."

Laney retrieves the completed arrangements from the cooler and places them on the table. "That's all you *can* do. Then you'll wake up one morning, and your future will seem brighter."

"You're lucky. You have your girls and a boyfriend and your business. I have nothing to add to my pro column."

"You will." Laney stops what she's doing and takes Hazel by

the shoulders. "You've put your life on hold for years, waiting to have children. You have much to offer the world. You'll discover your passion in time."

Hazel swallows past the lump in her throat. "I don't have much *time* left. I'm already thirty-eight years old."

"Stop!" Laney says, shaking her a little. "Plenty of women reinvent themselves at our age. Be open to trying new things. You'll know it when you find it. If I can do it, so can you."

Hazel feels overwhelmed by all the changes in her life. "I wish I had your optimism."

Laney places a soft hand on her cheek. "Give yourself a break, Hazel. It's only been a few days. Selfishly, I want you to continue working here, but I don't blame you for wanting to move on to bigger and better things. I'll even help you. With your many talents, you'll find that thing that fuels your fire."

Sucking in an unsteady breath, Hazel throws her shoulders back and holds her head high. "You're right. From now on, I'm going to explore all my options."

"Thatta girl." Laney drops her hand from Hazel's cheek. "Now. We'd better get these flowers over to Love-Struck."

They load up the back of Laney's suburban, lock up the shop for the day, and head out of town. On the drive over, Laney says, "Say a prayer we get the Vino Bistro account."

Hazel presses her hands together in prayer. "What would that entail?"

With eyes on the road, Laney explains, "Single stems for dining tables twice a week and a large arrangement for the entrance area. I count my blessings every day that the Love-Struck event planners haven't cut me from their supplier list."

"Why would they? You're the most talented floral arranger in town. Not to mention you're professional and reliable and the brides all love you."

"And I'm Hugh's soon-to-be ex-wife. He could insist they cut me off. I'll go bankrupt without the vineyard's wedding business."

"You should branch out. Having all your eggs in one basket is risky." Hazel pauses a beat. "There are plenty of potential clients in town we could solicit."

"We're stretched thin as it is. You and I can barely manage the business we already have." Laney turns off the highway and passes between the vineyard's stone columns. "But you might be right. I've been thinking of hiring a part-time assistant anyway. To keep the shop open on Saturdays while we're preparing for weddings."

"That makes sense. I doubt it would be that hard to find someone."

They arrive at the bistro to find Casey scurrying about, attending to last-minute details before the event.

"These are amazing," Casey says when she sees the arrangements. "This was supposed to be a small affair, but it's turned into a huge event. And I can't complain. I'm thrilled the locals are so enthusiastic about the bistro. I hope you two are planning to attend."

Laney's cheeks pinken. "You're sweet, but I'm not sure we'd be welcome."

"Of course, you're welcome. I'm inviting you." Casey pulls them out of the stream of traffic of workers hustling about. "Divorced or not, you are still members of this family. Maybe I'm naïve, but I think we can all get along if we try. Besides, it would mean a lot to Daniel if you came."

Laney's brow shoots up. "I sincerely doubt that. Daniel doesn't give two red cents about us." She glances at Hazel. "At least not about me."

"That's not true." Casey says. "Daniel's changed. His stroke, a near-death experience, has enabled him to see his life from a different perspective. He just wants everyone to be happy. What do you say? There will be plenty of food and wine."

"I'm sure the girls will have homework." Laney shoulder-bumps Hazel. "What do you think? Should we come for a little while?"

Hazel shrugs. "Why not?" She has nothing better to do than hang out in her apartment with empty memories from her night with Davis.

"Thank you both! This really means a lot to me." Casey starts off and turns back around. "By the way, Laney, can we talk about a permanent arrangement? I'd like you to provide biweekly bouquets for the bistro, tasting room, and winery. Flowers add a soft touch. I want our guests to feel welcome."

Laney beams. "Absolutely! I'll call you tomorrow, and we'll work out the details."

Hazel leans into her. "See! I knew you'd get the account." She's genuinely happy for her friend. How cool would it be to run her own business?

———

Hazel flips through the tired hanging clothes in her closet. She regrets accepting Casey's invitation to the opening. Exhausted from sleepless nights, she longs to order a pizza and watch a movie. But remembering what Laney said about trying new things, she puts on her favorite navy linen dress, styles her honey-colored hair in a loose updo, and touches up her makeup.

Why not? She thinks as she smears clear gloss on her lips. *Beats staying at home alone with my demons.*

Ten minutes later, she's waiting in the alley behind the building when Laney swings by to pick her up. Hazel studies Laney on the drive over. She appears much younger than her forty years, with layered auburn locks sweeping her shoulders and a splattering of freckles across her nose. Laney, aside from being stressed about her finances, seems happy with her new life. Hazel hopes she, too, will be in a better place in six months' time.

Casey, stunning in a coral jumpsuit that clings to her slim figure, is the first to greet them when they arrive. "I'm so glad you came! There is food everywhere." She sweeps an arm at the banquet tables set up on the terrace. "Appetizer stations and samples of our entrees and desserts. And Bruce is pouring our new Brut Blanc de Blancs. You must try it. I can't wait to hear what you think."

Laney's blue eyes travel the terrace, her expression softening when she finds Bruce. Is it possible Hazel will one day find love again?

Casey excuses herself to check on something in the kitchen. She's no sooner disappeared inside when Daniel approaches them, embracing each of his daughters-in-law. Hazel hasn't seen him since the stroke. She didn't expect him to look so tan and fit. Instead of aging him, his snow-white hair makes him appear more distinguished.

"It's wonderful to see you both. I feel sorry for Hugh and Charles. They are losing their better halves. I will always consider you two part of the family. You're welcome at Love-Struck anytime."

Laney mutters a thank you, but Hazel, unable to speak past the lump in her throat, merely nods.

"Enjoy your evening," Daniel says, turning away from them.

Laney and Hazel stare at his retreating back with mouths agape. "Did I hear him correctly?" Hazel asks when she recovers her voice.

Laney nods. "I've never known Daniel Love to say such kind words. The stroke must have positively affected the part of his brain that experiences emotion." She lowers her voice. "Do you see Hugh anywhere?"

Hazel scans the crowd. "Not on the terrace. Maybe he's inside."

"With any luck, he won't show up at all. I'm going to get some wine. Do you want some?"

"I'm fine, thanks."

When Laney leaves, Hazel makes her way to the edge of the terrace. While she recognizes several faces, she doesn't know any of the people well enough to strike up a conversation. When she notices Charles in the crowd, she looks around for somewhere to hide. But it's too late. He's seen her and is already heading her way.

"It's great to see you, Hazel. I'm glad you came," he says, kissing her cheek.

Hazel offers him a tentative smile. "Casey invited Laney and me. You guys have really outdone yourselves. The bistro is amazing."

Charles hangs his head. "I can't take any credit. I don't work here anymore. I resigned."

Hazel's blue eyes go wide. "What? Why?"

"Dad is appointing one of us his successor. He's having a competition to determine the best fit for the job. Since I don't stand a chance, I bowed out gracefully." He relaxes as the tension leaves his body. "I'm fine with it, honestly. I wasn't happy here. I only stayed because I felt obligated to Dad. He made the decision easy when he announced he's only promoting one of us."

"That's a bold move, Charles. What are you doing now?"

"Trying to find myself. At age thirty-eight, it's about time, don't you think?" He smiles softly at her. "I wish I had my best friend to help me."

His best friend? Does he mean her? For the second time tonight, she's rendered speechless.

"I'm talking about you, Hazel," he says with a twinkle in his pale olive eyes she hasn't seen in years. "I miss our friendship."

"But what about Stuart?"

"Stuart has chosen to stay with his family. They are moving to Nashville for a fresh start. My relationship with Stuart was volatile. We were never friends. Not like you and I are friends."

In a soft voice, Hazel says, "I miss our friendship too, Charles."

"Will you have lunch with me tomorrow? I'm considering a business venture, and I would value your opinion."

Hazel experiences a flutter of hope in her chest. Is it possible their friendship will survive the divorce? "I'll be swamped at work for the next few days with several parties in town and a wedding here on Saturday. How about Sunday?"

"Sunday would be even better. I have something I'd like to show you after lunch. I'll text you the time and place."

"Sounds good," Hazel says, relieved she now has plans for her long day off on Sunday.

An awkward silence settles over them, and Hazel excuses herself to use the restroom. When she emerges from the bathroom, Davis is waiting for her.

"Hey there, gorgeous." He props himself against the wall, preventing her from going past him. "I had a good time with you on Saturday night. Maybe we can do it again later." He thumbs her chin. "After the party."

"Don't touch me," she says, swatting his hand away. "I rarely drink, and I had three glasses of wine that night. I remember nothing after we left the Blue Saloon."

Davis pushes himself off the wall. "Really? That's a shame, because you seemed to enjoy yourself."

Hazel's face burns. "I'm not the kind of girl who sleeps around, Davis. I'd appreciate it if you'd keep this between us," she says and hurries away.

Tears blur her vision, and she stares at the ground as she returns to the terrace. She's not watching where she's going when she collides with Sheldon. He takes her by the arms to steady her. Noticing her wet eyes, he pulls her to his chest. "There now. Don't cry."

"I'm fine." She pushes away from him to find Ollie watching her. The sight of the baby in her arms brings on more tears. "I'm sorry. I'm not myself tonight."

Ollie places her free hand on Hazel's shoulder. "Of course, you're not. You're going through a tough time right now. Let's sit down while you pull yourself together."

Sheldon hands Hazel a red bandana, and she presses it to her eyes as he leads her to a grouping of vacant chairs.

"Do you wanna talk about it?" Ollie asks.

Hazel spots Davis standing close to Ruthie with a possessive hand on the small of her back. What a sleazeball. They're clearly here together, yet he was hitting on Hazel seconds ago outside the bathroom. She'd let her guard down on Saturday night by allowing herself to be attracted to his good looks and charm. But that mistake in her most vulnerable moment is not the end of the world.

Hazel shifts her gaze back to Ollie. "I'm okay. Really. I just had a weak moment." She looks down at the baby. "He's beautiful. I'm sorry I haven't been to visit him. Charles said we shouldn't disturb you. Can I hold him?"

"Of course," Ollie says, and gently places the sleeping baby in her arms.

Hazel lets out a contented sigh as she settles back in her chair. "How do you get anything done?"

Ollie laughs. "It's not easy. All I want to do is sit and hold him. Do you mind if I grab a plate of food real quick?"

Hazel gives her a dreamy smile. "By all means. Take your time. Take all night."

Ollie chuckles and Sheldon asks, "Can we get you anything?"

"No thanks. I'll wait until after you two eat."

When Ollie and Sheldon leave for the food tables, Hazel brings the baby's downy head to her nose, breathing in his sweet scent. He's so peaceful, so innocent, so pure. She's not a worldly woman, has never been ambitious. Since the time she was a little girl, all she's ever wanted is to be a mother. Laney's wrong. She doesn't need to reinvent herself. Her maternal instincts are the most fundamental part of her. She knows exactly what she wants from life. She'll get a baby. Or die trying.

CHAPTER 13
RUTHIE

R uthie feels like a clown in her frilly pink cocktail dress and silver Christian Louboutin sandals when the other women at the grand opening are wearing drab colors—mostly black and gray. Her dress may be a little summery for late April, but she feels more feminine wearing brighter hues. At least her attire doesn't appear to bother Davis. In stone-colored trousers and a navy linen blazer, he fits right in with the other gentlemen guests. His open-collared shirt, offering a glimpse of exposed bare chest, and his woodsy cologne make her swoon.

Davis's fingers graze her bare arm. "Excuse me a minute. I need to use the restroom. Can I get you something to drink?"

"Sure! I'll have whatever Bruce is pouring."

Confusion crosses Davis's face. "Who is Bruce?"

Ruthie dips her head at the auburn-haired man at the wine tasting table. "He's the head winemaker here."

"In that case, I'll be back in a few."

Ruthie watches him stroll toward the bistro, his broad shoulders and gently swaying hips ever so sexy. He is a fine specimen of a man. Such a shame he's way too young for her. At their age, ten years makes a big difference. Parts of Ruthie's body are drooping, and the lines etched in her face grow deeper every year.

Davis, on the other hand, is in his prime. Men, like good red wine, age well with time.

Oh well. The boy toy may not be a candidate for old-age partner, but where's the harm in a little innocent hanky-panky?

Ruthie scrutinizes the crowd. Over near the food tables, she spots Daniel deep in conversation with an attractive silver-headed lady. Even from the distance, Ruthie detects an air of old money and proper breeding about the woman. She's just Daniel's type. Unlike Ruthie, she will fit right into his social circles.

Ruthie grabs hold of Casey's arm as she passes by. "Girlfriend, you look amazing. You rock that jumpsuit."

Casey blushes. "You don't think it's too much?"

"Not at all. You're the most stylish woman here."

"Hardly. I'm afraid you have that honor. Are you here on a date?"

"A casual date. I'm here with Davis Warren, the new owner of Country Craftsman Hardware. He's the attractive man in the navy blazer over by the tasting bar."

Casey follows her gaze. "Whoa. He's a hottie. But what's going on between you and Daniel? I thought you two were back together. Didn't he—"

"Ask me to marry him? Yes, but I turned him down. It's too soon after everything that happened between us. I agreed to date him again, though. Unfortunately, it looks like he's found someone new."

Casey finds Daniel in the crowd. "That's Millie Mathis. She's not his date. She's our new event planner. Be sure to introduce yourself. Excuse me. I need to check on something inside."

Casey's abrupt exit confirms Ruthie's suspicions. Daniel *is* interested in Millie Mathis.

Ruthie wanders over to the appetizer table and loads up a plate with one of everything. She feels someone's breath on her neck and hears Davis's voice near her ear. "Are you gonna share some of that with me?"

When she turns to face him, he offers her a glass of sparkling wine. "Of course. Let's find somewhere to sit down."

They wander around a few minutes before snagging two wicker lounge chairs near the stone fireplace. "This place has a killer vibe," Davis says, snatching a fried pimento cheese bite off her plate. "I keep hearing mention of Daniel Love, the vineyard's owner. Which one is he?"

"The white-headed man standing at the bar with a glass of red wine," Ruthie says, relieved to see Daniel is no longer with the event planner.

"Do you know everyone in town?" Davis asks.

"Pretty much. Everyone eventually makes their way into my diner, some more often than others." Ruthie places the plate of appetizers on the armchair between them, and while they eat, she points out the town's most intriguing personalities.

"Who's the dame with the dark hair and legs for days?" Davis asks, his eyes on an attractive young couple emerging from the bistro.

"That's Ada Love and her new husband, Enzo. Ada is Daniel's daughter—correction. He raised her as his daughter," Ruthie says, aiming a pink lacquered nail at the evening sky. "But he recently found out she's not his biological child."

"Sounds like a scandal. Tell me more," Davis says with mischief on his lips.

"Well . . ." Ruthie settles back in her chair with legs crossed, revealing a shapely thigh. "Years ago, Daniel and his wife, Lila, were having marital problems, and agreed to take a break. Daniel flew off to Napa to spend the summer researching winemaking techniques. While he was gone, his wife had a fling with his best friend and got pregnant. The timing of Daniel's return enabled her to pretend the baby was his."

Ruthie shifts in her chair, her dress hiking even farther up her thigh. "Meanwhile, out in California, Daniel was having an affair with a big-time network's morning news anchor. She, too, became pregnant and kept the baby from Daniel until her death last spring. When Casey learned about her father, she came to Lovely looking for him. She's the attractive blonde in the coral, standing in the bistro doorway."

Davis's blue eyes seek Casey, and an appreciative smile appears on his lips. "She's a knockout."

Ruthie nods. "She's as sweet as she is pretty."

"Lovely sounds like the modern day Peyton Place."

"We have our share of drama for sure," Ruthie says as she sips her wine.

A loud and obnoxiously drunk Hugh gets their attention when he demands a drink from the bartender at the outdoor bar.

"I've met Hugh before," Davis says. "Who's the babe with him? I'm digging those crazy blonde curls."

"That's Miranda Wells, recently separated from her husband, Gray, who owns Valley View Vineyard down the road. Those two deserve each other."

"How so?"

Ruthie rolls her eyes. "Don't get me started." She places the empty appetizer plate on the coffee table and leans in closer to him. "You don't strike me as the do-it-yourself kind of guy. How did you end up in the hardware business?"

Davis crosses his legs, settling back in his chair. "I've always loved building things. Legos and wooden log cabins as a little boy and then furniture as I grew older. I studied architecture in college and worked for a commercial firm in Atlanta for twenty years. But my work grew stale, and I grew tired of the crime in the city. A friend, who came to Lovely for a wedding a few months ago, told me about the hardware store being for sale. I drove up for a visit and fell in love with the town and the business. If you've ever shopped there, you know Country Craftsman is not your typical hardware store."

Ruthie arches a brow. "Have I ever shopped there? Only all my life. I used to go in at least once a week with my father. He was the original DIY guy."

"Does that make you a DIY gal?" he asks, a smirk tugging at his lips.

Ruthie laughs. "I've done my share of home improvement projects."

"I find a tool-belt-wearing woman sexy." Davis looks past her, his eyes widening. "Wow! Check out that sunset. Why don't I grab us some refills and we can get away from this crowd to watch it?"

Jumping to his feet, he takes her empty glass and returns a minute later with fresh drinks. Taking her by the hand, he leads her to the edge of the terrace where they sit down on the knee wall to wait out the sunset.

"Did you ever marry?" Ruthie asks, sipping her bubbly.

"Nope," Davis says with a vehement shake of his head. "I never found the right girl, never really felt inclined to have a family. What about you? Do you have children?"

"No, but I wish I did. I married too young, to the wrong man. By the time I got the courage to leave him, my child-bearing years were over. I'm grateful to have the diner to keep me busy. It's all I've ever known. I've worked there since I was a child and inherited it when my parents passed away."

"Do you ever plan on retiring?"

"Actually, I've been thinking about that a lot lately. I'd like to enjoy my life while I still have my health. I don't plan to officially put the diner on the market anytime soon, but if the right situation comes along, I'll consider it."

They finish their drinks in silence as the sun descends below the horizon. When they stand and turn back toward the terrace, the other guests are bathed in soft lighting. "I see someone I should speak to," Davis says. "Will you excuse me for a minute?"

"Of course. I'll wait here," Ruthie says, once again lowering herself to the knee wall.

She's no sooner sat back down when Daniel appears. "I'm surprised at you, Ruthie. Robbing the cradle is beneath you."

"For your information, he's not that much younger than me. This may come as a surprise to you, Daniel, but other men find me attractive."

"Why would I be surprised? You have a lot to offer. You're beautiful, fun to hang out with, and smoking hot in bed. When you find the right guy, he'll be mighty lucky to have you."

The right guy? Has Daniel taken himself out of the running? What happened to him courting her with flowers and chocolates and elaborate dinners? What I am thinking? Millie, the event planner, happened.

"Anyway, I met some people I think you should know." He flags down an attractive middle-aged couple who are all smiles as they make their way toward them.

Daniel holds his hand out to them. "Ruthie, meet Mark and Marjorie McKinney. They just moved here from Philadelphia and are looking to buy a business. They've owned restaurants in the past, and since you've mentioned the possibility of selling the diner, I thought the three of you should talk."

"What kind of restaurant did you own?" Ruthie asks, toying with her fake strand of pearls.

"Most recently, a gourmet Philly cheesesteak joint," Mark says.

"But before that, when we lived in New York, we owned a diner," Marjorie adds.

Ruthie considers her response. *How ironic that I was just talking about this with Davis. Is this the right situation? Maybe I should hear them out.* "I'm open to having a conversation, but the diner isn't officially on the market."

"We understand," Marjorie says. "We're getting ahead of ourselves. Your place may not be suitable for our needs. We're still getting settled in our new house. How about if we stop by the diner one day next week for a tour?"

Ruthie smiles. "That would be fine."

"We'll call before we come," Mark says, as he and his wife walk away.

"They seem like nice, hard-working people. I hope it works out for you," Daniel says, before turning and leaving her alone at the edge of the terrace.

Ruthie goes in search of Davis. She finds him at the bar, flirting with a striking blonde young enough to be his daughter. She tugs on his coat sleeve. "Are you ready to go? I have an early morning tomorrow."

"Sure thing! I was just getting ready to come find you." If Davis is irritated at being interrupted, he doesn't let it show. Nothing seems to bother him. Ruthie isn't sure if that's a good thing or not.

On the way home, Davis chatters on about how fortunate the Love family is to own a spectacular property like Love-Struck. Ruthie agrees with him. As long as she can remember, she's dreamed of living on the vineyard as Daniel's wife. And she could've had that if she'd accepted his proposal. But he hurt her deeply, and she wanted to teach him a lesson. She gambled and lost. Now Millie Mathis, or a woman like her, will be the mistress of The Nest.

Davis parks in front of her pink house and puts the car in gear. "Can I come in for a nightcap?"

Ruthie hesitates. She enjoys his company more than she cares to admit. "As much as I would like to say yes, I'm not ready for what might happen after the nightcap."

"I respect that." Leaning across the console, he presses his lips against hers.

The bottom falls out of Ruthie's stomach. "Can I take a rain check?" she asks, her breath a whisper against his lips.

"You bet." He pulls her closer, his tongue finding hers. When the kiss ends, he rubs his nose against hers. "Is Friday night too soon?"

"Friday is perfect. I'll cook dinner for you, and we'll dine on my porch."

"That sounds nice. I'll bring the wine."

Ruthie gets out of the car and strolls up the sidewalk. As she locks up the house for the night, she contemplates what she'll cook for dinner and what she'll wear to seduce him into her bed. Davis might be just the man to help her forget about Daniel Love.

CHAPTER 14
SHELDON

L ate Friday morning, Sheldon strolls, with coffee in hand, across the road to Valley View Vineyard. He waits on the farmhouse porch while Gray finishes giving a tour of the winery.

"Can you spare a minute to talk?" Sheldon asks after the last guest has left.

"Sure! Let's go inside to my office."

Sheldon follows Gray through the house to a glass room that is handsomely decorated with a black lacquered desk, a worn oriental rug covering the brick floor, and a comfortable sitting area.

A set of sliding doors offers a sweeping view of the vineyard, and immediately attracts Sheldon. "This room is seriously cool, bro."

"Thanks. My grandmother was a musician and music teacher. She played and taught piano, violin, and the flute. My grandfather had this conservatory built for her, which is where she taught her students."

Sheldon imagines Ollie working here. Once they hire a nanny, she'll be able to get away for several hours at a stretch.

Gray gestures at Sheldon's cup. "Can I get you a refill on coffee?"

"I'm good. But thanks."

They sit down in comfortable chairs opposite each other. "Ollie and I would like to match the anonymous party's offer. I asked a Realtor friend to draw up a contract to include an escalation clause not to exceed a hundred thousand more than my price." Sheldon removes the folded contract from his back pocket and hands it to Gray.

Gray scans the contract. "This is great. I haven't received a formal contract from the other buyer. As far as I'm aware, he has not included an escalation clause in his offer."

"I'm almost positive Hugh is your anonymous buyer. I'm pretty sure he's up to something underhanded, and I'm afraid he's dragging Miranda down the dark alley with him."

Gray stiffens. "Miranda is usually the instigator, not the one being dragged. What makes you think they're up to something?"

"I overheard them talking the other day in Hugh's bedroom at The Nest." Sheldon tells him about eavesdropping on Hugh and Miranda's conversation and the mention of their dirty little secrets. "It sounded to me like they were blackmailing each other."

Gray furrows his brow. "Wonder if they are blackmailing each other with the same dirt. Do you think they're sleeping together?"

"That's a good question. The way they were talking in Hugh's room, they didn't sound like lovers. But they were drunk and all over each other at the Vino Bistro opening last night." Sheldon drums his fingers on the chair's arm. "Whatever's going on, I aim to get to the bottom of it."

"What can I do to help?"

"Buy me some time." Sheldon points at the contract in Gray's hands. "That is our best offer. I'm sure Hugh will come back with more money. I need a few days or a week to do some digging. If Hugh is up to something illegal, I intend to bring him down. For my family's sake and the sake of our vineyard."

"For the sake of my vineyard as well." Gray lets the contract fall into his lap. "I will hold off on presenting this offer to Miranda until the last minute. Let me know if you find out anything I can use against Miranda in the divorce."

"Will do." The men stand, and Gray walks him to the door.

Returning to Foxtail, Sheldon gets in his SUV and drives over to Love-Struck. He continues past the winery to The Nest. The coast is clear with no one in sight and no cars parked out front. He lets himself into the side entrance of the children's wing and tiptoes down the hall to Hugh's bedroom, not surprised to find the closed door unlocked. Daniel never allowed locks on bedroom doors when they were growing up.

Sheldon searches the room from top to bottom but finds nothing suspicious or incriminating aside from a locked desk drawer. Sheldon doesn't consider this a big deal. He keeps his own important documents locked in a desk drawer.

Leaving The Nest, he walks toward the winery and enters the security hut where he finds Jeremy McCoy, head of security, eating a banana and mayonnaise sandwich as he's done every day for all the thirty-some years Sheldon has known him.

At the sight of him in the doorway, Jeremy freezes with sandwich positioned near his mouth. "Sheldon, this is a surprise," he says, lowering his sandwich to the wax paper wrapper. "How is fatherhood treating you?"

"Excellent. Ollie loves being a mother, and the baby is thriving." Sheldon scrutinizes the new bank of monitors linked to surveillance cameras spread about the vineyard. "This is some fancy new equipment you've got here."

"Yep! Your father upgraded during the recent renovations. He spared no expense. What brings you my way?" Jeremy moans as he rises slowly from his chair. He's pushing seventy and out of shape, with a large gut bulging over the waist of his khaki pants. He should back off on the banana and mayo sandwiches.

"I was wondering if you've noticed anything unusual going on at The Nest lately."

"What sort of goings-on are you talking about?" Jeremy asks with pinched expression.

"I'm primarily interested in any strange behavior you might have noticed from Hugh."

Jeremy strokes his turkey neck. "Not that I'm aware of."

"I have reason to believe he's up to no good. Can you look into it for me? Maybe pull some of the footage from the surveillance cameras?"

"I don't think I can do that, Sheldon. Last I checked, you no longer work here. Besides, Hugh is my boss. Giving you information about him could get me into a heap of trouble."

Sheldon looks the security head in the eyes. "Hugh is not your boss, Jeremy. Daniel Love is still in charge of the vineyard. It's his safety I'm concerned about. If you need Dad's permission, I can get if for you, but I'd hate to worry him with the matter, considering his fragile health," he says, exaggerating the bit about Daniel's health to put pressure on Jeremy.

The security head reluctantly agrees. "All right. I'll see what I can do. But I'm not making any promises."

Sheldon claps him on the shoulder. "Thank you, Jeremy. You're a good man. In the meantime, for Dad's sake, please have your men keep a closer eye on The Nest."

"I can do that." Jeremy sits back down. "Give my regards to the missus," he says, and sinks his teeth into his sandwich.

"Will do. You have my number. Call me if you find something."

Sheldon is grateful when he encounters no one on his walk back to his car. Upon his arrival back at Foxtail, he spots Ollie attacking weeds in the vegetable garden behind the house while the baby, in his stroller, sleeps in the shade of a nearby maple tree.

Sheldon stands at the picket fence surrounding the garden. "Slow down, Ollie. You're going at it with a vengeance. What did those poor little weeds do to you?"

Ollie jumps to her feet, drops a handful of weeds in the wheelbarrow, and closes the distance between them. "I'm upset, Sheldon. I want you to walk away from Love-Struck and the Valley View deal."

Sheldon's skin turns cold despite the warm day. "What're you talking about? Valley View is our dream."

Tears well in her aqua eyes. "I'm freaking out. I haven't felt this anxious since we got married. Hugh is dangerous. If something happens to you, Henry will be fatherless. If something happens to me, he'll be all alone in the world. And that terrifies me."

Sheldon enters the garden and takes her in his arms. "Oh, honey. Why didn't you tell me your anxiety had come back?"

"I was fine until today," she sobs. "I saw you leave in your car, and I figured you were headed for Love-Struck. My imagination kicked into high gear. I envisioned you and Hugh getting into a fight and him going postal on you. He's dangerous. He'll stop at nothing to get Valley View. Buying that vineyard is not worth losing your life. We're doing just fine with the land we have here."

Sheldon strokes her back. "I understand what you're going through, babe. I've had my share of anxiety since Henry was born. Being a parent is scary stuff—introduces a whole new level of responsibility. But we're not alone. If something happens to me, my sisters, Casey and Ada, will support you. They're your family now."

"I know. Having them nearby is reassuring." She lifts her head off his chest and looks up at him. "I just feel like we're asking for trouble. We've been blessed with so much. Why tempt fate?"

Sheldon cups her cheeks, thumbing away her tears. "I can't let this go, Ollie. I can't shake the nagging feeling Hugh is up to something. I may no longer work at Love-Struck, but the Loves are still my family. I have an obligation to protect Dad and Casey."

The baby cries, and Ollie retrieves him from his stroller. "I understand you can't turn your back on your family. But why do you have to be the one to investigate Hugh? Why not hire a professional, like a private investigator?"

"It may eventually come to that. I'm just poking my nose around, to see if I come up with anything on my own. I spoke with the head of Dad's security team today. I told him I'm worried about Hugh, and he promised to be on the lookout for trouble."

Ollie lets out a sigh. "I guess we don't have any choice but to see this thing through. Just promise me you'll watch your back and won't try to be a hero."

"I promise I'll be careful. If all goes as planned, we'll be rid of Hugh for good and we can finally live in peace." Sheldon takes the baby from her, cradling him in his arms. He has his precious family to protect. He won't let anything happen to them.

His oldest brother has done some underhanded things in the past, but the stakes are higher for Hugh this time. His wife is divorcing him, and his daughters won't speak to him. The vineyard is the only thing he has left. Who knows what measures he'll go to in order to win the competition for head?

CHAPTER 15
HAZEL

At noon on Sunday, Hazel drives three miles out of town to Merchant's Row, a string of old row houses a local developer has recently converted into businesses. Just past the row, she turns into the parking lot for Traveler's, a rambling and rustic structure with a deck off the back overlooking the mountains. The new eatery is the talk of the town, and Hazel is excited Charles suggested it for lunch.

Hazel finds him sipping a Bloody Mary at a table on the deck's railing. She's no sooner sat down than the waitress appears.

"Would you like a Bloody?" Charles asks.

Hazel smiles up at the waitress. "I'll just have sweet tea, please."

"You got it." The waitress drops laminated menus on the table and scurries off.

Hazel looks around the deck at the collection of metal road signs from small and large cities across the country. "This place has a cool vibe. I feel like I'm in a tree fort on top of a mountain."

"Wait until you try the food. It's amazing."

Hazel's heart sinks. So this isn't his first time at Traveler's. Did he come here before with Stuart? When they were first married,

Hazel and Charles were among the first to try new restaurants. She can't remember the last time he took her to any restaurant.

"You look tired, Hazel. How're you holding up?"

"I'm surviving," she says, but truth be told, she's strung out from exhaustion. She wakes most nights in a cold sweat from nightmares. The dreams are always the same. She's stranded in a pit of darkness, searching for a way out. She interprets the pit of darkness as her lost memory of the night she spent with Davis.

The waitress returns with her tea, and when Charles orders the Californian Cobb salad for both of them, she glares at him in irritation. She'd never minded him choosing her food before. In hindsight, she'd allowed him to control nearly every aspect of her life. She shrugs it off. There's no point in causing a scene when the Californian Cobb would've been her first choice anyway.

"Tell me about your business venture," Hazel says, sipping her tea through a straw.

"Before we get to that, I'd like to clear the air. I owe you an apology. I treated you unfairly. I should've told you a long time ago about Stuart. I know how much you want children, and I led you to believe I did as well." He looks down at his drink. "It's not that I never wanted them. But I knew having our child would bind us together forever, and I couldn't continue holding you hostage."

"Then why—"

Charles holds his hand up to silence her. "Every morning when I woke up, I promised myself that would be the day I told you the truth. But every time I got an opportunity, I chickened out. I'm a coward, and I'm deeply ashamed of myself. I had no right to be angry about the social media post. I would've done the same in your shoes. I'm honestly relieved everything is finally out in the open."

"I'm as much to blame as you. I allowed you to string me along. I knew something was wrong between us, but I was too afraid of losing you to find out what it was." She smiles at him. "I have an appointment with an adoption counselor next week. I'm determined to get a child one way or another."

"That's wonderful news, Hazel. Are you hoping for a newborn?"

"A newborn would be ideal. I'd like to experience every aspect of motherhood, from birth to college. But I'll consider adopting an older child if the situation is right."

"Good for you," Charles says, his genuine tone letting her know he means it.

Their salads arrive, and they eat for a minute in silence. She sneaks a peek at Charles. He appears relaxed and his complexion has a healthy glow, reminding her of the young Charles she fell in love with. Considering they'd both made mistakes and can't turn back time, they might as well look toward the future.

"Are you ever gonna tell me about your business venture?"

"I'm procrastinating." Charles sets down his fork. "You're the first I've told, and I'm worried you'll think it's a stupid idea."

She dabs at her lips and returns her napkin to her lap. "You never know until you try me."

Charles sucks in a breath. "Okay . . . here goes. I had an ulterior motive in asking you to meet me here. The end unit on Merchant's Row is for sale, and I'm thinking of buying it."

Hazel's forehead wrinkles. "For what type of business?"

He grins like a little boy. "The one thing Lovely doesn't have. Can you guess what it is?"

"A movie theatre!"

Charles laughs out loud, a sound she hasn't heard in years. "This town definitely needs a movie theatre. But I'll leave that endeavor to someone else. I'm seriously contemplating a guide business for mountain sports—kayaking, rafting, biking, and fly-fishing."

Hazel's butt comes out of the chair. "That's a brilliant idea, Charles! I absolutely love it!"

Charles beams. "Do you really? I would never have considered it five years ago, but as fast as our town is growing, with the new boutique hotel scheduled to open next fall, we're attracting the type of tourists who are looking for outdoor adventures."

Hazel folds her arms on the table. "Tell me more."

"What do you think of the name Peak Adventures?"

Hazel gives a nod of approval. "Love it. Go on."

Charles talks about the equipment he would buy and the guides he would hire. "I'll start small this summer and use these next few months to determine how best to grow." He presses a hand against his chest. "My heart's pounding. I'm so relieved you approve of the concept. Stuart said it was the dumbest idea he'd ever heard."

"Then Stuart doesn't know you at all. Peak Adventures is right up your alley."

Charles's expression turns serious. "I'd like for you to be my partner, Hazel. The arrangement would be somewhat unconventional with us being divorced, but our love of the outdoors is the thread that has kept us together all these years."

Hazel is suddenly suspicious. "What are you really asking for, Charles? If it's money, you've come to the wrong place." Her brown eyes widen. "Oh, I get it. You want to sell the farm and use the proceeds."

Charles presses his lips thin. "Hold on a minute, Hazel. You're getting way ahead of yourself. My business venture aside, I figured we'd sell the house since neither of us want to live there. At least I assume you don't, otherwise you wouldn't be renting Laney's apartment."

"You're right. I have no interest in living at the farm anymore."

"I've built up equity over the years, and the house is almost paid for. With today's booming real estate market, we stand to make an enormous profit. We'll split the proceeds, and you can do as you please with your share." He leans into the table and lowers his voice. "This is not about money, Hazel. Contrary to what you think, I'm not strapped for cash. I have savings and my shares in Love-Struck. I plan to give you whatever you want in the divorce settlement."

Relief floods her. She was worried how she would take care of a baby on the meager salary she earns at Laney's Bouquets. "Thank you for that."

Charles signals the waitress for their check. "Let's get out of here. I want to show you the unit."

Charles pays the check, and they walk next door to the white two-story frame house. He gestures at the gravel parking lot extending behind the back of the house. "I'm thinking we could enclose this area with a privacy fence to store equipment."

Hazel imagines stands for kayaks and rafts and bicycles. "There's certainly plenty of room for that."

At the back door, he punches in the code on a combination lock and stands out of the way for her to enter. Other than drab gray paint on the walls, the space has enormous potential.

"A real estate firm previously occupied the unit," Charles explains. "As you can see, there's a reception area with three small offices and two generous-size public restrooms. Upstairs is a small apartment where I'll live for the time being. It's nothing special, but it's clean and the kitchen has been updated."

Charles waits in the reception area while Hazel circles the downstairs, poking her head in the offices and checking out the bathrooms. Returning to reception, she looks out the front window at an attractive man entering the store next door. "You're lucky to be so close to the outdoor sporting goods store. I imagine they'll bring in a lot of business for you."

"I think so too." He comes to stand beside her. "Well? Do you approve?"

"Wholeheartedly." She turns to face him. "It's perfect for *you*, Charles. But I already have a job at the flower shop."

"That's a job, Hazel. I'm offering you a career. Doing something you love."

"Doing *what* exactly? I can't see myself guiding rafting trips."

"For starters, you would book groups and be in charge of social media marketing. We both know how proficient you are at social media."

She play-punches him. "Haha."

"Or you could guide vineyard bike tours."

Excitement stirs inside of her. "Now you're talking." She turns away from the window. "Problem is, I'm not sure how this fits in with me having a child."

Charles follows her around as she tours the downstairs again. "You can bring the baby to work with you. I want the tour center to have a laid-back vibe where outdoor lovers come for adventure."

"Buying a house is my top priority. I'm not sure I can afford both."

"You can if we get what I think we can for the farm. Listen, Hazel. We don't have to be equal partners. I have the finances to start the business without you." He takes her by the arm. "You have always been the most important person in my life. I don't want to lose you. We can forge a future together as friends and business partners."

Her lips part in a soft smile. "It's good to see you so excited about this." His enthusiasm is infectious, and she's intrigued by his business concept, but something is holding her back. "This is a big move, Charles. I need time to think about it."

"I understand, and I promise not to pressure you." He opens the door for her. "Do I have your blessing to move forward with selling the farm?"

Hazel steps out onto the small back porch. "That's fine. We're entering wedding season, and I don't have a lot of free time, but I'll help when I can."

Charles closes the door behind them and returns the combination lock to the knob. "I'm not working right now. I can easily handle getting the house ready to put on the market."

"That would be great." They start off toward the Traveler's parking lot. "It's surreal to be talking to you like this. I feel like I'm reconnecting with an old friend. But part of me is still furious at you, Charles. You betrayed me in the worst way. As intriguing as Peak Adventures is, I may not be ready to embark on any kind of new partnership with you."

"That's totally fair. And I respect your feelings." They reach her car, and he turns toward her. "If I can help you with looking for a new home or finding a child to adopt, all you have to do is ask."

"You seem like a different person. You're practically exuding happiness."

"Because I am happy." Charles throws his arms in the air above his head. "I'm me! And I'm free! You have no idea what it's like to look in the mirror and not feel ashamed of who I am. For everyone's sake, I should've come out of the closet a long time ago."

"Does Daniel know you're gay?"

"Yes!" Charles falls back against her car. "He invited me to lunch a few days ago. Believe it or not, he apologized for not being the kind of father I could talk to about my sexuality. He says he wants what's best for me, and I believe him. I only hope he approves of Peak Adventures."

"I'm sure he will. He'll be proud of you for finding new direction in your life." Hazel kisses his cheek. She's genuinely happy for him. The ending of their marriage is the beginning of a new life for him. If only Hazel could figure out what it means for her.

CHAPTER 16
RUTHIE

Ruthie is a red-hot mess after five endless nights of making love with Davis. While her body is sexually satiated, her brain is on another planet. She burns toasts, spills coffee, and screws up customer orders. On Thursday, she's late for her meeting with Marjorie and Mark McKinney.

"I'm so sorry!" Ruthie says when she sees them seated at the breakfast counter. "My dental hygienist took longer than expected to clean my teeth."

After that remark, she feels Tanya, her head waitress, staring a hole in the back of her pink uniform dress.

Ruthie stuffs her purse under the counter and reaches for the coffeepot. "Can I offer you some fresh coffee?"

Mark holds up a white mug to show it filled to the rim with coffee. "I'm good." He gestures at the dirty plates in front of them. "We ate breakfast too. The food was delicious."

"Tasty, although lacking in originality," Marjorie says with a turned-up nose.

Mark shoots his wife a sharp look. "There was nothing ordinary about my spinach and bacon frittata. A minute ago, you were raving about your oatmeal Brulé."

Marjorie wipes her lipstick-smeared lips and tosses her napkin on her plate. "Once we agree on a price, we'll be making some changes."

Ruthie's skin prickles. *Agree on a price? I haven't agreed to sell the diner.* Her curiosity gets the best of her. "What sorta changes?"

Marjorie's brown eyes travel the room. "The retro theme isn't really my style. The black-and-white floor will have to go. I'm thinking something cozier with more wood and less pleather."

Ruthie loses control of her tongue. "Something more in line with cheesesteak joints?"

Marjorie lets out a loud humph. "Our menu may have centered on Philly's famous cheesesteaks, but our cuisine was gourmet and our decor upscale comfort."

Ruthie pours herself a cup of coffee. "Just so you know, retro isn't a theme for my diner. The decor is original from when my parents opened the place in 1954. Whenever something wears out, I replace it with the same."

"The location is ideal, right smack in the center of town." Mark stands abruptly. "Can we have a tour?"

"Of course." Ruthie gives them a brief tour of the dining room before leading them into the kitchen. After pointing out the spotless and updated commercial-grade appliances, she shows them the office, break room, and alley out back.

Marjorie, surprisingly, seems impressed. "I didn't mean to upset you earlier, Ruthie. I just have a different vision for the diner. Should we buy it, we'll want to make the place our own."

Ruthie gives her a curt nod. "I understand, but keep in mind, it took me years to build my brand. I have customers who come from miles away to purchase my specialty pastries, pies, and muffins. I've valued their business for decades. I would hate to disappoint them. And I would hate for you to lose the clientele."

"Pastries, pies, and muffins aren't the menu items I have in mind. Perhaps you should start a bakery in your home."

Ruthie levels her gaze on the woman. "The idea is for me to

retire. Operating a bakery out of my house is not my idea of relaxation."

"I plan to wow our customers with new menu items. They won't even miss your little old pastries."

Our customers. This woman has in mind to change everything. Ruthie's Diner would be no more. She must save *her* customers from this awful person. When she decides to sell, the price will need to be high and the new owners the right fit.

"I'm sorry for wasting your time, but I've decided not to sell." She ushers the couple back through the diner to the front door. "Thank you for stopping by."

Mark opens the door. "Let's step outside for a minute. I've studied the comps from recent sales of buildings on Magnolia Avenue, and I'm prepared to offer you an attractive price."

He holds the door for the women, and the threesome huddle together on the sidewalk out front. When Mark tells her the amount, Ruthie's eyes pop and her mouth falls open. With that kind of money, she could live lavishly for the rest of her life.

Mark continues, "We would take possession of the restaurant in sixty days, and we can't guarantee jobs for your current staff. Although we would like to interview all of them."

"I don't know what to say. I never dreamed my business was worth so much."

"We'd be buying the building, not the business," Marjorie snaps.

Mark rests a hand on his wife's shoulder, a warning for her to dial it down. "This town is growing by leaps and bounds. Real estate on Magnolia Avenue is a hot commodity. I understand if you need some time to think about it."

"But don't take too long," Marjorie warns. "We're looking at other properties."

"Can you give me the weekend?" Ruthie asks, and the McKinneys agree.

"But no later than Monday," Marjorie says as they climb into their black Cayenne.

Ruthie's head spins as she goes back inside. Has real estate in Lovely gone up that much in the past few years? She's in over her head. She needs professional guidance.

She retrieves her cell phone from her purse and types out a text to the only Realtor she knows, asking to meet with him as soon as possible. Jamie responds right away. *I'm in the neighborhood. I'll be there in a few minutes.*

Ruthie tidies up the dining room while she waits, collecting dirty dishes and throwing away trash. When she glimpses Davis in front of Laney's Bouquets next door, she moves closer to the window to get a better look. He appears to be having a heated discussion with Hazel. He tries to grab Hazel's arm, and she backs away, shaking her head as if to tell him no. No to what? Is he asking Hazel on a date?

With a sick feeling in her gut, Ruthie turns away from the window. Why does she care if Davis goes out with Hazel? Ruthie and Davis aren't exclusive. Their relationship is all about sex. He's too young for her. A temporary playmate. A distraction to help her forget about Daniel.

Ruthie refills her coffee mug and sits down at the breakfast counter to wait for Jamie. But she can't shake the feeling of impending doom. If Davis means nothing to her, why does she feel so down? Then it dawns on her that everything is changing. She's considering selling the diner. She's getting older, no longer a pretty young thing like Hazel. She'll soon be entering her twilight years, and now that Daniel is out of the picture, she'll be making the trip alone. While she's been out with every available man in town, she can't see herself in a long-term relationship with any of them. None of them are Daniel. He was the perfect man for her. But her mistrust of him drove him into the arms of another woman.

Ruthie is deep in thought when Jamie slides onto the barstool beside her. He nudges her arm, and her head spins toward him. "Oh. Hey, Jamie."

A smile crosses his boyish face. "What's up? Are you selling or buying?"

"Selling. Potentially. I'm not sure I'm ready, although I just received a very attractive offer." She tells him about the offer. "Do you think the diner is worth that much?"

His baby blues twinkle. "In this market, it might be worth more. You are sitting on prime real estate. I wouldn't jump into anything until you've done some research. If you're serious about selling, I can help you get the best price." He gives his spiel about the advantages of using a Realtor when selling property. "If you're interested in working with me, we'll start by checking comps."

"That would be great! How long will it take? I have until Monday to notify the potential buyers."

"I'll email them to you this afternoon. Call me after you've reviewed them." Jamie jumps to his feet. "Any chance I can get a cream cheese Danish to go?"

"Sure thing." Ruthie goes behind the counter, slips a pastry into a wax paper bag, and hands it to Jamie. When he tries to pay for it, she tells him it's on the house. "Thanks, Jamie. I'll be on the lookout for your email."

The lunch rush prevents her from checking her email until later in the afternoon, and she's stunned to see the recent selling prices of buildings on Magnolia Avenue. She clicks on Jamie's number. "These comps are remarkable."

"I told you. We can get way more for the diner than what your potential buyers offered. Would you like for me to negotiate with them?"

"I think I'll wait this one out. The McKinneys aren't interested in the business. They want the building to open a new eatery. Ruthie's diner is a cornerstone of our charming small town. For the sake of my customers, I'd prefer to find a buyer interested in keeping the diner as is."

"I'll poke around and see what I can find out. Are you in a hurry?"

"Not at all. Finding the right buyer is the most important thing." The weight of the world is lifted from her shoulders as she ends the call. She won't let anyone pressure her into anything until she's ready.

CHAPTER 17
HAZEL

Davis moves slowly toward Hazel. "Come on, Hazel, all I'm asking for is one drink. I want to get to know you better."

"I'm not interested," Hazel says, backing toward the shop's front door.

He cocks his head to the side. "How can you say that when you haven't given me a chance? You certainly seemed *interested* the other night." He wraps his fingers around her wrist. "Admit it, baby. We had fun together."

"Leave me alone." She jerks her hand away and closes the door, locking it behind her.

Hazel retreats behind the checkout counter and slides down the wall, cowering in the corner. Her memory bank explodes and flashbacks assault her. She buries her face in her hands as visions of her naked body in sexual positions she never thought possible burn her eyes. Davis was aggressive, but from what she remembers, he never forced her into doing any of those things.

Hazel doesn't move when she hears the back door open or when Laney kneels down beside her. "Hazel, honey, you're shaking all over. What's wrong?"

Hazel opens her mouth to confess her sin, but no words come out. She longs to unburden herself, but what she did is too awful to speak of. She's disgraced herself. She'll carry her secret to her grave."

Laney rubs circles on her back. "Did someone rob the store? Are you hurt in any way?"

Hazel shakes her head. "I'm fine. Just having a bad day."

"I know what that's like." Laney stands. "I'll get us some iced cappuccinos from Delilah's. Be right back."

Once Laney has exited the front door, Hazel grabs the counter's edge and pulls herself to her feet. She grips the counter until the dizziness passes before going into the back room. She's bundling wildflowers into bouquets when Laney returns.

"Feeling better?" Laney asks, setting the iced beverage on the stainless-steel worktable.

Hazel manages a smile. "Yes. Sorry. Just trying to figure out my life. How was your meeting with the Pratts?"

"Awesome. We're officially swapping houses. The Pratts go to Nantucket for the month of July. Before they leave, they'll move their stuff into storage so the painters can work their magic. Then I'll move into their house so the painters can finish my house before the Pratts come home."

Hazel laughs. "You just made my head spin, but I'm glad you've worked out all the details. How does Hugh feel about you selling the house?"

"He's relieved to be unburdened from the financial responsibility. Fingers crossed he starts making alimony payments." Laney drops several bricks of oasis in a bucket of water to soak. "Will you and Charles sell the farm?"

"Yes! Believe it or not, Charles and I had an amicable lunch on Sunday, and we've decided to put the house on the market. I'm hopeful we can get back to being friends. Charles is starting a new business venture. He asked me to go in with him. But I have some reservations."

"That sounds exciting. What kind of venture?" Laney asks, crossing the workroom to the metal shelves and surveying the collection of containers.

"A mountain sports business, offering guided bike, rafting, and kayaking tours."

Laney whirls around to face her. "That's amazing! Just what this town needs. It's the perfect occupation for you and Charles, as much as you two love the outdoors."

Hazel smiles, her eyes on the bouquets as she twists rubber bands around the stems. "Do you think so, really? It seems so touristy."

"Duh, Hazel. We live in a tourist destination."

"True." She wraps clear plastic around a bouquet and ties it with a lavender ribbon. "I love working with you, Laney. I'm not sure I want to leave."

Laney marches over to her and takes the bouquet out of her hands. "Talk to me, Hazel. Tell me what you're really afraid of."

Hazel shrugs.

"I'll never find anyone as dedicated as you, but I will manage somehow. I was already planning to hire one shop assistant. Why not hire two?"

Another wave of dizziness overcomes Hazel, and she leans into the table for support. "Having lunch with Charles felt like old times. What if we can't be friends again? What if we form a business partnership and end up fighting all the time?"

"Then he buys you out, and you come back to work for me." Laney brushes a strand of hair out of Hazel's face. "Too much has happened for things to ever be the same between you two. But the special friendship you guys once shared is at the heart of your relationship. You'll build on that."

Hazel inhales a deep breath. "I hope you're right. Talking to him again might help. Maybe I'll pay him a visit during my lunch hour."

Laney glances up at the wall clock. "You're almost finished

with the bouquets, and our orders for the afternoon delivery are ready. Why don't you leave now? Take extra time if you need it."

"Are you sure? I think I can catch him out at the farm."

Laney shoos her away as she gathers up the armload of flower bouquets. "Go! I'll put these in the display rack for you."

"Thanks, Laney. You're the best." Hazel grabs her purse and heads out the back door to her car. Since meeting with Charles on Sunday, her excitement over the prospect of investing in Peak Adventures has grown. She's even managed to forget about Davis for long stretches of time. A diversion like this is just what the doctor ordered. Now she needs Charles to reassure her it's the right move for both of them.

Hazel finds him upstairs in the baby's sunny yellow nursery, staring down at the empty crib. He's a million miles away, and when she says his name, he startles.

"Hazel! I didn't hear you come in. I was just thinking about how things could've been different if only . . ." His voice trails off as tears fill his eyes.

Hazel goes to stand beside him. "We can *if only* ourselves to death, but it won't change anything."

"Nope. You're right." He wipes his eyes with the backs of his hands. "How did your meeting go with the adoption counselor?"

Hazel's shoulders slump. "Not great. The chances of me getting a newborn are slim. But foster homes are overflowing with older children who need parents. I'm not sure that's the right choice for me, but I promised the counselor I'd think about it and call her in a few weeks."

"It's none of my business, but I think you should consider it. You would make a great mom to a child of any age."

Hazel smiles at him. "Thank you for your vote of confidence."

Charles turns his back on the crib. "So, what brings you out this way?"

"I've been thinking a lot about partnering with you in your business venture, but I have some reservations."

He tilts his head sideways. "Such as?"

Hazel moves over to the window. "I'm worried now isn't the right time, so soon after our separation."

She hears footfalls on the wooden floor behind her, followed by his voice near her ear. "I understand your concern. We can wait six months or a year. Whenever you're ready, the offer will still stand. Like I told you Sunday, I don't need your money. I value your judgement, and I appreciate your love of the outdoors. You're the ideal partner for me, plain and simple."

She turns to face him. "But what if we can't get along?"

"If I thought that would happen, I wouldn't have suggested a partnership. But if it does, I'll buy you out."

A month ago, she would've thrown her arms around him and kissed his lips. But that urge no longer exists. Their marriage has been on the rocks for so long, perhaps she was more ready for divorce than she realized. "I need a few more days to think about it."

"Take all the time you need."

Hazel looks around the nursery one last time. She spent countless lonely hours in here, praying for a baby. Now that day will never come.

Charles presses his hand against the small of her back as they leave the nursery together without so much as a backward glance.

"You shouldn't have to sort through all this alone," Hazel says about the boxes piled high in the kitchen. "If you want some help, I can come back after work today. We have a wedding this weekend, but I'm free on Sunday."

Charles smiles. "I won't say no to an offer like that. I've hired Jamie as our Realtor. I assume you approve."

"Of course. He knows everyone in town." Hazel removes a lavender glass vase from the windowsill, dumps the dead daisies in the trash can, and slips the vase into her purse.

"Jamie suggested we get our personal items out but leave enough furniture to make the house appear lived in without looking cluttered. I've rented a storage unit for my stuff. We can get a unit for you on Sunday."

"That would be great."

Charles walks Hazel to her car and kisses her cheek in parting. Her spirits soar on the way back to town. For the first time in years, she's hopeful about the future.

CHAPTER 18
CASEY

Daniel finger-whistles his approval of Casey's publicity campaign proposal. "Faith, family, and community are exactly what we should focus on. Bringing our small world closer together with good old-fashioned, wholesome fun."

A wide smile spreads across Casey's face. "I would like to kick off the campaign with a picnic on the afternoon of July Fourth for local families with young children. Nothing fancy. I'm thinking hot dogs, inflatables, and games—three-legged races and egg tosses and horseshoes."

"What's stopping you?"

"I'm worried it will interfere with the preparations for the evening party."

Daniel considers her concern. "We could host the picnic on the lower lawn out of the way of the preparations for the big event that night." He stands abruptly. "I love this idea of building community. But you'd better get on it. July Fourth will be here soon." He starts toward the door and turns back around. "I assume you'll have Hugh approve of the campaign before proceeding."

Casey's smile fades. "Not only did I send a calendar invite for today's meeting to his assistant, I reminded Hugh by text this morning. And he still didn't show up. I'll provide the slide deck for him to review, but as head of marketing, I'm making the executive decision to move forward."

A hint of appreciation appears on his lips. "You've worked hard on the campaign. You do what you think is best."

Casey waits for her father to leave the conference room before gathering up her things and hurrying back to her office. Closing the door, she sits down at her desk with her cell phone. There are no missed calls or texts from Luke. Not that she expected any. She hasn't heard from him since he moved to Washington.

She drops her phone on her desk, rests her head against the back of the chair, and closes her eyes. Her emotions have been in turmoil these past weeks, vacillating between intense anger and deep sorrow. She and Luke had something special, and they threw it all away in favor of their careers.

But Casey is determined to make the most of her sacrifice. She's channeling her frustration and disappointment into the fight for head position at Love-Struck. While the contest is far from over and she knows better than to let her guard down, Hugh, through poor judgement and rash decisions, is giving her plenty of opportunity to shine.

One of those instances happens on the third Friday in May. Casey is making her morning rounds through the facilities when she encounters a group of angry business executives and a flustered Sydney, their youngest event planner.

Casey whispers to Sydney, "Why is everyone so upset?"

"Hugh was supposed to give this group of tech executives a tour of the winery, but he's nowhere to be found. They're seriously pissed, and I don't blame them. They booked the tour months ago."

"I'll take care of it. Which one of them is in charge?" Casey asks.

"Him." Sydney dips her head at an older man with salt-and-pepper hair and dark eyes. "His name is Garrett Hudson."

Casey approaches the man. "Excuse me, Mr. Hudson. I'm

afraid Hugh has been unavoidably detained. If you'll allow me, I'd be delighted to give you a tour of the winery and tasting."

Hudson gives her a once-over. "And who are you?"

"Casey Hobbs, head of marketing and Daniel Love's daughter."

He nods his approval. "Fine. But let's get on with it."

"Sure thing. Give me one minute to make some arrangements," Casey says to Hudson and pulls Sydney aside. "Find Bruce. Tell him I need a VIP tasting right away. And book us a table on the terrace for lunch afterward. If you can get hold of Daniel, ask him to join us."

"I'm on it," Sydney says, scurrying off.

While she's never actually conducted a tour, Casey has been on countless ones since she started working at Love-Struck. Each time, she learned something new about the winemaking process and their varietals. She has studied the vineyard's history, and her knowledge shines through during the tour. They finish with an extensive tasting provided by Bruce in their most luxurious private tasting room. The tech executives, originally from California, are no strangers to wine tastings, but Bruce woos them with his expertise. All ten of the men are tipsy when the tasting is over.

Casey walks with Hudson back to the main building. "I booked a table for lunch on the terrace. I hope your party will join me. My treat."

"Lunch would be lovely." Hudson kisses her hand. "Thank you for your hospitality. I'm glad Hugh was unavoidably detained."

Casey's face lights up. "As am I."

They pass through Vino Bistro and emerge onto the terrace to find Daniel standing beside their table. Casey provides the introductions, and everyone sits down with Casey and Daniel at opposite ends.

They are halfway through lunch when Hugh appears wearing dark glasses and rumpled clothing. Daniel motions him over, whispers something to him, and then sends him away. If any of the executives notice Hugh, none of them say anything.

Hudson pushes back from the table when everyone has finished eating. "Casey, I believe a few of us would like to order wine to have shipped back to California. Can someone help us with that?"

"Absolutely!" Casey makes a call, and five minutes later, two members of the winery staff appear.

The executives purchase multiple cases of different varietals. Several even join their wine club. They make their exit with bids of gratitude and promises to come back soon.

Once they're gone, Casey turns to Scott and Barry, their waiters, who are clearing the table. "I comped the meal to make up for our mix-up this morning. I will take care of your tips."

"That's unnecessary," Barry says. "Mr. Hudson insisted on paying the tab. He didn't want me to tell you until after they were gone."

Casey smiles. "I'm not surprised. They are a pleasant group of gentlemen."

Daniel draws her in for a half hug. "You saved the day, young lady. Hugh owes you big time."

While Casey is curious why Daniel sent Hugh away, she doesn't ask. "I'm glad I was here to cover for him." She wanders off, hoping her words will sink in. She's on her A game and Hugh is failing every test.

Returning to her office, Casey is going through her emails a few minutes later when Hugh slams the door and marches toward her desk. "Are you deliberately trying to sabotage me?"

Casey doesn't bother looking up from her computer. "I don't need to. You're doing a fine job of that yourself."

Planting his hands on her desk, he leans toward her. "For your information, my alarm didn't go off, and I overslept. I'm positive I set it last night. My phone must have malfunctioned."

Casey glares at him. "Sounds like user error to me." Catching a whiff of alcohol, she waves her hand in front of her nose. "I can smell the booze on your breath from here. My guess is, you were up late partying and forgot to set your alarm. Regardless, your appointment with the tech executives was at ten o'clock. Late night or not, you should not have missed it."

Before Casey can react, Hugh rounds the desk and yanks her up from her chair by her hair. "You're really pissing me off, little girl. You don't belong here. Pack up and leave town before you get hurt."

Casey, despite the agonizing burning on her scalp, laughs in his face. She stomps on the top of his foot with the clunky heel of her sandal, and he cries out in pain. When he releases her hair, she shoves him backward, opens her top desk drawer, and pulls out a small handgun. The color drains from his face as she trains the gun's barrel on his head.

"You're too chicken to shoot me."

"Are you willing to take that chance? I'd be doing the world a favor by getting rid of you." She walks toward him and he stumbles backward. "This gun belonged to your mother. Sheldon insisted I have it to protect myself from you. He taught me how to use it on targets much smaller than your head."

Hugh scurries to the door and fumbles with the knob.

"You know what I've learned about bullies, Hugh? They are full of hot air, and they almost always back down."

He opens the door and flees her office, her laughter following him down the hall. She waits until he disappears around the corner before closing her door. Instead of returning the gun to the desk drawer, she slides it into her purse. This is getting old. Daniel's little competition can't end soon enough.

CHAPTER 19
SHELDON

Sheldon sneaks through the kitchen door and tiptoes across the porch. He's in the driveway, feeling confident he's escaped the house without his wife knowing, when the spotlight comes on and Ollie's voice stops him dead in his tracks. "Where do you think you're going in the middle of the night?"

He slowly turns around. "I need to check on something at Love-Struck. By the way, it's only eleven o'clock, not the middle of the night."

Pulling her robe tight around her, she steps down off the porch. "Why are you dressed in black?"

Sheldon feigns surprise as he glances down at his black jeans and polo shirt. "Just a coincidence. I didn't want to wake you, so I grabbed whatever I could find in the dark."

"Mm-hmm." She throws a thumb over her shoulder. "Your car's right there. Are you planning to walk?"

"I am, actually. I know the trails like the back of my hand. I told you I was best friends with the kids who lived here at Foxtail. We used to go back and forth between the vineyards all the time."

She spreads her arms at the night sky. "But it's pitch-dark out."

He tugs a flashlight free of his back pocket. "That's why I have this."

Ollie moves closer to him. "You're up to something. I have a feeling I'm better off not knowing what it is. But please be careful. You have a wife and child who need you."

He gives her a quick hug and a peck on the lips. "Nothing's going to happen to me, Ollie. I just need to check on something at The Nest. I'll be back in a flash."

"And I'll be waiting," Ollie says, and turns back toward the house.

Memories transport Sheldon back to his childhood as he navigates the dark trails through the woods separating the two farms. He's been fighting branches about ten minutes when the trees thin and The Nest comes into view. The mansion is dark aside from a few outdoor spotlights and a dim glow from his father's window. Daniel, who has a fetish for spy novels, often reads well into the night.

Continuing around the front of the house, Sheldon is relieved to find Hugh's car missing from the driveway. He waves at the security camera in the roof's eave where the main house connects with the children's wing. He's nagged Jeremy several times, but the security head has yet to pull recent footage from the surveillance cameras. Either Jeremy has grown lazy in his old age or he's hiding something. Regardless of the reason, Sheldon intends to fire him when all this is over.

Sheldon slips inside the children's wing to Hugh's room. Removing a screwdriver from his back pocket, he jimmies the lock on the bottom desk drawer. Inside, he finds plastic bags of pills in a variety of shapes and colors, as well as a bag of white powder he assumes is cocaine. He's reaching inside the drawer when a blow from behind knocks him out of the way.

Hugh's face is red and angry. "What're you doing, bro? This is my room. Who do you think you are breaking into my desk?"

"I was worried about Dad's safety. Are you trafficking drugs?"

Sheldon points his screwdriver at the drawer. "You have enough pills and cocaine in there to get all of New York City high."

Hugh slams the desk drawer shut. "It's not what you think. I needed to make some extra money, and I took a part-time gig repping for a pharmaceutical company."

Sheldon barks out a laugh. "Be real. I know Xanax bars when I see them."

Hugh expels a huff of air. "Look, Sheldon, I got in a bit of a bind, but I'm figuring my way out of it. Now go home and pretend you saw nothing."

"Like hell I will. You need to turn yourself into the police. Or I'll do it for you."

Grabbing Sheldon by the arm, Hugh wrestles him out into the hall. "Now beat it," he says, giving Sheldon a kick in the butt.

Sheldon stumbles a few feet before righting himself. "Not while you're dealing drugs out of Dad's house."

"I told you I'm taking care of the situation. I'm getting rid of the drugs. They are only here temporarily."

"I'm coming back tomorrow, and that drawer better be empty," Sheldon says, jabbing his finger toward Hugh's room.

Hugh's demeanor changes from hard ass to concerned big brother. "For your own good, Sheldon, stay out of this. You have a wife and kid to protect."

"I'm sorry, Hugh. But I can't leave this alone. Not while you're putting Dad's life in danger." Sheldon turns his back on Hugh and hurries out of the children's wing. He runs around the side of the house and down the lawn, not slowing down until he reaches the woods.

He removes his phone from his pocket and clicks on Casey's number. After four rings, she answers in a groggy voice. "The situation with Hugh is worse than we thought. But I can't tell you about it on the phone."

"You woke me up to tell me you can't talk about it?"

"I woke you up to make sure you're safe. Is your gun nearby?"

"In the top drawer of my nightstand. You're scaring me, Sheldon."

Guilt overcomes him at the sound of fear in Casey's voice. His snooping around has put all their lives in jeopardy. "I'm a little weirded out myself, honestly. I'll tell you everything in the morning. Can you come to the farm?"

"I'll stop by on my way to work around eight."

"I'll be waiting on the porch with coffee," he says and ends the call before she can interrogate him further.

Sheldon jogs the rest of the way home through the woods. He checks all the locks on the windows and doors before heading upstairs. The lights are out in their bedroom, but Ollie is still awake.

"Is everything okay?" she asks in a sleepy voice.

"Everything is fine," he lies.

Sheldon waits until Ollie is snoring softly before removing his handgun from his nightstand and sliding it under his pillow.

———

After a sleepless night, Sheldon rises at dawn, brews a tall tumbler of coffee, and rides his four-wheeler deep into the vineyard. When the fresh air clears his head, he weighs the situation from every angle and comes to one conclusion. He has no choice but to turn Hugh in to the police.

He's returning to the house to meet Casey when two dark-skinned men step from a row of vines into his path. He slams on the brakes to keep from hitting them. The bald man jerks him off the four-wheeler to the ground, and the man with the tatted-up face jumps on top of him, pummeling Sheldon with his fists. Excruciating pain tears through him when Baldie kicks him repeatedly in the ribs with his pointy-toed cowboy boot. Tattoo dude frees Sheldon's gun from its holster and presses the barrel to his forehead.

"Today's your lucky day. Your brother convinced us to let you live. But if you don't mind your own business, I'll come back and rape your pretty little wife and kill your kid."

Taking his gun with them, the men disappear into the vines. Sheldon lies still until he's certain they're gone. He tries to sit up, but the pain is too great. He pats his pockets for his phone but comes up empty. Turning his head to the side, he spots his phone on the ground over near the four-wheeler. Biting his lip against the agony, he slides on his back across the ground. His progress is slow. He's only gone a few feet when he hears Casey calling for him. He tries hollering back, but the pain takes his breath. He's close enough to the four-wheeler to pound on the metal fender. Fortunately, Casey hears him and comes running.

"Oh my god, Sheldon! Who did this to you?"

"Long story," he gasps out.

She pulls out her phone. "I'm calling 9-1-1."

Sheldon snatches her phone. "No. Not safe. Help me up." He holds out his arm. "Do it quick."

Casey stares at his arm. "I can't. I don't want to hurt you."

"Do it, damn it! I can take it," he says, and lets out a guttural scream when she pulls him into a sitting position. Holding onto the four-wheeler for support, he pulls himself to his feet. "You drive. I'll sit on the back. But go slow. And hand me my phone."

The pain is unbearable, and he vomits several times on the way to the house. Casey parks the four-wheeler beside the porch and kills the engine. "We need to get you to the emergency room."

"No way. There's no treatment for broken ribs anyway."

Casey throws her leg over the seat and helps Sheldon down. He leans against her as they climb the steps and cross the porch to the kitchen.

"How did you find me?" he asks, as she drags a wet dish towel over his face.

"You said you'd be waiting on the porch with coffee. When you weren't here, after your phone call last night, I got worried something had happened to you. Obviously, I was right. Where's Ollie by the way?"

"Took Henry for a doctor's checkup."

"Right." Casey opens the freezer and removes two bags of frozen peas, handing them to Sheldon. "Put these on your face. Anyway, I drove down to the barn. When I saw the door open and the four-wheeler gone, I figured you were in the fields."

Placing the peas against his cheeks, Sheldon says, "I'm in trouble here, Casey. These guys mean business." He tells her about finding the drugs in Hugh's room and his attackers warning him to mind his own business. "They said they'd come back and rape my wife and kill my kid. And now I've dragged you into it." He winces as he lowers himself to a counter stool.

Casey pops a K-cup in the Keurig machine. "You didn't *drag* me into anything. I was already here. What are we gonna do?"

"Call an old friend about security," Sheldon says, accessing his contacts and clicking on Brad's number.

"Let me talk to him." Casey takes the phone from him and sits down next to Sheldon with her coffee. When Brad answers, she introduces herself and briefly explains the situation.

Sheldon is close enough to the phone to hear Brad say, "Sit tight. I'm on my way."

Twenty minutes later, they hear cars in the driveway and Casey goes outside to greet Brad and bring him into the kitchen. Sheldon hasn't seen his old high school friend in several years. "You look good. You've lost some hair but gained some muscles."

Brad chuckles. "I have to stay fit in my line of work."

"What, exactly, is your line of work?" Casey asks, and Brad explains, "I own a private security firm based out of Hope Springs. Tell me what happened?"

Sheldon lets Casey do most of the talking as they bring Brad to speed about Hugh's criminal activities.

"I'm tempted to turn Hugh into the police," Sheldon says.

"That's the last thing you should do," Brad says. "These men warned you to mind your own business. And you need to heed that warning. At least for appearance's sake. Meanwhile, we'll hire a private investigator to get to the bottom of Hugh's drug trafficking."

Sheldon furrows his brow. "Where are we gonna get one of those?"

"Believe it or not, Kathy Sinclair, the best investigator in the state, lives in Lovely. She travels a lot on business but likes to come home to peaceful surroundings on the weekends." Brad thumbs off a text. "It may take Kathy a while to get back to me. I'll be in touch when she does. In the meantime, I'll station two patrol units outside your door. You should be safe here for now."

Sheldon salutes him. "Thanks, Brad."

Casey walks Brad out and returns with Ollie and the baby. Sheldon expects Ollie to be furious about Sheldon's beating, but she's understanding.

Ollie lifts her phone to her ear. "I'm calling the doctor. Bare minimum, you need pain meds."

"Don't call the doctor. Call Hugh. He has plenty of narcotics," Sheldon jokes, although neither Casey nor Ollie finds him funny.

Sheldon drops his smile. "Whatever you do, don't tell the doctor the truth about what happened. Tell him I had an accident on the four-wheeler."

Ollie nods as she walks outside to speak to the doctor's office.

"Are you okay?" Sheldon asks Casey.

Casey shakes her head. "Not really. I'm mad as hell at Hugh for dragging all of us into his problems. He deserves to be locked up in jail."

"That's exactly where he's going," Sheldon says, and makes a silent vow to put his brother away for a very long time.

CHAPTER 20
HAZEL

Hazel looks up from her flowers to find Davis waving at her from the checkout counter. She lets out a groan. She can't get away from him. She runs into him at every turn. In the grocery store. When she's out for her morning walks. And he comes into the shop regularly—conveniently, when Laney is not around. Which is the case today. Laney has taken the first round of table arrangements to Love-Struck for a wedding later this afternoon.

Hazel jabs the poet's laurel into the arrangement, wipes her hands on her apron, and pushes through the swinging door into the showroom. "What're you doing here? Didn't you see the Closed sign on the door?"

He glances at the door and back at her. "I didn't notice the sign. Why is the door unlocked if you're closed?"

"I forgot to lock it after a customer left with her arrangement." Hazel brushes past Davis and swings open the door. "You can leave now."

He runs his fingers down her arm. "Come now, Hazel. Playing hard to get is only making me want you that much more."

Hazel shrinks away from him. "I'm not playing hard to get, Davis. I've told you a thousand times, I don't want to go out with you. Or anyone else. My marriage just ended, and I'm not currently dating. Why can't you get that through your thick head?" she says, her voice nearing hysteria.

Neither Hazel nor Davis hear Laney come in, and they startle at the sound of her voice. "What's going on here?"

Hazel cuts her eyes at Davis. "He keeps asking me out, and I keep telling him I'm not interested."

Laney strides toward them. "What part of *no* don't you understand?"

"Hazel, here, is sending me mixed signals. She hooked up with me one night a few weeks ago. Didn't you, baby?" Davis runs his fingers down her arm. "You had no trouble telling me *yes* that night."

Hazel's cheeks burn as she smacks his hand away. "You're stalking me. If you come near me again, I'm calling the police."

Laney puffs out her chest. "And I'm a witness to this conversation. Consider yourself warned. You are not welcome here. Now please leave my property." Grabbing his arm, she walks him to the front door and locks it behind him.

Hazel's dam of emotion breaks, and she bursts into tears. In between gulps of air, she says, "I'm so embarrassed. It happened a few nights after I caught Charles with Stuart. On the Saturday night after Spring Fling. A few of us went to the Blue Saloon. You know I never drink much, but I had three glasses of wine. Next thing I know, I wake up on Davis's couch. I couldn't remember anything at the time, but I could tell we'd had sex. When the memories started coming back . . ." She sobs, her fist pressed against lips. "The things I let that man do to me . . . I'm so ashamed."

"Oh, honey." Laney grabs a box of tissues from under the counter and holds it out to Hazel. "None of this is your fault. You were vulnerable. He took advantage of you."

Hazel snatches several tissues from the box and blots her cheeks. "He's a snake, and I wasn't in my right mind. I'm trying to forget what happened, but every encounter with him brings on a fresh onslaught of memories from that night."

"If we could figure out a way to put him in his place . . ." Laney pinches her chin as she thinks. "Isn't he dating Ruthie?"

Hazel bobs her head. "I see them together all the time."

"You need to tell her he's hitting on you. She'll be furious at him. They'll have a big fight, and she'll insist Davis stay away from you."

"I've thought about telling Ruthie, if for no other reason than she's our friend. She should know what Davis is doing behind her back." Hazel glances through the window at the diner next door where Ruthie is wiping down tables. "There are hardly any customers there. I should go now while I have the nerve."

"No time like the present." Laney walks Hazel to the door. "I'll watch from here. If you get in over your head, signal for me and I'll rescue you."

Hazel takes in a deep breath. "Wish me luck. Here goes nothing."

Ruthie is carrying a bin of dirty dishes to the back when Hazel enters the restaurant. "Hey, Ruthie! Do you have a minute? I need to discuss a personal matter."

"Sure thing, hon." Ruthie dips her chin at the dish bin. "Let me put these down, and I'll be right back."

Hazel sits down at a table by the window, and Ruthie joins her a minute later with a pot of coffee and two mugs. "What's up?" she asks, pouring coffee into the mugs.

Hazel fidgets with the tissue in her hand. "I thought you should know Davis has been harassing me. I told him I don't want to go out with him, but he won't leave me alone."

"Have you given him a reason to hit on you?" Ruthie asks in an irritated tone.

Hazel repeats the story about the night at the Blue Saloon. "I'm pretty sure you weren't dating him at the time. Or were you?"

Ruthie softens. "No. Our first date was the following week. We aren't exclusive now, Hazel. Davis is free to see whomever he likes."

Hazel can tell Ruthie's upset even though she's trying to make light of it. "I hate making excuses for my behavior, but I was a mess that night, and I drank too much."

"Don't beat yourself up. These things happen." Ruthie runs her thumb around the rim of her coffee mug. "Did anything unusual happen that night?"

The strange question gives Hazel gooseflesh. "Like what?"

"Like maybe he took advantage of you in your drunken state."

Hazel looks away. "I'd rather not talk about it. I'm trying to forget what happened that night."

"I understand," Ruthie says, sipping her coffee.

The door bangs open and four boisterous young college girls, home for the summer, pile into the diner and sit down in a booth near them. The young women, seemingly oblivious to who's listening to their conversation, babble loudly about their wild time at the Blue Saloon last night.

"Oh. My. God." One girl lets out a squeal and drops her phone on the table. "Natalie just texted me. She thinks someone roofied her last night. She's freaking out. She thinks the guy might have date-raped her."

Hazel freezes. Is it possible Davis drugged Hazel the night they hooked up? Is that why Hazel was having trouble remembering? She risks a glance at Ruthie, whose face has gone white as a sheet. Is she worried Davis might have drugged Natalie? Was Ruthie with Davis last night?

Hazel, suddenly finding it difficult to breathe, stands abruptly. "I'm sorry, Ruthie, but I've gotta go. Laney and I are doing a wedding at Love-Struck this afternoon," she says and hurries out of the diner and back to the safety of the flower shop.

Laney is waiting for her by the window. "What happened just now with those girls?"

Hazel explains what she overheard. "Do you think it's possible Davis roofied me?"

With a slow shake of her head, Laney says, "I don't know, Hazel. That seems farfetched. Are you sure you had only three glasses of wine?"

"Positive. And I didn't order the third. Davis got it for me when I went to the restroom."

"Well now, that's an interesting twist. While three glasses are a lot for someone with low tolerance, I don't think it's enough to make you black out. Then again, I'm not an expert. You should talk to your doctor."

Hazel turns away from the window. "What difference does it make? I can't do anything about it now."

"If it was Davis, you can stop him from drugging some other unsuspecting woman." Laney's arm shoots out, finger pointed at the girls in the diner next door. "Like their friend."

"But I have no way to prove it. The drugs are long gone from my system. Let's forget about this for now. We have wedding flowers to create."

She feels Laney's eyes boring a hole into her as she heads to the back room. Laney expects her to do the right thing, but Hazel doesn't know what that is in this situation. Despite what she overheard from the girls at the diner, she feels unburdened, having confessed her sins to Laney and Ruthie. As awful as it sounds, the possibility Davis may have drugged her puts more of the blame on him, alleviating a bit of her guilt.

CHAPTER 21
RUTHIE

Ruthie eavesdrops on the college girls as she serves them breakfast. More texts come in from Natalie, and Ruthie learns the details about the alleged date rape. The guy was older, seriously hot according to the girls. Natalie claims she didn't drink much, but she can't remember anything that happened after she left the Blue Saloon. Natalie, terrified her parents will find out, is opting not to go to the emergency room for a sexual assault exam. Since she's on the pill, she's not worried about getting pregnant.

After the girls leave, Ruthie locks herself in her office and collapses in her desk chair. She removes a small white pill from her uniform pocket and studies it for identifying markings, but there are none.

Davis seemed like a good guy in the beginning. Full of himself at times, but harmless, nonetheless. As she's gotten to know him better, she's begun to have doubts about him. He routinely breaks dates at the last minute, rarely offering a valid excuse. Like last night when he texted to say he couldn't make dinner because of a work emergency. As the owner of a hardware store, what emergency could he have? Did he run out of tenpenny nails?

Davis claims to be an architect, yet he failed to identify the style of her house despite its Victorian features. He told her he worked for a commercial architect firm in Atlanta, but every time she asks him about his life in Atlanta, he changes the subject.

As for their sex life, she initially delighted in his passionate drive. But the things he's tried to do to her lately have been borderline kinky, making her wonder if he's some kind of sexual pervert.

Then there's his behavior. He's moodier than a woman on her period. He'll show up in a rotten mood, and seconds later, he's cracking jokes. He doesn't appear to have a drinking problem. But she worries he may have a different type of addiction. Two nights ago, when she got up to go to the bathroom, she tripped on his heap of clothes on the floor. She picked up his pants to fold them, and a mini baggie of pills fell out of the pocket. She took this one and returned the bag to the pocket.

Ruthie opens her top drawer and drops the pill inside. Maybe she'll ask him about it later.

Her phone vibrates the desk with a text from Davis. *I missed you last night.*

"I bet you did," she says to the phone screen.

Another text pops up. *Care to spend the afternoon in bed?*

Ruthie types out her response. *We need to talk. Meet me at my house in ten minutes.*

She grabs her purse and leaves the office. On her way out, she tells Tanya she has a headache and is going home to rest. The short walk helps clear her head and make the tough decision she knows is best for her. Her affair was fun while it lasted. Time to move on.

Davis is waiting for her on her back porch steps when she arrives home. Sitting down beside him, she blurts, "I'm sorry, Davis, but I don't want to see you anymore."

Davis appears genuinely wounded. "What? You can't mean that."

"I never say anything I don't mean." Ruthie massages her temples, feeling a legitimate headache coming on. "Let's be honest. We both knew our fling wouldn't last. Our age difference is too big an issue."

Davis's face hardens, his boyish good looks replaced by deep creases and a hard-set mouth. "What did that mousy little bitch Hazel tell you about me?"

A chill travels Ruthie's spine. "What do you mean?"

"Don't play dumb with me, Ruthie. Hazel told you about the night we hooked up, didn't she? I bet she didn't tell you she's been stalking me, begging me to go out with her."

Ruthie jumps to her feet. "Hazel is a friend of mine. And she's accusing *you* of stalking *her*. Given the choice of who I believe, I choose her."

He stands to face her. "Come on, Ruthie. Don't be like this. Our casual relationship works for both of us. We have fun together."

"We *were* having fun together. Until you got weird on me."

"What's that supposed to mean?"

Ruthie shakes her head in disbelief. "Give me a break. You know what I'm talking about. I shouldn't have to spell it out for you." She leans against the stair railing. "The truth is, Davis, I'm looking for something more lasting. I'm not getting any younger, and I want someone to enjoy retirement with."

Davis cups her cheeks. "Look, Ruthie, I don't blame you for being upset about the thing with Hazel. She lied to you, but you're friends, so obviously you'll believe her over me. And I'm sorry I broke our date last night. I had a work emergency." He kisses her lips. "Take a few days to cool off, and then we'll talk again."

Ruthie snickers to herself as she watches him get in his car and drive off. She won't hear from him in a few days. He's the type of man whose ego can't handle being dumped. The pea brain needs to believe he's the one who broke up with her.

Why was Davis ever interested in her in the first place? Is it because she provided a cover for his extracurricular activities? Ruthie knows everyone in town, and prides herself on her stellar reputation. If the town thinks she and Davis are in a relationship, no one will suspect him of drugging young women and taking advantage of them. Ruthie reminds herself he's innocent until proven guilty. But when it comes to Davis Warren, something doesn't add up.

Ruthie changes into lounging attire and stretches out on the porch hammock with a cold cloth across her forehead. Closing her eyes, her thoughts drift to Daniel. She hasn't heard from him in weeks. It's unlike him not to stop by the diner for coffee or sunny-side eggs. Has Millie taken Ruthie's place at the breakfast table? Do the lovebirds eat whatever Marabella serves them on the patio at The Nest? If Millie Mathis is the right woman for Daniel, then so be it. For her own sanity, Ruthie will take a break from men for a while. No more dates with guys she's not interested in. And no more casual hookups for the sake of satisfying her sexual desire.

Thank goodness she still has the diner to fall back on. The McKinneys have upped their offer several times, but no amount of money would entice Ruthie to sell to the couple from Philadelphia, who seem hell-bent on destroying her brand. She's worked hard to establish her diner, and will sell only if the right buyer comes along.

CHAPTER 22
CASEY

Kathy Sinclair's doe eyes and innocent smile belie her reputation as a hardened private investigator. She'll easily fit the undercover scheme Casey has dreamed up for her.

After taking Kathy on an extensive tour of the property, the young women stop in at Vino Bistro for a cappuccino.

"The vineyard is spectacular," Kathy says. "I can't believe I've never been here for a wine tasting. I need to get out more."

Casey's pale olive eyes dart about the terrace as staffers prepare for an afternoon wedding. "Why don't you? Are you worried someone will recognize you?"

Kathy laughs. "Not at all. I've never worked a case in Lovely, and I only know a few locals, most of them in law enforcement. This town is my happy place. When I'm here, I stay close to home."

"Surely you have friends."

Kathy sits back in her chair and crosses her legs. "I'm originally from Richmond. If I'm in the mood to socialize, I will go visit my parents. Actually, there is one guy I consider a friend. Evan Beck is a detective on the police force. You'll meet him, eventually. He's currently running a background check on Hugh."

"I can't wait to see those results," Casey says in a sarcastic tone.

"Don't hold your breath. I don't expect him to find anything earth shattering."

Casey spots Daniel on the far side of the terrace, watching the wedding tent go up. "There's my father. I'll call him over. Ready or not, it's show time!" she says, coming out of her chair as she waves Daniel over.

His attention remains glued to the tent as he makes his way toward them. "Afternoon, ladies. That's the biggest tent I believe we've ever had."

Casey nods. "Last I heard, the head count for the wedding is north of four hundred." She gestures at Kathy. "Daniel, I'd like you to meet my oldest childhood friend, Sally Winters. She's visiting from New York."

Daniel accepts Kathy's outstretched hand. "Very nice to meet you, Sally. What brings you to town?"

"To be honest, I just broke up with my longtime boyfriend, and I needed to clear my head," Kathy says with a somber smile and flushed cheeks. She plays her part well.

"Can you sit with us for a minute? I need to ask for a favor." Casey tugs on his arm, pulling him down to the chair beside her. "Do you mind if Sally and I stay at The Nest for a few days? You have way more room than my condo. Plus, the pool and the grounds to roam." She presses her hands together under her chin. "Please! We promise not to be any trouble."

"I'd be delighted to have you lovely ladies. But you'll have to fend for yourselves. I'm headed to Figure Eight Island in North Carolina for the holiday weekend."

Casey nudges him with her elbow. "Good for you. Do these weekend plans include a woman?"

"Several of them. They're all married to my fraternity brothers. We get together every Memorial Day weekend. I'm the only single man, but for some reason, they invite me back every year."

Kathy flashes him a dazzling smile. "Let me guess, you're in charge of bringing the wine."

"Bingo." Daniel pulls out his phone. "I'm texting Marabella now to let her know you'll be staying at The Nest. Make yourselves at home. If you need anything, just let her know."

"Thanks, Dad!" Casey says, and Kathy adds, "This is so nice of you, Mr. Love."

"Please, call me Daniel. If you're still here when I get back on Tuesday, the three of us will have dinner together." Daniel glances at his watch and gets to his feet. "I need to hit the road. Have a fun weekend."

"You too!" Casey calls after him as he heads toward the parking lot.

Kathy tilts her cappuccino cup to Casey. "You're good at this. If you decide to quit your day job, you can come work for me."

Casey's smile fades. She may very well be out of a day job soon. "I hate lying, but it's for a good cause. After what Hugh's goons did to Sheldon, I won't be able to sleep at night until they are all behind bars."

———

Casey and Kathy spend the afternoon loading up on groceries and settling in at The Nest—Casey in her usual corner room at the back of the house and Kathy in the guest room across the hall that offers a view of the courtyard driveway.

Early evening, they open a bottle of Love-Struck's new Viognier and take their salads from Delilah's down to the pool. Music from the wedding band at the winery lends a festive air as they kick off their shoes and stretch out on chaise lounges.

"I could get used to this life," Kathy says. "Why did you ever move out?"

"Don't you think I'm too old to be living with my father?" Casey asks, stuffing a forkful of kale into her mouth.

Kathy shrugs. "Depends on the circumstances." She jabs her

fork at Casey. "Hugh, for sure, is too old to be living with his father. But we're going to remedy that."

"I hope you're right," Casey says in a doubtful tone. "Getting rid of Hugh may be more difficult than you realize."

"Have faith in the process, Casey. Bad guys usually get what's coming to them."

Kathy and Casey have no sooner finished their salads and refilled their wineglasses when Hugh and Miranda stumble down the stairs from the upper terrace. They're too busy making out to notice Casey and Kathy.

"Watch this," Kathy whispers. When she clears her throat, Hugh and Miranda jump apart like teenage lovers discovered making out by their parents.

"Casey! What're you doing here?" Hugh says with hands covering his erection.

"We're staying at The Nest for a few days." She holds a hand out to Kathy. "This is my friend Sally. She's visiting from New York."

Hugh lets out a huff. "So Dad goes out of town, and you just help yourself to his house and pool."

Casey looks down her nose at him. "For your information, Daniel invited us to stay here."

"Well, beat it." Hugh flicks his wrist, waving her away. "Miranda and I want to use the pool in private."

Casey shakes her head. "Sorry. No can do. There's plenty of pool to go around."

"Have it your way." Hugh tugs his shirt over his head and drops his bathing suit, revealing a flabby belly and now limp penis.

Casey's mouth falls open. "Geez, Hugh. Spare us."

"You can either leave or stay for the show." Taking Miranda by the hand, he drags her into the pool with him. When they are waist deep, he unties her bikini and tosses it onto the pool deck. Taking her in his arms, he presses his mouth against hers while his hands roam her body.

Casey shields her eyes with one hand. "This is gross," she says to Kathy. "We should go."

"No way! We're not giving him what he wants. Besides, we were here first." Kathy pulls Casey's hand away from her eyes. "Stare at them. Make them uncomfortable."

"If you say so." Disgust fills Casey as she watches Hugh fondle Miranda's breasts.

Before long, Miranda pries herself away from him. "They are creeping me out, watching us like that. You promised me a good time. Let's go to your room. I wanna party."

A naked Miranda emerges from the pool, scoops up her dripping bikini, and saunters up the stairs.

Hugh flips Kathy and Casey the bird. "Thanks for nothing, bitches," he says, grabbing his clothes and going after her.

Casey and Kathy wait until he's out of earshot before bursting into laughter.

"He's a real piece of work. I will enjoy taking him down." Kathy drains the last of her wine and throws her legs over the side of her lounge chair. "Time to get to work."

"Am I allowed to help?"

"No. Sorry. We can't risk your safety."

They gather up their trash and head up to the kitchen.

"I don't think anything will happen tonight, but just in case, I want you to lock yourself in your room and stay there," Kathy says as they rinse their glasses and place them in the dishwasher.

"Can you at least tell me where you'll be and what you'll be doing?"

"It's better if you don't know. But you can trust me, Casey. I'm good at my job."

"I'm not worried. Your reputation precedes you." Casey leads Kathy up the back stairs. When they part in the bedroom hallway, she says, "I know you're a professional, but please be careful."

Kathy offers her a soft smile. "Don't worry, Casey. I've got this."

A feeling of doom settles over Casey as she locks the door and gets ready for bed. It's still early, and she's not yet sleepy. She tries reading, but her current novel doesn't hold her attention. This room reminds her of Luke. They slept together for the first time in this bed. Will she ever stop missing him? Is he home for Memorial Day weekend? Surely, he wouldn't come to town without contacting her. Unless he's met someone new. Maybe he brought the new chick with him for a romantic getaway. She could drive by his house tomorrow to see if his truck is in the driveway. Then again, maybe it's best if she doesn't know.

Casey falls asleep listening for sounds coming from distant parts of the house.

When she wakes around eight on Sunday morning, the house is silent, and no cars are parked in the courtyard. She makes coffee and takes her novel down to the hammock on the lower lawn. She's a million miles away, lost in her love story, when Kathy appears around eleven thirty.

"Move over," she says and falls into the hammock beside her. "I'm sorry I slept so late. I was up most of the night."

Casey closes her paperback. "What happened?"

Kathy places a hand behind her head. "Were you aware this house is a maze of secret passageways?"

Casey's eyes widen. "You're kidding."

"It makes it easy to move around without being seen or heard. There was a party in the game room in the children's wing. No one even knew I was eavesdropping on them."

Casey sits up straight. "You mean there was a party in this house last night? I never heard a thing."

"There were some sketchy-looking people here. They were coming and going all night long."

"Why didn't security bust it up?"

Kathy drags a hand down her face. "That's a good question. I need to look into it. Maybe Hugh is paying them to keep quiet. I didn't see any evidence of Hugh *using* drugs, but he's definitely dealing them. Miranda is a different story. She appeared to have serious substance abuse problems. We need to shut his operation down."

Casey shivers. "How do we do that?"

"We lie low today, hang out by the pool or whatever. For appearance's sake, we're old friends catching up. I'll do more surveillance tonight. This time, I'll use recording devices and take photographs for documentation."

"You'll call for help if you need it, right?"

"Absolutely. And I won't hesitate. No one is getting hurt on my watch. Including me." Kathy rolls out of the hammock to her feet. "Before I forget. We're meeting with my detective friend Evan at Sheldon's house on Tuesday morning at eleven. He discovered important information about Hugh's sexual assault trial."

Casey breaks out in a cold sweat. This isn't a game they are playing. Hugh is involved in nefarious activities with potentially dangerous criminals. And it's all happening under her roof. She'd pack a bag and hightail it back to her condo if the safety of her family and the success of the vineyard weren't at stake.

CHAPTER 23
HAZEL

After careful deliberation, Hazel agrees to partner with Charles in Peak Adventures. They meet at their new office space on Sunday morning for a day of painting. Although he isn't scheduled to close on the building until late June, the current owner has offered to rent to Charles so he can make improvements. They start in the main room and work their way to the outer offices, covering the drab gray walls in crisp white linen.

While they work, Charles talks animatedly about the kayaks, paddleboards, and rafts he's ordered. "Bikes are next. I'm meeting with reps from a couple of different brands this week. We'll start with a small fleet and buy more as we grow."

Hazel dips her roller into the paint and drags it down the wall. "This is all so exciting, I can hardly stand it. Laney has hired a new shop assistant, a spunky young woman who just graduated from college. Skye is an art major. Apparently, very creative. After we train her, I should have more time to help you get organized."

Charles smiles over at her. "I'll take all the help I can get. Oh! I forgot to tell you. The house officially goes on the market on Tuesday. Jamie already has two days of showings booked."

"That's excellent news." As much as Hazel misses her farmhouse, she's relieved to be leaving that part of her life in the rearview mirror.

She sets down her paint roller and brushes the hair out of her face with the back of her hand. "I'm parched. I wish I'd thought to bring some water."

"I packed a cooler. It's on the back porch." When she returns with the bottled water, Charles asks, "Are you okay? You look a little peaked."

"I'm not a hundred percent, honestly. Chef Michael gave Laney and me a to-go box of wedding food yesterday. I think maybe I ate a bad oyster or something."

Charles knit his brows. "I totally understand if you don't feel like painting."

"I'll be fine," she says. But at lunchtime, when Charles hands her a tuna salad sandwich, a wave of nausea sends her running to the restroom where she vomits the meager contents of her stomach.

She returns to the picnic table outside. "I don't know what's wrong with me. You know how much I love tuna salad."

"Try these," Charles says, handing her a small bag of chips and a can of ginger ale.

"Thanks." The combination of salt and carbonation settles her stomach, and she devours two bags of chips.

After lunch, Hazel and Charles go to separate offices to paint. When they take a break midafternoon, Charles's jovial mood from earlier has vanished.

"What's wrong? You seemed so happy earlier."

"My emotions come in waves. All the change I'm experiencing overwhelms me sometimes."

"I know that feeling, Charles. I try not to think about everything at once. Worrying about one problem at a time makes it seem more manageable."

"That makes sense." He pulls a beer out of the cooler. "Want one?"

"No, thanks. But I'll have another ginger ale if you've got one."

"No more ginger ale." Digging through the drinks, he holds out a green can. "How about a lime LaCroix?"

"That'll work. Can we go outside? I could use a break from the paint fumes," Hazel says, waving a hand in front of her nose.

She follows him out the back door, and they sit down on the steps, watching a storm system build in from the west.

Charles pops the top on his beer and takes a sip. "I can't explain this sadness that overcomes me sometimes. I'm thrilled about the business and relieved I no longer have to pretend to be someone I'm not."

"Maybe you're missing Stuart?"

Charles leans into her. "I miss you more."

She rests her head on his shoulder. "I miss us, the people we were when we first met. We got lost along the way, but we're finding our way back to our true selves."

"Well said. I hope we never lose sight of those selves again." Charles snickers. "I certainly don't miss Stuart's drama. I'm grateful he's gone, but I admit I'm lonely."

"Maybe you should look for someone new, someone who isn't married with a family." As painful as it is to admit, Hazel believes that she and Charles will one day find new significant others.

Charles sits up straight. "I'm not that lonely. Your friendship is all I need at the moment."

"Well, you've got it. Now that your secret is out in the open, we can work toward building a new friendship. Somehow, our mutual respect for one another appears to have survived our breakup."

Charles pulls his head back to get a better look at her face. "You mean, your respect for me didn't change when you found out I'm gay?"

"Not at all. If anything, I respect you for trying to please your father by living a straight life." Hazel sips her drink. "For the longest time, I felt guilty that I was the one responsible for our failing marriage. I'm relieved to know it wasn't just me, that you have flaws as well."

"I'm a deeply flawed man, Hazel. I will always be here to share your burdens, no matter how great or small," he says in a genuine tone.

"That goes ditto for me."

"Most couples hate each other when their marriage ends. Do you think it's strange how quickly we got over our breakup?"

"Not at all," Hazel says. "I think it speaks to the strength of our friendship."

Charles chugs the rest of his beer and crumples up his empty can. "Is there anything new on the adoption front?"

"Not really. I'm having a difficult time wrapping my mind around the idea of adopting a foster child. For so long, I have set my heart on having my own baby. I'm trying to summon the courage to schedule an appointment with a fertility specialist to discuss artificial insemination."

"Whoa. That would be a big move." Charles hangs his head. "I'm sorry I couldn't give you your baby, Hazel."

"It's not your fault. It just wasn't meant to be for us." She stands and pulls him to his feet. "Let's finish up before the storm sets in."

When she returns to painting, Hazel's mind wanders, and she tries to imagine what type of man she would pick as a sperm donor for her child. Would she be more concerned with looks or brains? Perhaps she'll find a man who has both. The sperm donor's genetics don't really matter to Hazel. As long as she can see something of herself in her baby.

———

Rain is coming down in sheets when Hazel arrives back at her apartment around five o'clock. Exhausted, she curls up on the sofa with a fake fur blanket and falls into a deep sleep. She wakes two hours later to a loud clap of thunder. She'd been dreaming about babies. In her dream, she was nine months pregnant and stranded in the middle of nowhere with thunderstorms threatening from every direction. A truck with tinted windows pulls up alongside her and the passenger window rolls down. From behind the steering wheel, Davis says, "Get in, babe. We can't let my baby get wet."

A lightbulb goes off in her head, and she sits bolt upright on the sofa. *So that explains the nausea and fatigue.*

Hazel darts up the stairs to the spare bedroom, where she stored some of her personal items from the farmhouse. Tearing open a box marked *toiletries,* she removes one of several pregnancy tests and takes it into the bathroom. Minutes later, she has her answer.

She punches the air and lets out a loud whoop. At long last, her prayers have been answered. No matter how she came to be pregnant, this baby growing inside of her is a gift from God. She doesn't even care if her baby daddy is a skank and potential date rapist. For as long as she can remember, getting pregnant is all she's wanted, and she'll shower her baby with all the love she has to give.

Her heart races as she stands at the window and hugs her torso. This baby belongs to her. She won't have to share custody with anyone. But what will she tell people when they ask who the baby daddy is? Will they automatically assume Charles is the father? Maybe she'll tell them she had artificial insemination with a random donor's sperm.

Hazel turns away from the window. She's too excited to keep this to herself. Many times over the years, she's longed to share news of her pregnancy with Charles. Even though their circumstances have vastly changed, he's still the person she most wants to confide in.

Grabbing her raincoat and purse, she drives back to Peak Adventures. Gripping the wooden railing, she ascends the slippery metal stairs to the second-floor apartment.

All thoughts of her pregnancy vanish when Charles opens the

door with swollen eyes and tear-stained cheeks. "Oh. I thought you were Stuart," he says in a meek voice.

"Why would Stuart be here? Isn't he in Nashville?"

"He came to town for his last load of furniture. He asked if he could see me, and I told him it wasn't a good idea, but he insisted. He's on his way over." Charles grabs her arm and pulls her inside. "Please stay. I can't face him alone."

Hazel isn't prepared to witness an intimate moment between her soon-to-be ex-husband and his gay lover. "What are you so worried about?"

Charles rubs his eyes with his balled fists. "Stuart was going on about how much he misses me on the phone. He'll try to rope me into a long-distance relationship. He can be very convincing, and I'm extremely vulnerable right now."

Hazel's heart goes out to him. So, this is how it's been all these years. Stuart has used Charles as his puppet, his plaything, to satisfy his homosexual desires. "You deserve better, Charles. Remember, he chose his wife and children over you."

A knock sounds at the door, and in a pleading tone like a lost little boy, Charles says, "Please, don't leave me."

"Fine. I'll stay if you're sure that's what you want."

He deflates with relief. "I'm positive."

"What should I tell him?" Hazel asks, one hand on the doorknob.

"Whatever it takes to get him to leave me alone." Charles's face lights up. "I know! Tell him we're working out our marriage."

Hazel sucks in a breath. "I can do better than that," she says, and swings open the door.

Stuart's jaw goes slack at the sight of Charles's wife in his apartment. "What're *you* doing here?"

Hazel turns up her nose as her eyes travel up and down his body. "I should ask you the same thing. Charles doesn't want to see you."

"I don't believe you," Stuart says, pushing past her. He aims a thumb at Hazel. "Get rid of her so we can talk."

Charles shakes his head. "She's right. I don't want to talk to you."

Hazel tugs her phone free of her raincoat pocket and holds it up to Stuart's face. "Say cheese! This time I'll save you the embarrassment and send the pics directly to your wife. I'll bet Bonnie doesn't know you're here. Or does she? Do you two have an open marriage now?"

When Stuart grabs at her phone, Hazel steps backward.

"You're such a pain in the ass, Hazel. Charles is lucky to be rid of you."

"Who says he's rid of me?" She loops her arm through Charles's. "Didn't he tell you? After years of trying, I'm finally pregnant. You can be the first to congratulate us. We're having a baby."

CHAPTER 24
CASEY

Casey is on her way to the break room for more coffee when she overhears someone in the accounting office next door mention her name.

"We have to tell Casey. We have no choice."

Her neck hairs stand to attention as she enters the office. "Tell me what?"

Renee and Marsha—the vineyards most top-ranking accounting personnel—exchange a look.

Casey plants a hand on her hip. "One of you better start talking."

Marsha gives Renee the nod, and Renee exhales a huff of air. "Our accounts are all overdrawn. We'll have to use the reserve account to make payroll at the end of the week."

"You've gotta be kidding me." Casey closes the door. "How on earth did this happen?"

"I'm done covering for him." Renee tosses her pen on the desk and sits back in her chair. "Hugh is responsible. He started making small withdrawals months ago. Now sizeable sums are leaving the account daily. He must be desperate, because he's not bothering to hide it anymore."

Casey hesitates, unsure of how to respond. Embezzlement is low, even for Hugh. "And you're sure Hugh is behind this?"

"I can print out the bank statements to show you," Marsha says.

"Please. Make several copies, if you don't mind."

Marsha's fingers fly across her keyboard and seconds later, paper shoots out of the printer. She separates the pages, staples them, and hands the stack to Casey.

"I'm sure you two understand that this is a delicate matter, and I need to decide how best to proceed. Don't do anything until you hear from me." Casey marches out of the office and down the hall, her coffee refill forgotten.

She drops the printouts on her desk and continues on for her morning tour of the winery. When she exits the building, she spots an angry-looking Bruce in the parking lot heading toward his car.

Running after him, Casey calls out, "Bruce! Wait up! Is something wrong?"

"Hugh just fired me," Bruce says, clicking his doors unlocked.

Adrenaline rushes through Casey's body. "That's absurd. On what grounds?"

"He says my services as winemaker are no longer needed now that we've reformulated the varietals."

Casey steps in his way, preventing him from getting in the car. "That's not true at all. The vineyard is growing by leaps and bounds. We need you now more than ever."

Bruce slumps against the car. "This isn't about the vineyard, Casey. Hugh blames me for breaking up his marriage."

"Hugh ruined his own marriage when he assaulted Laney. But none of that matters, because Hugh doesn't have the authority to fire you."

"Tell that to him. He offered me a month's severance and a letter of recommendation. Not that his word means anything in this industry."

"Look, Bruce. This is just a big misunderstanding. Take the rest of the day off while I sort this out."

Bruce stares at the ground as he shifts his weight from one foot to the other. "I don't know, Casey. I enjoy working here, but I've had enough of Hugh. Even if you sort it out with him, I'm not sure I can stay."

"There's a lot going on that I'm not a liberty to discuss. Can you give me a couple of days? If all goes as planned, Hugh will be the one getting fired."

"All right," Bruce says reluctantly. "But only because I don't want to leave Laney. There's not another vineyard in Virginia I would work for. If I want to continue as a winemaker, I'll have to move back to California."

"You shouldn't have to do that. We'll figure it out," she says, forcing a smile.

Casey watches Bruce drive away before turning back toward the bistro. When she opens the front door, she hears voices arguing in the kitchen. Bursting through the swinging doors, she finds Hugh wagging his finger at Chef Michael's red face.

"What's with all the yelling?" Casey asks.

"He just fired me," Michael says. "For no apparent reason."

Hugh lets out a grunt. "I gave you two reasons. You're over-paid, and your food sucks."

Moving in closer, Casey sees Hugh is sweating profusely. From the smell of him, last night's booze is seeping through his pores. "You're out of line, Hugh. Michael's cuisine is the best in town, and he's worth every penny we pay him."

"Correction. You don't pay me enough to put up with his horse manure." Michael takes off his apron and throws it on the counter. "I'm outta here."

"Good riddance," Hugh shouts at the chef's retreating back.

Casey hurries after Michael, working hard to match his stride as they cross the parking lot. "Please don't go, Michael. Hugh is a problem, and I will deal with him. But you're the face of Vino Bistro. Without you, the restaurant won't survive."

"I'm sorry, Casey. But I saw this coming a mile away. Hugh's been badgering me for weeks, and I've been looking for other jobs. I received an offer this morning at a startup restaurant in Richmond."

Near tears, Casey says, "What am I supposed to do without a chef?"

Michael arrives at his truck and opens the driver's door. "Rod is an excellent sous-chef. He can manage things until you find a replacement." He gets in the truck and drives off, leaving Casey standing alone and feeling helpless.

Twirling a strand of hair, Casey walks in circles as she decides what to do. Daniel is on his way home from North Carolina. She could call him for advice, but she can't run to him every time she has an issue. He's ready to retire. He needs to know she's capable of handling whatever problems arise, no matter how big or small.

She can do this. She'll tackle one problem at a time.

She pulls out her phone and taps on Bruce's number. He answers on the third ring. "I'm glad I caught you. I've been thinking. I'd like to expand our wine collection, and I want to start with a sparkling rosé. Can you get right on that, please?"

"But what about Hugh?"

"Let me worry about Hugh. If he gives you any more trouble, you come to me."

"Yes, ma'am," Bruce says with admiration in his tone. "I think a sparkling rosé will be an excellent addition to your collection. I'll get right on it."

Casey hangs up with Bruce and calls Fiona, her close friend and head chef at Ollie's tasting room cafe. She quickly tells Fiona about Hugh firing Chef Michael. "I'm in desperate need of a head chef. I figured you might know someone."

"I do. That someone is Rod, your sous-chef. What he lacks in experience, he makes up for in talent. I can put you in touch with a chef headhunter, but if I were you, I'd give Rod a chance first. He's truly gifted, Casey."

"That's high praise coming from you. I'll give him a shot.

Coincidentally, I'm bringing my friend from New York over later for lunch at The Foxhole."

"Cool! I can't wait to meet her. See you soon."

Pocketing her phone, Casey returns to the Vino Bistro kitchen and pulls Rod aside. "Are you capable of holding down the fort while I look for a replacement?" She's willing to give Rod a chance, but he has to ask for it.

"Yes, ma'am. I'd appreciate the opportunity to apply for the job myself. I have some special dishes I'd like to prepare for you."

"All right then. Work up a dinner menu, and I'll invite some friends over at the end of the week."

"Awesome! Prepare your friends to be wowed."

"If nothing else, I applaud your enthusiasm," she says, and exits the kitchen. One thing's for certain—Rod is much easier to be around than moody Michael.

Casey inhales a deep breath to steady her nerves. *Two problems solved. One to go,* she thinks and heads back upstairs to the administrative offices.

Hugh's door is closed, and when she enters without knocking, she finds him asleep in his chair with his feet propped on the desk. "Napping before noon? Must've been a rough night."

Hugh's eyes open wide, and he throws his feet off the desk. "Who do you think you are, barging in here without knocking?"

"I'm your business partner. Since you've been making some decisions without my approval, I'm returning the favor." She plops down in the chair opposite him. "I've rehired Bruce. For the foreseeable future, he'll be working on a new sparkling rosé varietal. And I'm allowing Rod, our sous-chef, to apply for the head chef position."

He glares at her. "And if I don't agree?"

"I'll show Daniel these." She holds up the printouts from the bank accounts.

Hugh squints as he tries to read the small print. "What is that?"

"Evidence of your embezzlement. Keep your greedy hands out

of our bank accounts." Casey stands and slaps the printout on the desk in front of Hugh. "I'll have accounting tally up these withdrawals. You have exactly one month to return the money to the accounts."

Hugh goes pale. "Or else what?"

"Or else I'll press charges," she says, and strides out of his office, feeling proud of herself for standing up to him.

CHAPTER 25
SHELDON

Sheldon is surprised to find Gray waiting on his porch early Tuesday morning.

"Dude! What happened to you? Did you get into a fight?"

Sheldon massages his jaw. "The bruises are actually fading. You should've seen me a week ago." He motions Gray inside. "Come on in. I'll make us some coffee."

Sheldon senses Gray watching him as he sets the Keurig to brew.

"You're really moving slow, bro. Who beat you up? Was it Hugh?"

Sheldon hands Gray a steaming cup of coffee. "I wish I could tell you, but there's some family stuff going down right now, and I'm not allowed to talk about it."

Gray furrows his brow. "That sounds serious, Sheldon. Be careful. If it was Hugh, I hope you give him what he deserves."

Sheldon makes a second cup of coffee, and the men go out to the wicker rockers on the porch. "You're here early. I assume you have an update on our purchase offer."

"I wish I had better news. Miranda finally admitted that Hugh is the anonymous buyer. He's matched your escalation clause and raised it by fifty grand."

A heaviness settles over Sheldon. He dreads having to tell Ollie. "That sucks for us. My offer was a stretch as it was. No offense, man, but only a fool would pay way more than a property is worth."

"I agree wholeheartedly. Miranda and I have been arguing about this for days. I don't trust Hugh one bit, and she's hell-bent on selling him the vineyard." Gray sips his coffee. "Something's up with her. I can't put my finger on it. The last few times I've seen her, she's been wild-eyed and strung out. I'd be willing to bet the dirty little secret you overheard them talking about has to do with illegal drugs."

Sheldon grunts. "Those dirty little secrets are actually big filthy lies."

Gray shakes his head in disgust. "Am I supposed to just turn my family's vineyard over to him?"

"Not necessarily." Sheldon shifts in his seat. "I'm hesitant to say too much. But I can tell you we have people looking into the situation. If I were you, I'd buy myself some time. Accept the deposit but tell Hugh you can't close until after the harvest in the fall."

"That's not a bad idea, Sheldon. It makes sense for me to see this growing season through anyway. How much time do you need?"

"I'm not sure. Hopefully, only a couple of weeks."

Ollie, with the baby nestled in the crook of her arm, appears in the kitchen doorway. "Morning, Gray. Can I offer you some breakfast?"

Gray stands to go. "Thanks, but I've already eaten, and I need to get to work. Let's stay in touch," he says, clapping Sheldon on the shoulder.

Sheldon winces.

"Sorry, man. Did I hurt you?"

"The guys that did this to my face broke several of my ribs as well."

Gray glances in Ollie's direction and lowers his voice. "You have a wife and kid to protect. Maybe you should leave town for a while."

"I'm hoping it won't come to that. Let me know if anything suspicious happens with Miranda," Sheldon says, seeing Gray to the door.

After his friend leaves, Sheldon gathers their empty coffee mugs and joins Ollie in the kitchen, taking the baby from her while she scrambles eggs.

"We didn't get the vineyard, did we?" she asks as she melts butter in a skillet.

Sheldon lowers himself to a barstool. "How'd you know?"

"Your long face."

"I'm not giving up. There's still hope," he says and repeats his conversation with Gray.

Ollie slides a plate of eggs in front of him, and then takes the sleeping baby from his arms so he can eat. She brews a cup of Earl Grey tea and joins him at the counter.

Sheldon shovels a forkful of eggs into his mouth. "What do you think about us taking the baby and driving up to Maine for a couple of weeks?"

Ollie arches an eyebrow. "What's in Maine?"

"Not Hugh." He washes his eggs down with orange juice. "It doesn't have to be Maine. Just somewhere far away from my brother and his goons."

"We can't let Hugh have that kind of power over us. Besides, I feel safe here with the security company protecting us. Hugh's going down, and after all he's done to me, I want to be here to witness it," Ollie says, her eyes cold with vengeance.

"We have to think of Henry's safety. Let's wait until after our meeting to decide."

————

Detective Evan Beck—mid-thirties with dark hair and bulging muscles—is the first to arrive at eleven, followed shortly thereafter by Casey and Kathy. They gather around the pine table in the kitchen with a pitcher of sweet tea in front of them.

"Where's Ollie?" Casey asks, pouring everyone a glass of tea.

Sheldon points at the ceiling. "Upstairs with the baby. The less she knows, the better. She's a nervous wreck as it is."

"We have a lot to discuss," Evan says, planting his elbows on the table. "The court records from Hugh's assault case have been sealed. But we did some digging and discovered he paid an enormous sum of money to make the charges disappear."

Sheldon frowns. "Who did he pay? A judge?"

Evan shakes his head. "I'm not sure. And I honestly don't want to know. We believe Hugh got in over his head financially with the payoff and started dealing drugs."

"I learned this morning he's in even deeper financial trouble," Casey says. "The vineyard's accounts are overdrawn, and we have evidence Hugh's the one making the withdrawals. Question is, Why is he stealing from the vineyard when he's making all this money from selling drugs?"

"I may have the answer to that," Sheldon says. "Hugh and I have been in a bidding war for Valley View Vineyard. Hugh's latest counter is way more than the property is worth. I withdrew my offer this morning."

Casey toys with a lock of golden hair. "Why would he be skimming money out of the accounts to buy Valley View? Wouldn't he make the offer on behalf of Love-Struck?"

"Unless he plans to purchase it in his name," Sheldon suggests.

"We'll look into it and let you know what we find." Evan pulls an index card out of his pocket and scribbles a note to himself. "We've launched a widespread investigation into his drug-related activities. We have enough evidence to bust him now. However, we'd prefer to go after the ringleader."

Casey stares at him with mouth agape. "You're gonna allow

Hugh to continue selling drugs out of The Nest? While our father is living there?"

"It won't be for long," Evan says. "A few days. A week, tops. We're already making progress."

Kathy chimes in. "If it makes you feel better, Casey, I've committed to seeing this operation through. I'll be working closely with Evan's team."

Evan offers to place two undercover DEA agents at Love-Struck. "As dishwashers or fieldworkers or valet attendants. Wherever you can find a place for them."

Sheldon looks across the table at Casey. He can see the fear in her eyes, and his heart goes out to her. "Why don't you come stay with Ollie and me until this is over? We have private security guards around the clock."

"I'll be fine. But shouldn't we tell Daniel? For his own safety."

"I would advise against that," Evan says in a warning tone. "Parents instinctively want to protect their children, no matter how old they are. If Daniel thinks Hugh is in trouble, he could interfere with our investigation."

Sheldon nods. "I agree with Evan. Dad will do anything to keep Hugh out of jail."

"Are you saying you wouldn't do the same?" Kathy asks. "After all, Hugh is your brother."

Sheldon looks away. "Hugh dug his grave. Now he has to lie in it."

Kathy places her hand on Casey's. "Don't worry. I won't let anything happen to Daniel. To either of you. I promise."

Casey falls back in her chair. "Whatever. The sooner we get this over with, the better."

Evan rises from the table. "All right then. We have a plan. I can hardly believe all this is happening in little old Lovely. Our town has never had a drug problem until a few months ago. But things have quickly spiraled out of control. Several young women claim to have been drugged at the Blue Saloon. Every weekend, local police are raiding parties where a wide range of drugs are being abused. Many of these parties involve our youth, and we need to protect them from themselves."

"Is there anything we can do to help?" Casey asks.

"Just remain vigilant. Kathy will be your contact. You see or hear anything, you tell her. If you need anything, you let her know. Thanks to her diligent undercover work over the weekend, we're already surveilling several key suspects. With luck, we'll wrap this investigation up by week's end." Evan turns to Sheldon. "If I may have a word with you alone."

Out on the porch, Sheldon says, "What's up? Not more bad news, I hope."

"Nothing like that." He grabs Sheldon's arm, pulling him close. "I'm sure I don't need to say this to you, but no matter what happens, don't go anywhere near Love-Struck until this is over. Your wife and baby are your priority."

Sheldon nods. "I get it. You have nothing to worry about."

After Evan leaves, Sheldon returns to the kitchen to find Kathy consoling a crying Casey. "That's it. I'm taking you, Ollie, and the baby. And we're going on a little vacation until this is over."

Casey jumps to her feet, wiping at her eyes. "No, Sheldon! We have to see this through. I'm mostly worried about Dad. But I understand the need to keep him out of the loop." She pulls Kathy to her feet. "Besides, I have my personal bodyguard here to protect me."

"All right. We'll stay and fight." He engulfs Casey in a bear hug, lifting her off the floor a little. "Hugh will soon be out of our lives, and our town will once again be safe."

Sheldon goes to the bottom of the stairs and calls up for Ollie. "Come on, honey. Let's go eat. I'm starving."

On the way to The Foxhole, Ollie and Kathy walk the baby stroller ahead of Casey and Sheldon. "Are you sure you're okay, Casey?"

"I'm handling it. Hugh is growing increasingly desperate." Casey tells him about Hugh firing Bruce and Michael.

Sheldon stops walking. "Did you tell Dad?"

"No, and I'm not going to."

"You're making a mistake, Casey. These are things Dad needs to know."

She loops her arm through Sheldon and drags him onward. "It's hard not to run to Daniel every time there's a problem. I feel like a little girl walking in her daddy's big shoes. I'm making these huge decisions that affect *his* vineyard. But he needs to trust that whoever takes over the vineyard can handle it."

"I don't agree with you, but it's your decision." They walk for a minute in silence. "You realize it's game over if Hugh gets arrested."

"I'm banking on it. I feel guilty. He's making it easy for me. I wish you had stayed in the competition. You belong at Love-Struck."

"A part of me does. The other part is happy here. I've never felt so torn in my life." Sheldon shoves his hands in his pockets. "Let's get through the next few days, and then we'll figure everything out once the dust settles. I have faith in Kathy, but I want you to promise you'll call me if things get out of hand."

"Don't worry. I will."

How can Sheldon not worry when his family is in danger, and he's not allowed to help them?

CHAPTER 26
HAZEL

Hazel emerges from the examining room and continues down the hall to where Charles is waiting for her in the reception area. On Sunday night, after Stuart left Charles's apartment, Hazel confessed about her one-night stand with Davis, omitting the part about the possibility he may have drugged her.

Charles had seemed genuinely excited for her. "What difference does it make how you got pregnant? You're finally getting the child you've always wanted."

Hazel had smiled at him. "I think so too. I'm glad to hear you say that."

Charles tosses a *Fit Pregnancy* magazine on the coffee table and stands to greet her. "Well?"

"It's official. I'm pregnant. The baby is due on January twenty-first."

"Congratulations, Mama. Why don't we go to Traveler's to celebrate? My treat."

"Let me check with Laney. The new girl started this morning. I need to make sure they don't need me." She types off a text to Laney, who responds that everything is going well and for Hazel to enjoy her lunch.

Hazel and Charles, arriving ahead of the lunch crowd, are rewarded with a secluded table in the deck's corner.

"I have a proposition for you, Hazel," Charles says, once waitress has taken their order. "Hear me out before you respond. I'm not at all suggesting we get back together, but I would like to raise this child as my own. I am as excited about this baby as I was when we first talked about starting a family. Somewhere along the way, I got too wrapped up in my toxic relationship with Stuart, and my desire to be a father waned. But I can provide emotional and financial support to you. After all, being a member of the Love family has special perks."

"There are also high expectations and responsibilities associated with bearing the name. You know that better than anyone else." She sips her tea. "Your offer is incredibly generous, but I'm not sure you know what you're getting into. I suspect there's a lot we don't know about Davis Warren. This baby could carry some unscrupulous genes. I'll deal with whatever God gives me. But I wouldn't want to saddle you with burdens brought on by the sins of my baby's father."

"Don't go there, Hazel. This baby will be born with a clean slate. With the enormous amount of love you'll give the child, I'm confident he or she will become a well-adjusted little human being."

Hazel focuses her attention on tearing her paper napkin into tiny pieces. "Ruthie and Laney know about what happened with Davis. They might suspect he's the father. What would we tell them?"

Charles places his hand over hers to stop the napkin shredding. "That we got a paternity test that proves I'm the father. No one ever has to know any different."

"You're not suggesting we live together, are you?"

"Not at all. Although I'd like to help you find a house, preferably one with a guest room for me. I envision myself helping with middle-of-the-night feedings in the beginning."

She looks away, staring out at the mountains. "I was all set to raise the child on my own. I like the idea of not having to answer to anyone."

Charles places a hand over his heart. "I promise to never interfere in any major issues regarding the child. I simply want to provide love and support."

She stares at him with eyes aglow. "I'm touched by your generosity. But I need some time to think about it."

"I understand. This is an important decision, and you should take as much time as you need. I promise not to pressure you."

The waitress brings their meals—a grilled chicken sandwich with sweet potato fries for him and a salmon kale salad for her.

"I have good news," Charles says as he dips a fry in ranch dressing. "Jamie texted while you were in with the doctor. The showings are going well. He expects several offers by the end of the day tomorrow."

"That's exciting. I have good news as well. Starting next Monday, I'll be part-time at Laney's. I'm looking forward to working at Peak Adventures."

"Outstanding! I've hired a guide to help with the water excursions. The kayaks and rafts arrive tomorrow and bicycles at the end of the week. I was hoping you would take charge of the vineyard bike tour."

Hazel's eyes grow wide. "I would absolutely love that. Do you trust me with something so important?"

Charles looks at her as though she has two heads. "Wholeheartedly. There's no one better for the job. I figure we'll wing it as best we can this summer. My goals are to book as many tours as possible and get our name out on social media. After Labor Day, we'll regroup and establish our direction going forward."

A mischievous smirk appears on Hazel's lips. "I'm great at social media."

Charles chuckles. "I remember all too well." He points a fry at her. "Consider yourself in charge of social media."

"Cool. Action photos will be way more exciting to work with than wedding flowers."

Charles smiles. "Don't let Laney hear you say that."

While they finish eating, they discuss ways to promote their business. By the time Charles pays the check, they've developed a manageable plan to get the word out about Peak Adventures.

When he drops Hazel off at the flower shop, Charles says, "Think about what I said. I would love nothing more than to be your baby's father. We can talk about it more if you have questions."

"You're a good man, Charles Love." Hazel leans over the console and kisses his cheek. "I like how our new friendship is developing."

His lips curve into a smile. "So do I."

The phone is ringing when Hazel enters the shop. "I've got it," she calls out to Laney and Skye, who are busy creating arrangements in the back.

She answers the phone and takes a large order for an upcoming dinner party. She replaces the phone receiver and looks up, surprised to see Davis standing across the counter from her.

Hazel's heart skips a beat. What's he doing here? Did he find out about the baby somehow?

"What do you want?" she murmurs.

"To order some flowers for Ruthie."

Hazel's shoulders sag with relief. "Fine," she says, reaching for her order pad. "What did you have in mind?"

"Two dozen red roses." When Hazel rolls her eyes, he says, "What's wrong with red roses?"

"They're cliche. Why not go with pink roses? After all, pink is Ruthie's favorite color."

"Geez . . . you say it like I'm supposed to know her favorite color."

"In Ruthie's case, how can you not? Her house is pink. She wears bright pink lipstick and hot pink fingernail polish. Her uniforms are pink. Her name is written in pink on the diner window."

Davis's hand shoots up, motioning for her to stop talking. "Okay. I get it. Make it pink roses."

Hazel scribbles on the pad. "How about mixing in some pink peonies and tulips?"

"Whatever you think is best," he says in a curt tone.

"How much did you want to spend?"

Davis shrugs. "I don't know how much flowers cost. How about four hundred dollars?"

"We can do a lovely arrangement for a hundred and fifty," she says, writing the amount on her order.

"Then why'd you ask?"

"Because I figured you for a cheapskate." Hazel grabs an enclosure card and envelope. With pen poised over the card, she asks, "What would you like the card to say?"

"I'll do it," he says, snatching the card and pen from her.

While he fills out the card, she processes the charge. "When would you like these delivered?"

"As soon as possible." He slides the sealed envelope across the counter to her. "I gather that won't be a problem, since she works next door."

"No problem at all," she says, planting a fake smile on her lips.

She waits until he leaves before collapsing against the counter. That was close. In a few weeks, he'll be able to see her baby bump. Gossip spreads like wildfire in small towns. Now that everyone knows Charles is gay, people will wonder if he's the baby's father. If Davis thinks the baby is his, he might demand she have an abortion. Or worse. He might insist on being part of her child's life.

Hazel remembers what Charles said about a paternity test. Maybe she should take him up on his offer. Having a partner to help parent her child isn't a bad thing. Unless they get in a fight and Charles tries to take the child away from her. The same is true for their joint business venture. Should she risk everything with this man who lied to her about his sexual orientation for the entirety of their marriage? Clearly, she didn't learn her lesson the first time. But things are different this time. She has to follow her heart. And it's leading her toward a future with Charles as her best friend.

CHAPTER 27
RUTHIE

Ruthie's heart flutters when Daniel enters the cafe midafternoon on Tuesday. She hasn't seen him in weeks, and he's the picture of health with bright eyes and sun-kissed skin. He's no longer using his cane, and his limp is hardly noticeable. A sharp pain rips across her chest as she realizes she still loves him. If she doesn't get him back now, she'll regret it for the rest of her life.

She presses a hip against the counter and uses her sexiest voice to entice him. "Hey there, stranger. What brings you in?"

"I'm on my way home from the beach in North Carolina. I've been obsessing about your apple pie all weekend. Please tell me you have some."

"I just took one out of the oven a few minutes ago. Would you like that à la mode?"

"Absolutely," Daniel says, rubbing his toned gut.

Ruthie notices his new six-pack abs. Who is he trying to impress? Millie?

"I'll be right back." Ruthie disappears into the kitchen, and when she returns with the pie, Hazel is making her way through the front with an enormous arrangement of flowers.

Ruthie hollers across the diner to Hazel, "Those are gorgeous. Who are they for?"

"You," Hazel says from behind the bouquet.

Ruthie's heart does a somersault. They must be from Daniel. How like him to have flowers delivered while he's here.

Navigating the maze of tables, Hazel sets the arrangement on the counter next to Daniel. "They're from Davis."

Ruthie drops her smile. "Oh."

Hazel turns toward Daniel. "You're looking well. Where have you been to get such a tan?"

"Thank you. I was down at Figure Eight over the weekend. Charles told me about your business venture. I hope you two know what you're doing. The arrangement is unusual considering your marital situation."

"I have faith in us. Turns out, that marriage license was getting in the way of our friendship." Hazel's gaze shifts to the window behind Daniel. "Oops! There's a customer entering the shop. Laney and Skye are up to their eyeballs in flowers, and I'm supposed to be manning the showroom," she says, and hurries out of the diner.

Ruthie removes the enclosure card from the arrangement. Her face warms as she reads Davis's message. *I miss you. Give me another chance. Have dinner with me on Thursday night.*

When she looks up from the card, Daniel is watching her with a quizzical expression. "Love agrees with you, Ruthie."

"I'm not—"

"I lied about the pie." He drags his fork through the vanilla ice cream. "I stopped by to see you. We left things somewhat unsettled between us, and I wanted to clear the air. Hazel and Charles are an inspiration. If they can be friends, so can we, now that we're both dating other people." He smiles up at her. "Besides, I miss coming here for breakfast."

The earth falls from beneath her. Daniel doesn't miss her. He misses her sunny-side-up eggs.

Ruthie returns the card to the envelope and slips it in her uniform pocket. "Are you and Millie serious?"

"Millie and I have a lot in common," he says nonchalantly.

Of course they do. They're both cut from the same designer fabric.

Tears sting Ruthie's eyes, and she turns away from him. Over her shoulder, she says, "Excuse me, Daniel. I need to check on something in the oven."

Locking herself in the bathroom, she wills herself not to cry. She should've accepted his proposal when she had the chance. She gambled and lost. And now their relationship is over for good.

Removing her phone from her pocket, she thumbs off a message to Davis. *Thank you for the gorgeous flowers. I would love to have dinner with you on Thursday.* She isn't interested in getting back together with Davis. She just needs someone to soften the blow of losing Daniel.

When she returns to the dining room, Daniel is gone. She pockets the ten-dollar bill he left, and she's on the way to the back with his empty plate, when Jamie bursts through the door.

"Ruthie! I'm glad I caught you. I've found a buyer for the diner."

"Give me a second. Let me put this in the back." Ruthie retreats into the back, dropping the plate in the sink and pausing to steady her breath. The diner is all she has left. No way is she selling it now. But after all his hard work, she'll have to find a way to gently break the news to Jamie.

Wiping her hands on her apron, Ruthie returns to the front. "So tell me about this potential buyer."

"She's a middle-aged woman from Texas. She moved here to get away from the undocumented immigrants flooding the southern border. She's eaten here several times this past week."

A lightbulb goes off in Ruthie's head. "She's the attractive redhead who sits alone at a table by the window. I wondered why she always ordered several menu items as though she's eating for ten instead of one."

"That's Trixie. She loves everything about the diner. The food and the decor. The only thing she wants to change is the name. From Ruthie's to Trixie's."

Ruthie absently wipes the counter with a damp rag. "Trixie's Diner has a nice ring."

Jamie hands her a file. "I printed out her contract. She's offering full asking price with a closing date of July thirty-first."

"I'm sorry, Jamie, but I'm taking the diner off the market," Ruthie says, and spins away from his astonished expression.

"What is wrong with you, Ruthie? You won't get a better offer than this." He jabs a finger at the file in her hands. "That contract is clean."

"For personal reasons, I've decided not to sell. It's my prerogative."

Jamie's face flushes red with anger as he snatches the file out of her hands. "You can't jerk people around like this, Ruthie. I've worked hard for you. The next time the wind blows, and you decide to put it back on the market, don't call me. I don't represent flakes like you." He storms out of the diner, the front door banging shut behind him.

Ruthie goes after him, catching up with him on the sidewalk. "Jamie, wait! I'm sorry. I'm having a bad day. The diner is all I have. My parents started the restaurant, and I've worked here all my life. I'm afraid of letting it go."

Jamie softens. "I get that. But you can't keep changing your mind." He hands her back the file. "Trixie is offering you a boatload of money. You'll be set for life. You have to at least consider it. I'll figure out a way to stall her for a few days."

Ruthie flips through the contract to the money page. "There *are* a lot of zeros behind that number." She lets out a sigh. "You're right. I probably won't see this kind of money again. Let me think about it. I'll get back to you by the end of the week."

CHAPTER 28
CASEY

Casey has only been at her desk a few minutes on Wednesday morning when Daniel summons her to his study at The Nest. Fear and uncertainty overcome her. Daniel reserves his inner sanctum for all his serious talks. Has she done something wrong? Is he going to lecture her?

She leaves her office and race-walks across the lawn to the mansion. When she arrives, instead of waiting for her in his study, Daniel is having breakfast on the back terrace.

He rises out of his chair to greet her. "Good morning, sunshine. Care to join me for breakfast?"

Casey pats her stomach. "Sally and I ate earlier. I'm still stuffed. Now I understand why you always rave about Marabella's *famous* French toast."

Daniel chuckles. "What is it you youngsters call it, a food coma? I'm headed in that direction for sure."

Casey slides into the chair opposite him, and Marabella appears with a pot of coffee. "Back for seconds?"

"Haha. No. I was just going on about your French toast, but I couldn't eat another bite." She eyes the coffee pot. "I'll have some coffee though, please."

Marabella fills her cup and disappears inside.

Casey studies her father. He's the healthiest she's seen him since before his stroke. "How was your trip?"

"Relaxing." He looks at her over a forked sausage link. "A little birdie told me you encountered some monumental problems while I was gone."

Casey wrinkles her brow. "I'm guessing this little birdie is your youngest son."

Daniel nods. "Sheldon was singing your praises. He says you have things under control. But he wanted me to be aware of what's going on, and he thought you should be the one to tell me."

She sits back in her chair with her coffee mug. "Hugh fired Bruce. He told him his services as winemaker are no longer needed since we've reconstituted our varietals."

Daniel lowers his fork. "He can't do that without my approval."

Casey wraps her hands around her mug. "That's the part that confuses me, that you never made clear. Isn't the point of our competition to prove we can manage the vineyard without you?"

"To a certain extent. But if one of you fires key personnel, I need to know about it. Please tell me Bruce didn't leave."

"He's still here. I hired him back. I have him working on a sparkling rosé varietal for us."

Daniel points his fork at her. "Smart thinking! Sparkling rosés are growing in popularity."

Casey sips her coffee. "Hugh also fired Chef Michael, claiming we were overpaying him. Unfortunately, I wasn't able to convince Michael to stay."

"That's not good," Daniel says as lines appear on his forehead. "What're we doing about a chef?"

"Rod, our sous-chef, is currently managing the kitchen. He asked to be considered for the head job. What he lacks for in experience, he makes up for in talent. He's creating a special menu, and I'm putting a table together for sampling tomorrow night. I hope you can come."

Daniel doesn't hesitate. "I wouldn't miss it. May I bring Millie?"

"Absolutely! I invited the whole family, including Ada and Enzo. They have news to share, which could be interesting."

Daniel's face lights up. "Do you think she's having a baby?"

Casey shrugs. "What else could it be, since they already bought a house and started their own business?"

"How exciting! I'm going to be a grandfather again. Who else is coming to the dinner?"

Casey ticks off the guests on her fingers. "Charles asked if he could bring Hazel. Not sure what that's about, but I guess we'll find out soon enough."

"Charles and Hazel are going into business together. I think it's too soon after the divorce, but who am I to argue? Who else is coming to dinner?"

"Sheldon declined. He doesn't go out much these days with an infant at home. Hugh hasn't responded. And Sally. I hope you don't mind if she stays until the end of the week. Being away from New York has given her the reset she needed."

"I don't mind at all. Both of you are welcome to stay as long as you'd like. I enjoy having young people in the house again." He looks over at the new construction next door. "Speaking of houses, mine is almost finished. Would you like to see it?"

Casey has a full morning ahead, but she hasn't yet broken the news to Daniel about Hugh's embezzlement. "Sure! But I can only spare a minute."

On the short walk next door, Casey broaches the subject. "There's something else you should know. Marsha and Renee in our accounting department found some discrepancies in our bank accounts."

Daniel stops walking. "What sort of discrepancies?"

Casey faces him. "For several months now, Hugh has been withdrawing sizeable sums of money. I'm honestly not sure what's going on. Maybe he's stretched thin because of the divorce and assault charges. Maybe it has to do with the bidding war he's in with Sheldon for the purchase of Valley View Vineyard. Hugh countered Sheldon's latest offer with a price that's way more than the property is worth."

Daniel's expression turns grim. "Do Marsha and Renee have evidence of these withdrawals?"

"I have copies on my desk. I'll email them to you when I get back to my office."

Daniel looks away, staring over at The Nest. "Did you confront Hugh about the missing money?"

"I did. I told him he has a month to pay back the money, or I'm pressing charges."

Her words hang in the air between them. Thirty days is also the deadline for Daniel to choose his successor.

Daniel proceeds to the house, fumbling in his pocket for the key. He opens the door and steps out of the way for Casey to enter. The small foyer opens into a large living area with massive windows. Off the living room is a screened porch leading to a stone terrace on the level below.

They stand at the windows, looking out over the mountain range. "I've decided to build a pool," Daniel says. "Whoever takes over The Nest doesn't want me hanging around the pool all the time."

Whoever takes over The Nest? Is he serious? Is Daniel still considering Hugh for the head position after everything she just told him?

Turning her back to the windows, Casey goes to the adjacent kitchen, inspecting the handsome hunter-green cabinets and commercial-grade appliances. Dragging her fingers across the quartz countertops, she asks in a teasing tone, "Are you taking Marabella with you when you leave? Or will Millie be cooking for you?"

"I can cook for myself, thank you very much. I enjoy Millie's company, but we aren't serious. I was using her to make Ruthie jealous. Unfortunately, it isn't working. Ruthie is in love with her hardware store boy toy."

"It won't last. That guy is creepy."

"So, what do you think?" Daniel asks as they leave the kitchen and migrate back toward the front of the house.

"You're definitely downsizing. Are you sure you won't feel cramped over here?"

"Maybe a little at first. But it's time to pass the baton."

Daniel locks the door, and they stroll back across the yard.

As they approach The Nest, Casey wonders what living here all alone would be like. With no husband or children, only herself to rattle around in the vast rooms. She suddenly feels overwhelmed at the prospect of the upkeep. "It must be a massive job to take care of an estate this size."

"The Nest is a well-oiled machine. We have maintenance and grounds crews to handle most everything."

"It seems like a lot for one person."

"The house is intended for a family. Generations of Loves have raised large broods of children here. Speaking of which, have you heard anything from Luke?"

"Not a word. I assume he's waiting for me to make my decision about my career, because obviously he's not changing his mind about his."

They reach the pool level, and Daniel turns toward her. "Have you thought about whether you'll stay on at the vineyard if Hugh wins the promotion?"

Casey's brow hits her hairline. Has he lost his mind? Then she notices the corners of his mouth twitching. He's goading her. He's intentionally getting under her skin to see how she'll respond. As if she hasn't already shown him how tough she is.

She looks him dead in the eye. "No. Because I have no intention of losing the competition."

"Good answer. But remember, despite Hugh's flawed judgement, he's still my son. I can't turn my back on him, any more than I would turn my back on you."

"I hope you know what you're doing. Because Hugh's *flawed judgement* may very well result in the downfall of this vineyard."

Casey whirls around and strides off in the opposite direction, toward the winery. For the first time since this ridiculous competition started, she doesn't care if she wins or loses. If Daniel is stupid enough to pick Hugh, then father and son can wallow in their *flawed judgements* together.

CHAPTER 29
HAZEL

Charles is waiting outside Hazel's apartment when she gets off work at six o'clock.

"Jamie has received five offers on the house. He's on his way over to present them to us. Can we meet in your apartment?"

"Sure!" Hazel says with the key already in hand. They've barely reached the top of the stairs when Jamie arrives with two large pizzas and his work satchel slung over his shoulder.

Hazel grabs paper plates and napkins for the pizza and beers for the men. Gathered around the small dining table, they carefully read through each contract. Narrowing it down to the two offering the highest price, they choose the one with no contingencies and a requested closing date of June thirtieth.

"Out of curiosity, do we know anything about the buyers?" Hazel asks and stuffs the last bite of pizza crust in her mouth.

Jamie flips through his notes. "He's a young doctor, and she's a nurse. They have three children under the age of six."

"Perfect," Hazel says, a satisfied smile spreading across her lips. The joyful sounds of children's laughter will finally fill her beloved farmhouse.

Jamie gathers up the contracts. "That's it then. I'll notify the other agent. Congratulations," he says, and grabs one last slice of pizza on his way out.

Charles collects the trash while Hazel stores the leftover pizza in two Ziplock bags. She hands one bag to Charles. "Here. For your lunch tomorrow."

"Are you kicking me out already? I was hoping we could take a walk. I have something to show you."

"A walk sounds nice." Hazel removes a lightweight sweater from a hook beside the door. "Can we get gelato on the way to wherever we're going?"

Charles's brow shoots up. "Are you having cravings already?"

"I wouldn't call it a craving. But I'm hungry all the time."

"Better than morning sickness, I guess."

"I like your positive thinking. What flavor should I get?" As they lock up and walk around to the front of the building, Hazel debates between salt caramel, pistachio, and strawberry cheesecake.

Charles laughs. "You're seriously excited about this gelato."

"I can hardly wait." But when they encounter the line of people streaming out the door at Delilah's, her spirits deflate. "Never mind. I don't need gelato that badly."

"The line's moving quickly. I've got this. You wait here," Charles says and motions her to a nearby park bench.

"Are you sure?"

"Positive. What's the winning flavor?"

She grins. "Surprise me."

Easing down to the bench, Hazel watches Charles progress up the steps and into the gourmet shop. Now that the farmhouse has sold, she allows herself to consider where she might live when she moves out of the apartment. She's so lost in thought, she doesn't notice when Davis slides onto the bench beside her.

He rests an arm behind her. "Hey, gorgeous. Why are you sitting all alone?"

She inches away from him. "I'm not alone. I'm waiting for my husband to bring me gelato."

"You must be joking. You're getting back together with that fag."

Hazel cuts her eyes at him. "Homophobia is not a good look, Davis. Not that it's any of your business, but Charles and I are still friends. Some couples have relationships after they divorce."

"You're a buzzkill, Hazel. I don't know what I ever saw in you." Davis gets to his feet. "By the way, I convinced Ruthie to have dinner with me on Thursday. If you try to sabotage our date, I'll . . ." His voice trails off.

"You'll what, Davis? Are you threatening me?"

Davis looks around, as if checking to make certain no one is nearby, before leaning in close. "Screw up my relationship with Ruthie, and you'll leave me no choice. I'll post images from our hookup on social media. You were awfully naughty that night. You don't want anyone to see them." He hunches a shoulder. "Or maybe you do. If you decide to quit your job at the flower shop, you'd be a shoo-in for the lead in a porn movie."

Chills travel Hazel's spine. "You're bluffing."

A smirk tugs at his lips. "Are you willing to take that chance?"

Hazel glances toward Delilah's, hoping to see Charles heading her way. But he's still at the checkout counter, paying for the gelato. When she turns back, Davis has disappeared. Did she imagine the encounter? She sniffs, smelling the lingering scent of his patchouli cologne. She'll never get away from him as long as they live in the same town.

Charles returns with their gelato. "They only had three flavors. Lucky for you, one of them was strawberry cheesecake."

She takes the cup from him.

Charles narrows his eyes. "Do you feel all right? You're as pale as a ghost."

"Let's just go." She starts off toward the sidewalk, and when he steps in line beside her, she says, "What did you want to show me?"

"You'll have to see for yourself. It's this way." He leads her across Magnolia Avenue and down a side street away from the center of town. They weave their way in and around the blocks of the picturesque neighborhood until they come to a Cape Cod with gray siding, black shutters, and a wide front porch.

"Who lives here?" she asks.

"No one at the moment. But an old high school buddy owns it. He's been renting it for the past couple of years, but his tenants have moved out, and he's putting it on the market in a few weeks. It'd be perfect for you and the baby. As long as your offer is competitive, Drew promised to give you special consideration."

Hazel closes her eyes, but when she tries to imagine living in the house with the baby, all she sees is Davis lurking behind the bushes. He will be a constant threat. The only way to get rid of him is to leave town.

"I'll think about it." Hazel turns away from the gray Cape Cod and begins retracing their steps.

Charles is slightly out of breath when he catches up with her. "Talk to me, Hazel. I can tell something happened while I was inside Delilah's."

Hazel increases her pace. "I ran into Davis. He claims he has inappropriate pictures of me from our night together. He threatened to post them on social media. If he does, people will suspect he's the baby's father."

Charles stops in his tracks. "What a jerk. We'll fix him. Hold this." He hands Hazel his gelato and removes his phone from his pocket.

"What're you doing?" she asks, watching his thumbs fly across the screen.

"Googling, to see how soon we can get a paternity test. This says a blood test at seven or eight weeks of pregnancy can determine who the father is. That's next week. So, we lie and tell everyone I'm the father."

She hands him back his gelato, and they start walking again. "I'm having some reservations about passing my baby off as yours."

"What reservations?"

"If you're listed on the birth certificate, you'll legally be the baby's father. What if we get in a fight and you try to take my child away from me?"

"That won't happen, but if it makes you feel better, we'll have a legal agreement drawn up."

"I guess that could work." They reach Magnolia Avenue and Hazel dumps the rest of her now-melted gelato in the trash can. "But what do I do about Davis? As long as he has these incriminating images, he's never going to leave me alone." She stares down at the ground. "This is so embarrassing."

"You can't let him get away with it. Next thing you know, he'll be bribing you. Report him to the police, Hazel."

"If I press charges, the case will go to court and the entire world will know what happened."

"An old high school buddy of mine is a detective with the Lovely Police Department. I can arrange for us to meet with him in private. You can tell him you wish to remain anonymous."

Hazel's lip quivers. "I haven't told you the worst of it. I think there's a chance Davis may have drugged me that night." She tells him about overhearing the college girls talking at the diner. "At first, I couldn't remember anything that happened after we left Blue Saloon. Then bits and pieces started coming back." She chokes back a sob. "You know me, Charles. I'm not into kinky sex. I must have been under the influence of something to do the things I did with him."

Charles lets out a sigh. "Come here," he says, pulling her to him. "I know it won't be easy, but you could save another young woman from the same fate by going to the police."

Hazel presses her forehead against his chest. "You're right. I should've done it a long time ago. But I'm afraid."

He whispers in her ear. "You can trust me, Hazel. You're not alone in this."

Despite all they've been through, Hazel trusts him more than anyone else in the world.

———

A terrified Hazel leans on Charles when they enter the police station the next afternoon at four o'clock. A rookie officer shows them to an interviewing room and tells them the detective will be with them soon.

"How much did you say to this detective?" Hazel asks when they're alone.

"Not much. I wasn't able to get him on the phone. But I texted him we had a delicate matter to discuss with him."

Hazel snatches a tissue from the box on the table. "We need to make sure the understands the need for secrecy. For the baby's sake."

"Leave that to me," Charles says with a definitive nod.

When Evan Beck enters the room a few minutes later, Charles exchanges pleasantries with his old high school friend before explaining they have a delicate matter to discuss. "We want to make you aware of the situation, but for personal reasons, we won't be pressing charges."

"Understood." Evan focuses his attention on Hazel. "What's this about?"

Evan appears impatient at first, as though ready to be done with the interview, but he snaps to attention when Hazel says, "I met a man at Blue Saloon. I believe he may have drugged and date-raped me."

Evan slides his chair closer to the table. "Several other women have made similar allegations. When did this happen?"

"The last Saturday in April."

Evan removes a stack of index cards from his pocket. "Start at the beginning and tell me everything you remember," he says, and scribbles notes as she recounts the events of the night.

"I rarely drink much, but that night I was an emotional mess."

Charles interjects, "She'd just found out I was having an affair with another man."

If Charles's bluntness surprises the detective, he doesn't let it show. "I remember hearing about that." He turns back to Hazel. "How much did you drink?"

Hazel holds up two fingers. "I ordered two glasses of wine. I went to the restroom, and when I came back, a third was waiting for me on the table. I don't remember whether I finished it."

"What can you tell me about the man's identity? The other women can't remember much, only that he's older, in his mid-to-late forties, and nice-looking with wavy hair."

"I know exactly who he is. His name is Davis Warren. He's the new owner of the Country Craftsman hardware store."

Evan's blue eyes pop. "You know this for certain?"

"I'm absolutely positive." Hazel stares down at her hands, wringing the tissue as she talks. "I woke up on his sofa. Before I snuck out of his apartment, I peeked into the bedroom and saw him sleeping. He's been hitting on me since then, trying to get me to go out with him, but I've been ignoring him. I ran into him last night in front of Delilah's. He claims he has photographs from that night, and he threatened to post them on social media."

Evan taps his pen on the table. "I thought that guy was seeing Ruthie from the diner."

Hazel shrugs. "I tried to warn her about him. She broke up with him, but I think they're back together."

Evan pushes his chair back from the table. "Thank you for coming in today, Hazel. Can I contact you if I have further questions?"

"I'm happy to speak with you directly, Detective, but I don't want my name associated with this situation."

"I'll do my best to honor your request," Evan says and flees the room.

Hazel looks over at Charles. "That didn't sound very promising."

"Evan is one of the good guys. He will protect your identity."

Hazel feels spent as they find their way out of the police station. "I'm not sure I'm up for dinner with your family tonight."

"Are you sure? Because you'd be doing me a huge favor. Dad

seems skeptical about my business venture and us becoming partners. I'm hoping to ease his concerns."

"Ah-ha. So that's what this dinner is about."

"Not only that, it will be a fun time. The assistant chef is vying for the head chef position. He's preparing a special meal to showcase his talents. *And* Dad says Ada has exciting news to share."

"She's having a baby," Hazel says without hesitation.

"That's what I think too. Our children will be cousins."

Hazel likes the sound of that. With Charles as the father, her child will have plenty of family around—a grandfather along with multiple aunts, uncles, and cousins. But if she raises it alone, Hazel and her child will only have each other. What if something happens to Hazel? If she gets cancer or dies in a car accident? The child will have no one.

They get in Charles's truck, and he starts the engine. "Since Laney gave you the rest of the afternoon off, why don't we stop by Peak Adventures? I want to show you the new equipment, and you can meet Jared, our new guide."

"That'd be great! I'm dying to see the bikes." Excitement stirs inside of her. Peak Adventures continues to provide the distraction she desperately needs.

He drives away from the police station. "If you want to change before dinner, we can stop by your apartment on the way to Love-Struck. Although you're fine with what you're wearing."

Hazel laughs. Charles is not taking *no* for an answer. "All right. I'll go to dinner with you. As long as you promise not to keep me out too late. I'm sleeping for two now, remember?"

CHAPTER 30
RUTHIE

Ruthie takes advantage of the afternoon lull by treating herself to a glass of freshly squeezed lemonade. Seated at the counter, she opens her iPad and searches the internet for the best small towns in the United States. She spends thirty minutes reading about charming places in faraway states like Maine and Colorado. If she sells the diner, with nothing keeping her in Lovely, she can finally fulfill her dream of traveling. She'll put her house on the market and rent a storage unit for her furniture. Combined with the profits from the diner, she'll have enough money to comfortably live on for the rest of her life.

Her mind wanders, and she imagines herself driving across the country in a pink vehicle. Something sporty, like a Jeep Wrangler or a Mini Cooper, customized in the exact shade of hot pink. She'll tour every state from Virginia to Louisiana to Wyoming, hitting all the popular small towns. If she finds one she loves, she'll buy a house and start a new life. Lovely will always be her home. If things don't work out, she can always come back here.

Ruthie is so lost in her daydream, she doesn't hear Jamie enter the diner until he's seated beside her. "I can't hold Trixie off any longer, Ruthie. She's on her way over. Can you at least let her inspect the kitchen?"

Ruthie snaps shut the cover on her iPad and spins the stool to face Jamie. "I was just going to call you. I've—"

The front door bangs open and a tiny woman with a beehive of auburn hair enters the diner and strides toward Ruthie with an outstretched hand. "Hey there, hon. I'm Trixie Bell. You've waited on me before, but I was incognito." She barks out an obnoxious laugh that Ruthie thinks is wonderful.

"It's nice to officially meet you." Ruthie shakes Trixie's callous hand, an indication of her work ethic.

"I'm so sorry to be such a pest. I've hounded poor Jamie to death. I can't help myself, I've fallen in love with your diner. I'm hoping to ease your reservations about selling."

Ruthie smiles. This woman is a younger version of herself. "I'm sorry it's taking me so long to decide. This place means the world to me." Her throat thickens. Is she really going to sell her diner?

Trixie places a hand on Ruthie's shoulder. "Oh, honey. I know how you feel. I had to get rid of my diner in La Joya, Texas. We're right on the southern border, and I was concerned for my safety with all the illegal immigrants coming across."

Ruthie makes a mental note not to tour the southern border on her trip across the country. "How awful for you. I'm sorry to hear that."

"I'm sorry for our country." Trixie dabs at her wet eyes with a tissue. "I promised myself no more boohooing. I just can't help myself."

Ruthie gives Trixie's shoulder a reassuring pat. "No worries. This is a difficult time for you."

"For all of us. Our country will never be the same," Trixie says, blowing her nose.

Ruthie casts a nervous glance at the Realtor. "Jamie mentioned you'd like to see the kitchen."

"Yes! Please!" Trixie says, dropping the wadded tissue into her cross-shoulder bag.

As they tour the kitchen, Ruthie explains about the upgrades to the appliances she's made in recent years.

Trixie gives a nod of approval. "I can tell you've kept everything in good working order."

When they reach the office, Ruthie pulls Trixie inside and closes the door on Jamie. "Jamie won't approve of us having this conversation, but we're gonna have it anyway. I never got married, and I never had children. My customers are my family. They mean the world to me. They count on certain items being available to them. People come from miles away for my cream cheese Danishes. I can't ask you not to change the menu, but can you promise you'll keep at least a few of the more popular items?"

Trixie draws an X over her heart. "You have my solemn word. I may add to the menu, but I have no intention of getting rid of anything. As long as you share your secret recipes." She giggles. "The diner is perfect as is. If you accept my offer, I'm hoping you'll allow me to shadow you for a couple of weeks, to show me how you do things and introduce me to your customers."

Ruthie's shoulders sag as the tension leaves her body. This is the right choice for her. The diner will be in expert hands with Trixie Bell. "I would like that very much. And I've decided to accept your offer."

"Really?" Trixie says, bouncing on her toes. "That's amazing. I'm beyond thrilled. Does the end of July work for you to close?"

"That date works fine. Let's tell Jamie. He'll be thrilled." When Ruthie opens the door, Jamie falls into the office. "Were you eavesdropping?" she asks with fists buried in hips.

He straightens, smoothing back his hair. "Just looking out for my clients." He produces a file folder. "Now sign this contract before you change your mind again."

Trixie and Ruthie burst out laughing.

"Give me that." Ruthie snatches the contract and scrawls her name on the designated lines.

The threesome discusses details of due diligence as they walk to the front door together.

"Toodle-oo!" Trixie flaps her hand in parting. "Call me when you're ready for me to shadow you. I'm available, just sitting around twiddling my thumbs."

"Will do," Ruthie says with a cheek-to-cheek grin. The woman's enthusiasm is infectious.

Jamie kisses her cheek. "Congratulations, Ruthie. You made the right decision."

"I think so too. Now that we've settled that, I'd like to discuss putting my house on the market."

Jamie drops his smile. "Are you leaving town?"

"Yes! I'm going on an extended adventure. I may come back." She hunches a shoulder. "Or I might not."

"There will be a lot of people with long faces around here. You're the heart and soul of this town."

"You know that's not true. But thanks for saying it anyway." She opens the door and gives him a shove. "Now get out of here before I cry."

———

Ruthie is in the mood to celebrate. Too bad she agreed to have dinner with Davis. But since he's the best she's got, she'll have to make do. She fastens her hair in a sophisticated updo and puts on her least sexy dress—a pink sleeveless frock with a high ruffled collar. No point in enticing him when she has no intention of sleeping with him.

She's waiting out front when he picks her up. She slips into the passenger seat of his Porsche. "I sold the diner. I hope you're in the mood to celebrate."

"Heck, yes!" He punches the accelerator and speeds off down the road. "I never need an excuse to party. Although I think you're crazy for selling your business when it's thriving."

She pats his arm. "You're too young to understand."

The hostess at Vino Bistro seats them in the least desirable corner of the terrace with a view of the parking lot. "Do you have something available overlooking the mountains?" Ruthie asks.

"Sorry," the hostess says, gripping the menus to her chest. "We have a full house tonight. I may be able to seat you inside."

Ruthie spots Daniel and Millie sipping cocktails with his family on the lawn. Nearby, at the outer edge of the terrace, a rectangular table is set for a large party, presumably the Love family. Daniel won't see her if they move inside. Since she's stuck with Davis, she might as well flaunt her handsome date. And he's looking especially hot tonight in a pink checked shirt and dark washed jeans.

"This will have to do." Ruthie waits until the hostess leaves to complain to Davis. "We might as well be eating in the bed of your pickup."

Davis looks at her from behind the wine list. "What pickup? I drive a Porsche."

"Now that you mention it, why don't you drive a truck? You're the owner of a hardware store."

His blue eyes go cold. "Driving a truck is not a prerequisite to owning a hardware store, Ruthie. What's with you tonight? First, you complain about the table, and now you're giving me a hard time about my car. I thought you wanted to celebrate."

Chill out, Ruthie, she tells herself. "You're right. I'm sorry. I'm just on edge. Lots of changes in my life."

"No worries." He places his hand on top of hers. "Let's start over."

Davis orders a bottle of Veuve Clicquot, and when the waiter pops the cork, every head on the terrace turns toward them. Feeling Daniel's eyes on her, Ruthie flashes the waiter her most brilliant smile. "We're celebrating," she says without telling him the occasion.

As she sips her Champagne, she watches the Love family migrate toward their table. Irritation crawls across Ruthie's skin when Daniel takes his place at one end, with Millie seated to his right in the place of honor. What difference does it make? Ruthie will be leaving town soon to travel the country.

When she returns her attention to Davis, he is scowling at his phone as his thumbs fly across the screen.

"Is something wrong, Davis?"

"More problems at my warehouse. This may turn into something serious. Fingers crossed we don't have to cut our evening short."

Ruthie doesn't cross her fingers. She wouldn't at all be opposed to going home. And she won't have to invent an excuse not to have sex with Davis. She could take the Champagne with her. She longs to curl up on her porch swing with her iPad and begin charting her cross-country trip. There's nothing left for her in this town. The time has come for her to move on.

CHAPTER 31
CASEY

After an hour of cocktails and canapés on the lawn, Casey herds her party toward their table on the terrace. "I've created place cards so everyone can easily find their seats," she explains to her guests.

"What about Hugh and Miranda?" Daniel asks.

"They're already forty-five minutes late. We'll have to start without them. Maybe they'll be here soon." Casey is torn between hoping Hugh won't show up and wanting him to cause a scene. Either way, Daniel's high opinion of his eldest son would take a hit.

Casey smiles to herself. She purposefully seated Hugh and Miranda near Daniel and Millie at one end of the table. Their vacant seats are a sore reminder of Hugh's rudeness.

As soon as everyone is settled, two waiters appear with the first course—cold avocado soup paired with a Spanish Albariño wine. Casey's antenna goes up when Ada places her hand over her glass, politely refusing the wine. She'd noticed earlier when Ada turned down the offer of a cucumber martini.

Daniel, who has also been watching Ada's every move, says with a devilish smile, "I can't believe you're turning down an Albariño. It's one of your favorites."

Ada bursts into laughter. "Okay, fine! I'm busted. I was going to tell you all tonight anyway." She takes hold of her husband's hand. "Enzo and I are having a baby in early January."

The table erupts in cheers and whistles. Daniel holds his glass up to the beaming couple. "Congratulations! I'm thrilled for us all. You and Enzo will be wonderful parents."

Everyone is busy peppering Ada and Enzo with questions about the baby when Hugh arrives at the table. "I'm sorry, everyone. Miranda's not feeling well. She won't make dinner."

Casey studies Hugh from afar. Other than glassy eyes and an untucked shirt, he appears subdued, not his usual drunk and obnoxious self.

Daniel leans toward Hugh and nods in Ada's direction, obviously telling him about the baby. Hugh smiles down the table at Ada and Enzo. "Congratulations, you two."

Charles places an arm around Hazel, drawing her in close. "Now seems as good a time as any to break the news. Hazel and I are also having a baby in late January."

Hazel gives Charles a swift elbow to his rib cage as she mutters something to him no one can hear.

Charles lets out an awkward laugh. "Oops. I'm in trouble. I spoke out of turn. I promised Hazel we wouldn't tell anyone until she's further along."

"Does this mean you two are back together?" Daniel asks.

Charles holds his head high. "No, sir. It means we've salvaged our friendship from the wreckage of our marriage. Who better to be business partners and co-parents with than your best friend? Hazel is getting the child she's always wanted, and I've promised to be a better father than I was husband."

Daniel's smile spreads from ear to ear. "That's truly wonderful, son. I'm delighted for you both. I'm ordering bubbly for those of us who can drink," he says and summons one of their waiters.

Casey's eyes travel from Daniel to Kathy, who discreetly nods at Casey's phone on the table in front of her. She picks up the phone and reads Kathy's text. *We have a situation. Is there somewhere we can talk in private?*

Casey responds. *In my office. I'll leave the table first.* Pushing back from the table, she says, "Excuse me a minute. I need to check on things in the kitchen."

Casey hurries through the restaurant, out the front door, and up the stairs to her office, leaving the light off to avoid being spotted by the diners on the terrace below.

She paces the floor until Kathy arrives five minutes later. "What's wrong? Is this about Hugh? He seems uncharacteristically chill tonight."

"He's on something. Xanax would be my guess. But this has nothing to do with him. At least not directly."

Kathy checks in the hall to make certain no one has followed her before closing the door. "Hazel has blown our investigation wide open," she says in a low voice. "She and Charles requested a meeting with Evan at the station today. Evan promised to protect their identity, so this goes no further than this room."

"Understood," Casey says, dragging an imaginary zipper across her lips.

"Hazel claims a man named Davis Warren may have drugged and date-raped her back in late April."

Casey's mind spins as she remembers Hazel's big news. *The timing is right. Could her baby be Davis's?* "Go on."

"Several other women have made similar claims in recent weeks. But none of them remembered much about the man who assaulted them. Do you know this Davis Warren?"

"I met him once. At the Vino Bistro grand opening. He's dating Ruthie. They're actually here tonight. I saw them from afar earlier." Staying close to the wall, Casey moves over to the window and peeks down at their guests. "Yep. There they are."

Kathy joins her at the window. "Where?"

Casey taps the window. "Back corner table on the left."

"I'll let Evan know he's here," Kathy says as she types out the message. "Suspicious activity has been reported at Davis's supply warehouse. Until now, the police have had no cause to investigate. But based on the information Hazel gave them, Evan was able to obtain a search warrant. His team is searching the warehouse as we speak."

"This is crazy. What does Evan think is in the warehouse?"

"Drugs." Kathy glances at her phone screen and lifts the phone to her ear. "This is him calling me now," she says and speaks briefly into the phone. "Mm-hmm. All right. I understand."

Kathy ends the call and pockets her phone. "We need to get back to the table. The police are on the way over. They found 30 grams of cocaine, a large number of pills, and a pill press in his warehouse. It's illegal for him to have one with DEA's knowledge."

"Why are the police coming here?" Casey asks, trailing after Kathy down the hall.

"To grab Davis before he hurts someone else."

"You mean arrest him? Here, in front of all my patrons?"

"Apparently. That's not a decision I would've made. But I'm not calling the shots."

When they exit the building, Kathy stops walking and turns to Casey. "We'll watch closely for Hugh's reaction when Davis is arrested. If he leaves the table, I'll go after him. Your job is to keep everyone calm. Business as usual. Remember, we have under-cover DEA agents on the premises."

"Do you think Evan will arrest Hugh tonight?"

Kathy shrugs. "I have no idea. He didn't say."

They return to the table, and a pair of police officers arrive a few minutes later. The officers approach Davis, have a brief word with him, and lead him away, leaving Ruthie gaping at their retreating figures. It happens so fast, and because their table is tucked away in a corner, hardly anyone notices. Except Daniel, who, despite being on a date with Millie, hasn't been able to take his eyes off Ruthie all night, and Hugh, who appears extremely agitated but makes no move to leave the table.

Daniel gets out of his chair and moves to Casey's end of the table, kneeling down beside her. "Did you see what just happened to Ruthie's date? The police took him away. Do you think they arrested him?"

"I'm not sure. Maybe so." Casey glances over at Ruthie. "She looks like she's about to cry. Maybe you should offer to take her home."

"That's a good idea. Cover for me. If anyone asks, tell them I left to help a friend."

Casey watches him cross the terrace to an embarrassed-looking Ruthie. She has a sneaking suspicion they have a long night ahead of them. For his safety, she's glad her father will be away from the vineyard in case more action goes down.

CHAPTER 32
RUTHIE

Ruthie's butt is glued to the chair. Sensing the other diners staring at her, she keeps her gaze lowered while she tentatively sips Champagne. Why did the police ask to speak with Davis? Is he in some kind of trouble? Is he coming back? How will she get home if he doesn't?

A pair of black Gucci loafers enter her line of vision, and her eyes travel up gray flannel pant legs and a blue seersucker sport coat to Daniel's face.

"Are you all right?" he asks, and she fakes a smile and a cheerful tone of voice. "Sure! I'm fine. Why wouldn't I be?"

Daniel looks at her as if she's lost her mind. "Because your date was just hauled off by two police officers. Do you know where they've taken him?"

Her smile fades. "They said they needed to speak with him about an urgent matter. He was having trouble at his warehouse earlier. I assume it has something to do with that. Maybe it caught on fire or something."

Daniel moves to the knee wall behind her and surveys the parking lot. "I don't see a police cruiser. What kind of car does your boyfriend drive?"

Ruthie stands at the wall with him. "His is the black Porsche parked near the door."

Daniel's jaw tightens. "Right. In the handicapped spot. Does he have mobility issues?"

Ruthie's cheeks burn. "Oops. I didn't notice the sign when he parked."

"It's a pet peeve of mine." Daniel rakes his hands through his snowy hair. "The point is, his car is still here and there's no police cruiser in sight. Which leads me to believe they've taken him to the police station to discuss this urgent matter."

Ruthie exhales a loud sigh. "Whatever. I really don't care where they've taken him. Davis and I are not technically together anymore. I broke it off with him two weeks ago. I agreed to have dinner with him tonight in a moment of weakness."

Daniel's lips part in a soft smile. "In that case, can I offer you a ride home?"

Relief overcomes her. She longs to put this night behind her. "Is your car here?"

"Yes. In my reserved spot in the parking lot. I drove to pick up Millie earlier."

Of course. Millie. "I hate to ask you to leave your date, but I'm desperate."

"I don't mind at all." He removes his key from his pocket. "Town is only a few minutes away. I'll be back in a flash."

Ruthie grabs her purse and the Champagne bottle and follows him out to a shiny gray Jaguar in the parking lot.

"Did you trade in your Range Rover?" she asks, sliding into the passenger seat of the sleek new sedan.

"Millie thinks I need something sportier now that I'm retiring. I feel a bit like James Bond driving it. But it gets much better gas mileage than the Range Rover."

Ruthie takes a pull off the Champagne bottle. "Sounds like you and Millie are serious."

"I started dating Millie, hoping to make you jealous, but . . ." His voice trails off.

"You've fallen for her," Ruthie says to the window as she stares out at the passing landscape.

"No one can replace you, Ruthie," he says in a wistful voice.

They ride the rest of the way in silence. He parks in front of her house, but she makes no move to get out.

Turning away from the window, Ruthie says, "I sold the diner today for an amazing price. The buyer, a woman named Trixie from Texas, is not planning to change much except the name."

"That's wonderful news, Ruthie. Congratulations. What's next for you?"

"I'm going to travel, like you and I always talked about." Ruthie holds her breath. If he's going to suggest they give their relationship another chance, this will be the moment.

But instead of offering to take a trip with her, he chuckles and says, "You were the one always talking about traveling. I've told you a thousand times, I have the best view of the world from my back porch."

Ruthie never remembers hearing him say that. Is it because she refused to admit they weren't as perfectly suited as she thought? "When I turned down your proposal, you said you'd fight for me, that you would court me with flowers and chocolates and elaborate dinners. But after that night, I heard nothing from you."

"Because you jumped into a relationship with Davis before I had a chance."

"I started dating Davis as a test to see if you really had changed. Can you blame me after what you did?"

Daniel ignores her question. "You turning down my proposal was a pretty clear signal you wanted nothing more to do with me."

Ruthie huffs. "You and I weren't even together when you asked me to marry you. Don't you think that's getting the cart before the horse?"

"I thought that's what you wanted, Ruthie. Remember, nine months ago, you broke up with me because I refused to marry you? Everything was fine in our relationship until you started hearing wedding bells."

"Correction. Until you lied and told everyone you were dying from cancer."

"Here we go, round and round like a merry-go-round." Daniel places his hands on the steering wheel. "I see no point in rehashing all of this now. I need to get back to my dinner guests."

Ruthie's phone pings in her purse with an incoming text. She removes the phone and reads the message from Davis. *I'm in a little trouble, Ruthie. The police found large quantities of illegal drugs in my warehouse. I'm losing my mind. I know nothing about the drugs. One of my workers is clearly responsible. I'm sorry. I won't be coming back. You'll have to find a ride home.*

Ruthie grits her teeth. Whatever. Davis is no longer her problem.

When she looks up from her phone, Daniel is watching her. "Is that Davis?"

"Nope. Just a spam text." Sliding the phone back into her purse, she opens her car door. "Thanks for the ride, Daniel. I hope you and Millie have a nice life together." She gets out and hurries inside to the safety of her pink house. The end of July can't get here soon enough. She's ready to be rid of this town and everyone who lives in it.

No longer in the mood to celebrate, she pours the Champagne down the drain and goes upstairs to her room where she changes into her nightgown, powers off her phone, and crawls into bed with her sleep mask covering her eyes.

CHAPTER 33
SHELDON

Sheldon looks up from staring into his Mount Gay and tonic to find Ollie watching him. "What's wrong?"

"You've been studying your drink for fifteen minutes without taking a single sip."

Sheldon shudders. "I can't shake the feeling something bad is about to go down at Love-Struck. I should be there when it happens."

"No, you shouldn't," Ollie snaps. "You haven't yet recovered from the last beating. Trust the professionals to handle it."

"I do trust the professionals. But it's not the same. Their family isn't in danger."

Ollie's arm shoots out, her finger pointed toward Love-Struck. "Then go. If *they* mean more to you than Henry and me." She gets to her feet. "I'm going to put the baby down."

"Are you coming back?" he asks, craning his neck to glimpse her retreating form.

She responds by slamming the kitchen door.

A pang of guilt grips his chest. He hates upsetting her, but he can't help feeling an allegiance to his father and sister. If they need him, he should be there.

He checks his phone, but there's no word from Casey. He

hasn't heard from her since yesterday evening. She's understandably upset with Daniel for being so blind about Hugh. Sheldon only hopes their father's preferential treatment to his oldest son doesn't drive Casey away.

Five minutes later, Sheldon's still sitting on the porch, staring into the dark night, when Gray's pickup truck speeds down the driveway and screeches to a halt beside the porch. The driver's window rolls down and Gray calls out, "Miranda called. She's over at Love-Struck. She's in trouble. I'm going to check on her. Will you come with me?"

Sheldon jumps up and hurries outside to Gray's truck. "Did she say what kind of trouble?"

Gray shakes his head. "I could barely understand her. She was talking in a soft voice and her words were really slurred. She's sick or something. I offered to call 9-1-1, but she refused. Apparently, Hugh isn't answering his phone."

Sheldon considers his options. Ollie will be furious if she finds out he went next door. He should report the incident to Kathy and Evan and let them handle it. But he would hate to bother them if nothing is seriously wrong. Where's the harm in checking on Miranda? This is the excuse he's been looking for. Confirming that everything is in order at Love-Struck will give Sheldon peace of mind, enabling him to sleep tonight.

He slaps the hood of Gray's truck. "Kill the engine. Let's go on foot. I'll get some flashlights."

He retrieves his keys off the kitchen counter and two flashlights from the junk drawer, and the two men set off through the wooded trails toward Love-Struck.

From behind him, Gray whispers loudly, "Hey, man. Why are we sneaking around in the dark? What aren't you telling me?"

Over his shoulder, Sheldon says, "I can't explain now. You'll have to trust me."

As they draw near the winery, he sees his family having dinner on the terrace at Vino Bistro. "There's Hugh, but I don't see Miranda. Maybe she went to the restroom."

"I'm telling you, man, she's in no condition to go to a dinner party."

"Then she must be in Hugh's room at The Nest," Sheldon says, and motions Gray on.

They sneak around the rose garden and up the hill to the children's wing. The main door is locked, but Sheldon has a master key that fits all the exterior door locks. They slip inside the children's wing and listen for the sound of voices, but all they hear is the loud hum of an air-conditioning unit on the brink of dying. Down the hall, they discover Hugh's bedroom door locked.

Sheldon inspects the knob. "This is new since I was last here. We'll have to bust it down. Stand back." Sheldon kicks open the door, and they barge into the empty room. "She's not here."

Stepping back out into the hall, Gray says, "She's gotta be somewhere."

"Let's try the game room." With Gray on his heels, Sheldon runs to the end of the hall.

On the coffee table is a small mirror with white lines of powder and a rolled-up paper bill. Miranda, her clothing soaked with vomit, is passed out on the floor between the coffee table and the sofa.

Gray moves the table out of the way and drops to his knees beside her, two fingers pressing against her throat. "Her pulse is weak, but she's still alive. I'll call for a rescue squad." He pulls his phone out and punches in 9-1-1.

"Make sure they send the police as well. I'll go outside and wait for them."

Sheldon calls Casey on his way out to the courtyard. When she doesn't answer, he tries two more times until she does. "We have a problem. Can you step away from the table?"

"Give me a sec." A rustling sound follows, and she's back on the phone. "What's wrong? Where are you?"

"I'm at The Nest. Miranda appears to have overdosed. Gray is calling an ambulance and the police. They'll be passing by the bistro any minute."

"Great!" Casey says in a sarcastic tone. "With sirens blaring and lights flashing to scare away our customers. When will this ever end?"

"Tonight, Casey. This ends tonight. I'm going to insist the police search Hugh's room."

"All right. Let me talk to Kathy. She'll know how to handle the situation."

Sheldon has no sooner ended the call when a black Prius speeds down the road and slams on brakes in front of Sheldon. The two dark-skinned men who broke Sheldon's ribs jump out of the car. He reaches for his holstered handgun at the small of his back, then remembers he put it in the lock box when he showered after work.

"Hold your hands up where we can see them," the bald guy demands.

Tattoo Face says, "I thought we warned you to stay away. You obviously didn't learn your lesson."

Sheldon, with his hands in the air, says, "I have a right to be here. My father lives in this house. This is my family's home."

"Where's Hugh?" Tattoo Face asks.

"I have no clue. But his girlfriend is inside. She overdosed. First responders are on the way. If you know what's good for you, you'll leave. And fast. Shit's about to go down."

"You're lying." Baldie pins Sheldon against the Prius, holding a switchblade at his neck.

Sheldon's life flashes before his eyes. This jackass will slit his throat, and he'll bleed out right here in the driveway. Ollie will become a widow and Henry fatherless. If only he'd listened to her and stayed at home, where he was safe.

"Freeze!" Two pistol-yielding men appear from around the corner of the children's wing, one wearing jeans and an apron and the other dressed like a server in black pants and a white shirt.

Tattoo Face pulls a gun out and trains it on them. "Beat it, whoever you are! This has nothing to do with you."

"The guy wearing jeans flashes a badge. We're undercover

DEA agents. Put your weapons down now. There's no way out. An army of officers will descend upon you any minute."

Tattoo Face and Baldie drop their weapons, and Sheldon doubles over, gulping in air. He narrowly escaped death this time. He's had enough of living on the edge.

CHAPTER 34

CASEY

C asey ends her call with Sheldon, waves at Kathy to get her attention, and sends her a text. *Miranda has apparently overdosed. Ambulance and police on the way. How should we proceed?*

She watches Kathy pick up her phone and type out her response. *I'll alert Evan. Come back to the table and follow my lead.*

Casey returns to the table, but instead of sitting down, she remains standing beside Kathy's chair.

"Listen up, everyone," Kathy says and waits for the chatter at the table to die down. "We have a situation at The Nest. Hugh's girlfriend is having a medical emergency. First responders are on the way. The lights and sirens will undoubtedly concern the other diners, so let's remain as calm as possible."

The table erupts into questions for Kathy, which she ignores. "Here's how this will go down. Hugh and I will leave first, followed by Casey and Daniel. The rest of you will remain seated. For appearance's sake, try to enjoy your meal."

Daniel gives Kathy an icy stare. "Why are you suddenly in charge of my family?"

"I'm not Casey's friend from New York. My name is Kathy

Sinclair, and I'm a private investigator, working undercover to bust a drug ring."

Daniel shakes his head in confusion. "I don't understand. What does this drug ring have to do with my family?"

"I'll explain everything later. Let's go, Hugh." Kathy hauls him out of his chair and holds on tight to his arm as they leave the terrace.

Casey waits until Hugh and Kathy have disappeared into the darkness before helping her father up.

"You have some explaining to do," Daniel says as they hurry to catch up with Kathy.

Casey stabs her chest with her thumb. "Not me. You need to talk to Hugh. He's the one with the answers."

"You should've come to me, Casey. Instead of involving the police."

"I didn't contact the police. Sheldon did, after Hugh's goons roughed him up, a beating which included breaking several of his ribs," Casey says and increases her pace to avoid further interrogation.

They arrive at The Nest to find chaos in the courtyard. An ambulance and four police cruisers are parked haphazardly in the driveway. Spotting Sheldon near the children's wing entrance, they rush over to him. "Where did Hugh and Kathy go?" Casey asks.

Sheldon throws a thumb over his shoulder. "Inside."

Casey opens the door. "The two of you stay here." But they follow her into the children's wing anyway, stepping out of the way when the paramedics wheel Miranda's gurney past.

Sheldon pulls a dazed Gray out of the line of passing people. "How is she?"

Gray shakes his head. "Not good. The paramedics are afraid the cocaine was laced with fentanyl. I'm gonna ride with her to the hospital in the ambulance."

Sheldon squeezes Gray's shoulder. "All right, man. I'll be praying for her. Call me if you need a ride home."

"Did he say fentanyl?" Daniel whispers to Casey.

"Yep. Unfortunately, it's all over our country."

Daniel's pale olive eyes widen. "Kathy mentioned a drug ring. Is someone trafficking drugs out of my home?"

"Another one of those questions you'll need to ask Hugh," Casey snaps.

The threesome continues down the hall to Hugh's bedroom where Kathy and a handcuffed Hugh are waiting outside while a team of officers searches within.

"Check the desk," Sheldon calls to them, and Hugh glares at him.

An officer pries open the locked desk drawer and pulls out two large bags, one with pills and the other cocaine. "Well now. What do we have here?"

Evan makes a timely appearance on the scene. "You've been a busy man," he says to Hugh and to the officer standing next to him, "Take him down to the station and book him."

Daniel steps between Hugh and the officer. "On what charges?"

"Charges related to drug trafficking," Evan says. "The list will be long."

Daniel appears crestfallen. "May I speak to my son alone in my study first?"

When the detective hesitates, Daniel says, "I give a healthy donation to your organization every year."

"Fine. I'll give you five minutes. But I insist Officer Rogers accompany you."

With a nod of approval, Daniel starts off down the hall with the officer and Hugh on his heels.

"Come on. This will be good." Taking her by the hand, Sheldon leads Casey out the back way and around the children's wing to the main part of the house. They press themselves against the wall in the hallway outside Daniel's study to eavesdrop on Daniel and Hugh.

"Tell me the truth, Hugh. Are you addicted to drugs? I can

send you to rehab, to get you the help you need, and potentially keep you out of jail."

"I'm not addicted to drugs, Dad. I have a gambling problem. The attorney's fees for the assault charges nearly bankrupted me. I started gambling . . ." Hugh's voice trails off and the sound of loud sniffling comes from inside the study.

Sheldon whispers to Casey, "I know this tactic. He's fake crying to make Dad feel sorry for him."

Casey rolls her eyes. "By attorney's fees, he means bribing the judge."

Hugh clears his throat. "It was innocent enough at first. Online slot machines and that sort of thing. I was doing all right too. But then I met a bookie who encouraged me to place larger bets on major sporting events. The thrill was exhilarating, and I got sucked in, but I hardly ever won any of my bets. Before I knew it, I was in major debt. The bookie introduced me to his boss, that dirtbag Ruthie is dating. Davis agreed to let me pay him back the money I owed him by distributing drugs."

"I can't believe you were doing all this under my roof. How did you get past security?"

"I paid Jeremy to look the other way."

Sheldon grimaces. "That explains a lot."

"You've got yourself into one helluva a mess this time, Hugh. Although I'm uncertain of the laws, I imagine if your girlfriend dies, they could charge you with involuntary manslaughter."

Casey gasps, her hand clamping over her mouth. "Is that possible?" she whispers to Sheldon.

Sheldon shrugs. "I have no idea."

"I'm sorry, Dad. I really screwed up this time."

"I will always love you, son. But this time, I won't come to your rescue."

"I understand, Dad. And I don't blame you."

Footfalls on the hardwoods precede Hugh's appearance in the hallway. He cranes his neck to give Casey and Sheldon the death stare as Officer Rogers leads him out the front door.

Daniel's voice booms out and echoes throughout the house. "Sheldon! Casey! I know you're out there. Get in here now."

Daniel is standing at the wet bar, pouring himself a whiskey, when Casey and Sheldon enter the study and sit down side by side on the sofa.

Daniel brings his drink over to his favorite leather chair. He squints at Sheldon. "Are you okay, son? Your face is green."

Sheldon touches his finger to his cheek. "These are bruises. Souvenirs from Hugh's thugs."

"Casey mentioned that. How long have you two known about all this?"

"A few weeks," Sheldon says.

"And you never thought to tell me about it?"

"Would you have listened?" Casey asks.

Daniel's eyes narrow. "Are you blaming me for Hugh's problems?"

Casey meets his gaze. "If the shoe fits. I think you're an enabler."

Sheldon's head jerks toward her. "Ouch! That's harsh, Casey!"

"But it's true," Daniel says. "I've made excuses for Hugh's downfalls and shortcomings all his life. I bailed him out every single time he got into trouble. I kept hoping he'd get his act together. I guess he's just rotten to his core." He turns to Casey. "For the record, you were always my number one pick for the head position. I created the competition to highlight Hugh's weaknesses. He and I never shared the same vision for Love-Struck."

"Hugh knew what you wanted," Sheldon says. "He just insisted on doing things his way."

Daniel offers Sheldon a sad smile. "I wish you hadn't dropped out of the race, son. My choice would be for you and Casey to run the vineyard together."

Casey leans into Sheldon. "I'm working on him. He knows how much I want him as my partner."

"Now that Hugh's out of the picture, I'll consider a part-time gig." Sheldon's phone rings, and he glances at his screen. "This is Ollie. I should take it. I'm sure she's worried."

Daniel waits for Sheldon to leave the room before moving to the edge of his seat. "I owe you an apology, honey, for putting your life in danger. I felt indebted to Hugh for seeing me through my recovery. If I had known what was going on, I would never have allowed such criminal activities to take place under my nose. Hopefully, there won't be a next time, but you must promise never to keep something so important from me again."

"As long as you promise to keep an open mind when it comes to your other children."

Daniel squeezes her knee. "Deal."

Casey places her hand on top of his. "I know you love Hugh, and I realize how difficult this is for you. I would gladly give up the head position in exchange for a more positive outcome for this family."

"We'll survive. We've weathered worse storms. I'm grateful to have you in my life to help ease the pain."

CHAPTER 35
SHELDON

heldon accepts Ollie's call as he makes his way outside to the back terrace. Her voice is tight with worry. "Sheldon! Thank goodness! Are you okay?"

"I'm fine, sweetheart. I'm at The Nest with Dad and Casey."

"What on earth happened over there? I saw the flashing lights and heard the sirens from here."

"Miranda overdosed, and Hugh was arrested, as were the two men who attacked me. It's a long story. I'll tell you the rest later."

Ollie's breath hitches. "That's awful. Is Miranda going to be okay?"

"I'm not sure. Gray rode with her in the ambulance to the hospital. I'm so sorry, Ollie. I—"

"I'm the one who should apologize. Your devotion to your family is one thing I love most about you. I was unfair to make you choose between them and me."

"There is no them and me, Ollie. Only us. You all own a piece of my heart."

"I know that. I guess I'm still a little freaked out about the attack."

"Understandably so. But I'm fine. And we'll soon be able to put all this behind us."

Sheldon's line beeps with an incoming call. "This is Gray. Let me grab it. I'll let you know what he says. I love you, Ollie."

"And I love you, Sheldon."

Sheldon clicks over to Gray's call. He can hear a loudspeaker in the background, paging a doctor to the emergency room stat. "How's Miranda?"

"I can't believe it, Sheldon. She died in the ambulance on the way to the hospital."

Sheldon falls back against the side of the house. He's at a loss for words. He never cared for Miranda, but he didn't wish her dead. "I don't know what to say, man. I'm so sorry."

"It sucks, but these things happen when you live on the edge like she was doing. I hate to ask you, but can I take you up on the offer of a ride?"

"Absolutely. I'm still at The Nest. Let me see if I can borrow a car. If not, I'll have to run home and get mine."

"Take your time. The doctors are still doing paperwork."

"I'll text you my ETA."

Sheldon ends the call and returns to his father's study. "I have bad news. Miranda didn't make it."

Casey gasps and Daniel says, "This could be devastating for Hugh."

His father's comment strikes him as insensitive. A woman has died, and his son is partially responsible. Who knows? Maybe Sheldon would react the same way in Daniel's shoes. He makes a silent vow to be a better father to Henry than Daniel was to his sons.

"Can I borrow one of your cars? I need to pick Gray up from the hospital."

Daniel fishes his keys out of his pocket and hands them to Sheldon. "You can take mine." He snatches them back. "On second thought, no, you can't. My car's at the bistro. In all the confusion, I forgot about poor Millie. They've probably finished eating by now. I should check on her. I'm sure she's ready to go home."

"Take mine." Casey jumps up. "I'll go get my key from upstairs." She darts out of the room and is back in a flash with her car key.

The threesome migrates from the study to the courtyard where law enforcement officers are still roaming around.

"Do you want to ride with me?" Sheldon asks Casey as he unlocks her car doors.

"I don't think so. One of us should stay here until the chaos dies down."

"Right. Be sure to tell Kathy and Evan about Miranda." Sheldon motions his father to the passenger side. "Get in. I'll drop you off at the bistro on my way past."

After adjusting the driver's seat, Sheldon heads off toward the winery.

Daniel says, "I love you, son. Our family has been through a lot these past couple of years. Now that everything is out in the open with Hugh and Charles, I hope we'll have the opportunity to heal."

"I hope so too, Dad. Despite what's happened with Hugh, we have much to be thankful for."

After dropping his father at the Vino Bistro, Sheldon watches his slumped figure in the rearview mirror as he drives away. He can't imagine what his dad must feel right now, knowing his son's crimes might send him to prison for the rest of his life. He vows to carve out more time for his dad in the months ahead.

Gray is waiting in front of the emergency room. When he gets in the car, he covers his eyes with his hands. "I can't believe she's gone. Despite everything, I still loved her. Somehow, I knew her risky behavior would one day catch up with her. I have to call her parents. How do I break this kind of news?"

"I don't know, Gray. I wish I had some advice to offer. Just be honest, I guess. Tell them she was struggling with some problems."

"They already know."

"Maybe that will soften the blow."

After a minute of awkward silence, Gray removes his hand from his eyes, draws in a deep breath, and holds his head high. "The vineyard is yours. We'll revert to the original asking price before Hugh entered the picture."

Sheldon glances over at him. "Are you sure about that?"

"Positive. I'm sorry Miranda was jerking you around. But that's not my style. If you can find a place for me, I would love to stay on."

"If Ollie agrees, I'd like to offer you the position of vineyard manager."

Gray's face lights up. "Seriously? That'd be awesome."

Sheldon grins. "Awesome for everyone involved. We're going to need extra help. Between you and me, Ollie has her heart set on having another baby."

"That's exciting, man. I'm truly happy for you."

"Fingers crossed," he says, ecstatic about the possibility of another baby. Maybe two. Another boy and a little girl who looks just like Ollie.

Sheldon loves working the land at Foxtail, but now that Hugh is no longer involved, the possibility of returning to Love-Struck intrigues him. He and Casey would make a good team. But is it too much of a commitment?

His mind drifts to thoughts of Hugh. When it comes to his oldest brother, he feels no guilt and no sorrow. Only sadness for the people who love Hugh. Even if he weasels his way out of these charges, Hugh will never again work at their family's vineyard. The rotten apple has been removed from the orchard. Now maybe the remaining fruit trees will thrive.

CHAPTER 36
HAZEL

Hazel and Charles are on the way home from dinner when Daniel calls. "Hey, Dad. In the interest of full disclosure, you're on Bluetooth and Hazel's in the car with me."

"That's fine. I want you both to hear the news from me. Hugh has been arrested on drug charges and his girlfriend, Miranda, died a little while ago from an apparent drug overdose."

Covering her mouth, Hazel says into her hand, "Oh my god."

"Will Hugh go to prison?" Charles asks, his eyes on Hazel.

"Probably so, son. We can talk more later, but I'm just calling now to apologize for putting you in a precarious position with my competition for vineyard head."

Charles's expression softens. "Actually, Dad, you did me a favor. You gave me the push I needed to leave the vineyard."

"I'm proud of you for forging your own path. I have no doubt but what you and Hazel will make Peak Adventures a success."

"Your support means a lot, Dad."

"And I couldn't be happier about the baby. I'm looking forward to being a grandfather to your little boy or girl. Let me know if there is anything I can do to make things easier for either of you."

Charles winks at Hazel. "Thanks, but we've got things covered for now. It's time I figured things out on my own."

"You're off to an excellent start."

Hazel interjects, "Thank you for your kind words, Daniel. I'm curious about what happened to Ruthie's boyfriend. Do you know where the police took him?"

"I don't know for sure, but based on what I heard from Hugh, I imagine he will also be charged with drug trafficking."

Charles glances over at Hazel. "What exactly did Hugh say about him?"

"In so many words, he gave me the impression that Davis is the ringleader of the local drug cartel."

Hazel sinks down in her seat. And this drug dealer is her baby's father. All the more reason to put this unpleasantness behind her. She'll see a shrink if necessary. But she won't let this be a black cloud over her baby's head.

Charles tightens his grip on the steering wheel. "I'm sorry things turned out this way for Hugh. But Lovely is a safer town tonight with them locked up."

"You're right, Charles. Hugh got in over his head and now he'll have to pay the price." Daniel clears his throat. "But things are turning out well for you. I haven't seen you this happy since you were a boy. Keep up the good work."

"That's the goal, Dad."

The threesome says goodbye, and Charles ends the call.

Hazel's fingers graze his arm. "This must be devastating for you. I know how close you are to Hugh."

"We're not as close as you think. We don't bear our souls to each other or anything close to that." Charles hesitates a beat. "I've never admitted this to you, but I was a sissy as a kid. Hugh, the big brother bully, was my protector. That relationship continued into adulthood. It was easier to let him fight my fights than stand up for myself."

"That explains a lot. I wish you'd told me sooner."

"I wish I'd told you a lot of things sooner," Charles says with a sad smile. "Hugh has been more irritable than usual these past few months. I sensed something was wrong, something other than his divorce, but I never suspected he was involved in criminal activity. He caused a young woman to die. He deserves whatever he gets."

"Daniel won't be able to bail him out this time."

Charles turns down the alley and parks in front of Hazel's apartment. He puts the car in gear and shifts in his seat to face her. "It was wrong of me to tell my family I'm the baby's father when you haven't yet decided how to handle paternity."

"Actually, I'm glad you did. Their excitement about the baby really moved me. Instead of being raised by a single mom, this little boy or girl will have a whole village of family and friends to support him or her."

Charles's face lights up. "So I can be the baby's father?"

Hazel grins. "You can be the baby's father."

He punches the air. "Yay me! We'll have an attorney draw up the documents we discussed regarding paternity rights."

"Do you really think that's necessary?"

"I'm not worried about me. I have no intention of ever infringing upon our agreement. But I think you'll be more comfortable with the situation if we have our agreement in writing."

Hazel thinks about it before responding with a nod. "I've decided to help the police convict Davis. If I need to pick him out of a lineup or whatever. We don't live in a safe world, and we must stand up for ourselves and protect one another as much as possible."

"You're making a brave choice, Hazel. I'll be beside you every step of the way."

A moment of silence passes between them. "Can you believe how far we've come? Six months ago, we were miserable, stuck in a failing marriage that neither of us knew how to get out of."

"We were waiting for life *to* happen to us instead of making it happen *for* us."

"You made life happen *for* you by starting your own business. But what have I done?"

Charles chuckles. "You posted the picture of Stuart and me on social media, for starters."

Hazel looks down at her lap. "That doesn't count. I reacted out of anger."

"The old Hazel would never have considered raising a child on her own."

Hazel tugs at a loose thread on her blouse. "And the new Hazel just chickened out on doing that by agreeing to let you be the father."

"Make no mistake about it. You'll be doing the heavy lifting when it comes to raising this child. My job is to offer support and to spoil the child rotten with toys and cars and ponies."

Hazel cuts her eyes at him. "Don't you dare."

Charles laughs. "I'm just kidding. My point is, you're underestimating yourself. However, if you feel the need to prove yourself, you can be in charge of the bicycle tour division of Peak Adventures. Not only would you guide them, you'd be responsible for designing the tours and making the division grow."

She jerks her head up. "Really, Charles? Do you mean it? I've been thinking about it, and I have some great ideas for tour packages."

"Have at it. I'm thrilled to hand this project over to you. I have my hands full with kayaks and rafting."

Hazel throws her arms around his neck. "Everything's working out the way it was meant to."

Charles holds her tight. "You bet. We took a major detour, but we're finally headed in the right direction."

CHAPTER 37
FOURTH OF JULY
CASEY

Casey, dressed for the Fourth of July party in the white halter dress she saw in the window at Faith's Fashions, stands at her bedroom window, looking out over the landscape. Daniel has encouraged her to redo the master suite to her liking. And she'll eventually get around to it. But for now, she's comfortable in the room she's come to think of as her own.

Guests are already approaching the tents on the lawn at the winery next door, but after a hectic afternoon at the picnic for young families, she needs a moment to collect herself before heading over.

She spots Daniel and Millie walking hand in hand across the backyard toward the party. Millie cut back her work hours to spend more time with Daniel. She's helping him put the finishing touches on his new house, and he's teaching her to fly-fish. Hugh's legal problems have taken their toll on Daniel. But, while there's a lingering sadness about him, he seems to improve every day, thanks largely to Millie's companionship.

Grabbing her clutch, Casey heads over to the tent where she takes a glass of Champagne from a passing waiter. Ollie and Sheldon are the first family members she encounters. She kisses both their cheeks. "Where's Henry?"

"At home with his new nanny," Sheldon says. "This is our first outing together without him."

"You picked a good night." Casey nudges Sheldon. "Are you ready for the big announcement? It's not too late to back out."

"No way!" Sheldon says with a vigorous head shake. "I'm 100 percent committed to the success of this vineyard."

Casey turns to Ollie. "And you're okay with this arrangement?"

Ollie nestles close to Sheldon. "I couldn't stop him if I wanted to."

Casey narrows her eyes at Ollie. "Are you okay? You don't seem like yourself."

Ollie and Sheldon exchange a look she can't interpret.

Casey's heart pounds in her chest. "What is it? I don't think I can handle more bad news."

"It's not bad news." Sheldon digs his chin into the top of Ollie's head. "You can tell her."

"I'm expecting another baby. If I don't seem like myself, it's because the morning sickness is way worse than last time." Ollie grabs Casey's arm. "Please, don't tell anyone yet. I'm not very far along."

"I won't say a word. Congratulations. I'm thrilled for you both." She notices Fiona and Jamie at the edge of the terrace. "Excuse me a minute. I want to speak to Fiona."

Casey makes her way through the crowd to her friends. "I'm so glad you two could make it."

"Are you kidding? I've been looking forward to this for weeks. Guess what? We're engaged." Fiona holds up her left hand to show Casey the sparkling solitaire diamond.

Casey lets out a squeal. "Yay. How exciting!" She hugs Fiona and Jamie in turn.

Fiona loops her arm through Jamie's. "We're getting married at The Foxhole on Labor Day Weekend. I hope you'll be my maid of honor."

"I'd be honored. I can hardly wait."

Someone calls her name, and Casey spins around to find Ada and Enzo standing with Charles and Hazel. "If it isn't the expectant couples. Are you guys comparing notes on pregnancy dos and don'ts?"

Everyone laughs.

"The women are." Enzo elbows Charles. "We men are discussing how to avoid middle-of-the-night feedings."

Casey bites her tongue to keep from blabbing the news about Sheldon and Ollie's second baby. "Just think, soon there will be lots of little Love cousins chasing one another around." She starts off and turns back around. "By the way, Hazel, both tourists and locals are loving your bike tours. Drop off some more brochures when you get a chance."

A broad smile crosses Hazel's face. "Will do! I'm proud to report we're already booking tours for fall."

Giving her a thumbs-up, Casey moves through the crowd toward the stage where Daniel is motioning for her to join him. She's almost at the stage when a hand stops her. She turns to face Laney, who is dazzling in a sky-blue silk dress.

"I wanted to congratulate you ahead of time on your promotion. You've worked hard and you deserve it."

Casey embraces her. "Thanks. That means a lot. I've been thinking a lot about you and the girls. How are you holding up?"

Laney flaps her hand in the so-so gesture. "The girls' friends are teasing them relentlessly about their father's criminal activities. Fortunately, it's summertime and they don't have to see them every day at school. You may not have heard, but Hugh has agreed to testify against Davis, which means Davis will be charged with Miranda's death."

"I didn't know that. Will Hugh be charged with anything?"

"His trafficking charge will be reduced to possession, but he will still serve time. And that's all that matters. I hope he uses this time wisely to get his act together."

"For everyone's sake." Casey looks around. "Are you here with Bruce?"

Laney smiles. "Yes! He went to get drinks from the bar. I'm grateful for him. He loves spending time with the girls, and they are really warming up to him. He's just what the three of us need right now."

"I'm so happy for you." Casey kisses her cheek. "I predict all good things for your life."

"For you too, Casey."

She hears Daniel's voice calling her name. "Let me run. Daniel's waiting for me. I'll talk to you after the announcement."

She's slightly out of breath by the time she reaches her father. "Sorry. I kept running into people I needed to speak with."

Daniel glances at his watch. "It's almost time. Are you ready?"

"I'm ready. Where's Sheldon?" Casey asks, looking around.

"He ran to the restroom." Daniel pulls Casey out of the way of the stage stairs, where band members are hustling up and down as they prepare for their first set. "I just want to say how blessed I am to have you in my life. I'm sorry we got off to a rocky start, but I hope we'll have smooth sailing from now on. I missed out on your childhood, but God willing, I'll have plenty of time to make up for it in the years ahead." He kisses the top of her head. "Have a magical night, sweetheart."

She gives him a quizzical look. "I'm excited about the announcement, but magical exceeds my expectations. What—"

Sheldon's arrival interrupts her attempt to question her father.

"We're all here. Let's do this thing." Daniel climbs onto the stage and approaches the microphone. "Can I have your attention, please?"

Silence spreads across the crowd, and they gather near the stage.

"Welcome! And thank you for joining us for what I hope will be a fun-filled evening. We have plenty of food and booze." He gestures at the musicians tuning their instruments. "The band will strike up momentarily, and a professional fireworks display will light up the sky at nine thirty."

"Before the dancing begins, I'd like to take this opportunity to make an important announcement." Daniel motions for Casey and Sheldon to join him onstage. "As you're aware, our family has experienced many hardships this past year. But tonight, we're looking toward tomorrow. I have officially retired as head of Love-Struck vineyards. I envision much fly-fishing and fox hunting in my future."

He pauses while everyone laughs.

"I'm proud to announce that my daughter Casey and youngest son, Sheldon, will cohead the vineyard going forward. I have faith in their talents and abilities, and I look forward to watching the vineyard flourish under their supervision."

Cheers spread across the crowd.

"As for my son Charles,"—Daniel sweeps an arm in Charles's direction—"I'm delighted he is following his passion for outdoor activities with his new business, Peak Adventures, which caters to guided rafting, kayaking, and biking adventures. I am confident Charles and Hazel will provide many hours of enjoyment for locals and tourists in the years ahead."

Another round of applause.

"And now, the moment you've been waiting for, the Dave Drummond Band," Daniel says and steps out of the way as the lead singer makes her way to the microphone.

As Casey is exiting the stage, she spies a familiar-looking head of sandy hair above the crowd. The sea of people parts, and Luke appears wearing the naughty smile that makes Casey's heart flutter. Is this what her father meant by *magical*?

The crowd disappears, and Casey floats on a cloud toward him. "What're you doing here?"

"I'm back. For good this time. Turns out Washington isn't for me." Taking her by the hand, he leads her away from the noise of the band. "On the first day at my new job, I realized something important. I don't need a flashy career. I only need you. I've missed you something awful these past two months. I'm so happy to be back, I'm never leaving Lovely again, not even to go on vacation."

Tears pool in her eyes. "Why didn't you call me?"

"My pride wouldn't let me. Not until I was ready to make things right. My new bosses weren't thrilled with me, and I felt obligated to stay at the EPA until they could find my replacement."

"Where are you working now?"

"The partners at my old firm gave me my job back. I will start next week. It's as though nothing has changed."

"Everything has changed, Luke. My life is completely different. I have important responsibilities now. I assume you heard Daniel's announcement. I'm cohead of the vineyard and also mistress of The Nest."

Luke brushes her hair off her shoulder. "I know. Daniel told me. I stopped by to see him earlier today."

So, this is what Daniel meant when he told her to have a magical night. "What did you need to see Dad about?"

"To make sure he still approves of me marrying you." He drops to his knees. "Marry me, Casey. We'll grow old together, living in The Nest and raising our brood of children."

Her pale olive eyes twinkle. "Those words have a familiar ring to them. Didn't you write a song once about me marrying you?"

Luke straightens. "I did. Wanna hear it? I brought along my saxophone."

Before she can object, he sweeps her off her feet and carries her onto the stage. The band goes silent, and the guests stop dancing. One of the band members hands Luke his saxophone. He presses his lips to the instrument and his beautiful music fills the night air.

When the song ends, he sets down his saxophone and removes the ring box from his pocket. He takes the engagement ring out and holds it up. The audience erupts in loud cheers and whistles.

"Marry me, Casey." He leans in close and whispers, "Please don't turn me down in front of all these people."

Casey gazes into his piercing blue eyes. "I have no intention of turning you down. I want nothing more than to be your wife. Yes, Luke, I will marry you."

"Yes!" Taking her hands, Luke twirls her around and into his arms. "I promise to never leave you again."

"You'd better not," Casey says in a scolding tone.

"Tightening his hold on her, he presses his lips to hers and the world falls away around them.

———

If you enjoyed the Virginia Vineyard series, please consider reading my Palmetto Island and Hope Springs series as well. Watch the trailers and learn more on my website @ashleyfarley.com

And . . . to find out about my new and upcoming books, be sure to sign up for my newsletter@ashleyfarley.com/newsletter-signup/

ACKNOWLEDGMENTS

I'm grateful for many people who helped make this novel possible. Foremost, to my editor, Patricia Peters, for her patience and advice and for making my work stronger without changing my voice. And to my cover designer, Damon and his team @ Damonza.com for their creative genius. A great big heartfelt thank-you to my trusted team of beta readers who are always available to read a manuscript, discuss plot issues, or help with cover selection. I'm always grateful to Kathy Sinclair, criminal investigator with the Bartow County Sheriff's Office, for her expert advice. And special thanks to my publicist, Kate Rock, for all the many things you do to manage my social media so effectively.

I am blessed to have many supportive people in my life who offer the encouragement I need to continue the pursuit of my writing career. Love and thanks to my family—my mother, Joanne; my husband, Ted; and my amazing kiddos, Cameron and Ned.

Most of all, I'm grateful to my wonderful readers for their love of women's fiction. I love hearing from you. Feel free to shoot me an email at ashleyhfarley@gmail.com or stop by my website at ashleyfarley.com for more information about my characters and upcoming releases. Don't forget to sign up for my newsletter. Your subscription will grant you exclusive content, sneak previews, and special giveaways.

ABOUT THE AUTHOR

Ashley Farley writes books about women for women. Her characters are mothers, daughters, sisters, and wives facing real-life issues. Her bestselling Sweeney Sisters series has touched the lives of many.

Ashley is a wife and mother of two young adult children. While she's lived in Richmond, Virginia, for the past twenty-one years, a piece of her heart remains in the salty marshes of the South Carolina Lowcountry, where she still calls home. Through the eyes of her characters, she captures the moss-draped trees, delectable cuisine, and kindhearted folk with lazy drawls that make the area so unique.

Ashley loves to hear from her readers. Visit Ashley's website @ ashleyfarley.com

Get free exclusive content by signing up for her newsletter @ ashleyfarley.com/newsletter-signup/

Lightning Source UK Ltd.
Milton Keynes UK
UKHW012110281222
414549UK00008B/90